PRAISE
RENE GUTTERIDGE

"Gutteridge creates suspenseful tension from the start of the story and doesn't let up until the end. Twists and turns will keep the reader guessing, and the sweet faith of a child is a refreshingly appropriate counterpoint to the action."

ROMANTIC TIMES ON *POSSESSION*

"From its captivating prologue to its powerful ending, Rene Gutteridge has written an engaging and memorable story. *Listen* concerns a theme of immeasurable importance to us all. Don't miss it."

RANDY ALCORN, bestselling author of *Safely Home* and *Heaven*

"Fascinating and tightly crafted—a story that explores a town's journey toward redemption with humor, grit, and heart. Rene Gutteridge's skills are evident in the snappy, realistic dialogue, and her talent for suspense keeps the pages turning."

LIZ CURTIS HIGGS, bestselling author of *Bad Girls of the Bible*

"*Possession* perfectly captures the essence of the intense world of a homicide detective—and the awful toll the job can exact on a soul. Rene Gutteridge's remarkable storytelling ability shines through in this nonstop suspense masterpiece, and it will keep you turning the pages well into the night. Highly recommended!"

MARK MYNHEIR, homicide detective and author of *The Corruptible*

"Clever novelist Gutteridge (the Storm series) has consistently upped the ante of Christian storytelling by offering her readers intelligent and entertaining texts. Her newest work delves into the deepest recesses of the human heart via the spoken word. . . . Gutteridge's skillful handling of the power of words will have every reader quietly introspective."

PUBLISHERS WEEKLY ON LISTEN

"This is a solidly plotted novel. . . . Gutteridge does a nice job of building suspense."

BOOKLIST ON POSSESSION

"Gutteridge makes her characters wrestle with right and wrong amid shades of gray. In a tightly wound, tension-filled plot, characters consider weighty issues while under extreme duress. . . . *Possession* is an entertaining yet thoughtful read for adrenaline junkies."

CROSSWALK.COM

"Current fans will certainly enjoy this offering and I'll bet that new readers with a penchant for suspense will have found a new author to put on their must-read list."

TITLETRAKK.COM ON POSSESSION

MISERY LOVES COMPANY

hroughout
directed, “E
and your b
en a footb
lightly. I don't
about prisoners of
and were able to play
prior to their solitary
they had merely

misery loves company

RENE GUTTERIDGE

Tyndale House Publishers, Inc.
Carol Stream, Illinois

Visit Tyndale online at www.tyndale.com.

Visit Rene Gutteridge's website at www.renegutteridge.com.

TYNDALE and Tyndale's quill logo are registered trademarks of Tyndale House
Publishers, Inc.

Misery Loves Company

Cover designed by Erik M. Peterson

Interior designed by Dean H. Renninger

Edited by Sarah Mason

Published in association with the literary agency of Janet Kobobel Grant, Books & Such,
Inc., 52 Mission Circle, Suite 122, PMB 70, Santa Rosa, CA 95409.

ISBN 978-1-4143-4933-6

Printed in the United States of America

19	18	17	16	15	14	13
7	6	5	4	3	2	1

For Cheryl McKay and Andrea Nasfell

Two mighty talented gals and wonderful, dear friends

PROLOGUE

IN THE EARLY MORNING HOURS, with the stars dotted across a fading black sky, the air was still and thick and shadowless. Turning on a lamp, he walked toward her and then stood over her, his thin shadow stretching across her body. She lay motionless, as fragile as a locust shell. It seemed if he touched her, she would crumble into dust.

He could not tell if she was cold. Her hands had been icy since she was in her thirties. But he pulled the blanket to her chin anyway. It was like tucking in a child. Except there would not be any wishes for sweet dreams. The dream was ending, slowly and painfully.

In another room, his dinner was long since chilled. He had no appetite, and she couldn't insist he do anything anymore.

"I haven't eaten," he said aloud suddenly. "Not a bite."

She stirred and let out the faintest breath, a hiss that sounded like a deflating bicycle tire.

He looked at the clock. In a little under an hour, the nurse would arrive, the only other person besides the two of them to come to this place. She'd agreed to work off the books.

Another hiss. Then her eyes opened, wide, as if she'd been dropped out the window of an eight-story building. Her gaze frantically searched the ceiling.

"Looking for someone?" He smiled gently.

She tried to lift a hand, but the weight of the sheet and the blanket kept it tucked away.

"Why am I still here?" Her voice was raspy and unkind, weighed down by spite.

He couldn't answer. He didn't have the answer.

"Why am I still here?" Her eyes had turned cloudy. They used to be blue and clear, like an afternoon sky. Now they were gray as gravel.

"You have no right," he said. "No right at all." He was not a man easily driven to anger, but it was the only emotion he felt these days.

"I have every right," she said, her watery eyes looking into his.

He stepped away from the bed, stared at her from a safe distance. Was he capable of this? He dropped to his knees, pressing a fist against his mouth to keep himself from screaming.

It was horrific pain either for her or for him. Which would he choose? Because ultimately, in a quiet, empty corner of his mind, he knew he believed that a soul could be damned.

The misery of it all was more than he could take. He had not understood until now what it meant to suffer.

She called his name, angrily, in a tone he'd never guessed

she was capable of. Over and over she called out to him, then cursed and cursed again. In the thirty-five years he'd known her, she had not uttered a curse word once.

His legs were shaky from age and burden, but he managed to stand again.

She turned her head when he stepped in front of the bedside lamp, sensing he'd returned. Her hair was stringy and clumped, what was left of it. At the crown, it was wispy, her white scalp showing like she had mange.

All the memories they shared were gone. They meant nothing now. He couldn't have imagined it, but the meaning of their love had trickled through his hands, puddling at his feet like dirty water. And even though he'd known her for most of his years, her foul mouth repulsed him, and her request had rendered her unrecognizable to him.

He thought he heard someone at the door. He checked his watch and listened. *Margaret? Please. Margaret.*

But it was silent again.

She'd managed to get her hand out from the covers and was grasping the air, clawing at it with her gnarled fingers. Her nails had grown thick and rough and yellow. The veins in her arms, blue and rigid, appeared to sit atop her skin instead of underneath.

"I know you're nearby," she whispered.

"I'm always nearby," he replied.

"I have done everything for you. Everything. Given you every dream. Offered you every opportunity. Asked nothing in return."

It was true. All of it.

"And then you cut down my tree. And you let the raccoon out, you ignorant menace. Do you think I didn't know you cut my tree down?"

It was often like this. She'd seem clear-minded and then slip into nonsense and crudeness. So he wasn't sure if her only request came from a clear mind or not. And even if it did, he didn't know if he loved her enough. Or too little.

"The nurse will be here soon," he said but probably not loud enough for her to hear because she was screaming and grunting now, thrashing about as much as she was capable, her head whipping from one side to the other.

"Are you in pain?" he asked.

She cursed him.

Tears streamed down his face. He could see her pain in the way her eyes bulged and how her hands suddenly clenched the sheets.

"Margaret is coming. Soon. Very soon."

She cursed Margaret.

Then, to his surprise, her hand grasped his shirt, so tightly that he heard a seam rip in the shoulder. She yanked at him and he stumbled, his bad knee hitting the railing of the bed.

"Don't ever say you love me again," she snarled. "There is no decency in you."

He took her hand and with little effort put it back under the covers, just as she slipped into unconsciousness. He pulled the covers to her chin once again. He brushed the wisps of hair out of her face. He checked his watch. The nurse would be here soon because she was almost always early.

A few minutes and it could all be over.

Including any decency he might have.

A heaviness pressed into his heart muscle, tearing at the fibers that held it together. There was only so much a human being could be expected to overcome. If there was a God, surely He was merciful enough to understand. Surely there was no sin too big.

But he wasn't certain.

He *was* certain, however, that he loved her.

And love could drive a man to do terrible things.

AT THE AGE OF THIRTY-FOUR, Jules Belleno couldn't believe how much routine comforted her.

She remembered watching her grandparents in their old age, wondering how anyone could be so set in their ways, so satisfied with uneventfulness. They rose at the same time every morning—an ungodly hour like 4 a.m. They ate the same thing for breakfast: half a grapefruit (always split and sprinkled with Sweet'N Low), a cup of decaffeinated coffee—hers with cream, his black. They'd walk the dog as soon as the sun rose. Lunch at eleven, errands or chores in the afternoon. TV dinners were served at 4 p.m., and their last and favorite thing was to watch *Wheel of Fortune* before they found themselves in bed by seven.

It had seemed like such a ridiculous life to her. She couldn't fathom why they wouldn't go to a movie in the evening or to the jazz festival or do anything outside their little world. They had so much freedom and never used it.

Of course, she was in her late teens at the time and also couldn't fathom that life was going to be anything but remarkable and spectacular. How naive she was.

Her grandparents had died within six weeks of each other, and Jules remembered thinking that was so sad. Now she understood what a gift it was. A gift that was rarely given.

She rose every day, without the help of a clock, at precisely 5:57 a.m. She never could figure out why her body chose that time, but it was where she'd landed.

By seven she'd already exercised and showered, and by seven thirty, she was cooking herself egg whites or having a bowl of cereal. Breakfast provided the most variety in her day.

A few minutes past eight, she was at her computer, logged on to her blog and her Facebook page.

Hoping the rain moves out today! A lame status update for today, but it was all she could muster.

Within minutes, she'd gotten eight thumbs-ups and a few remarks about the weather.

She'd dreaded this day, but dread never kept any day from coming. It was also the first Tuesday of the month, the day she reviewed a book on her blog. Readers expected it. She'd missed it once due to the flu and been surprised at how many inquiries she received about why her review wasn't posted.

On the far corner of her desk, the book sat, looking like it was in a time-out. Jules stared at its glossy cover, its embossed-gold, royal-like lettering. She'd watched over the years how his name had grown and his titles had shrunk. It meant he was platinum to the publisher.

But this one, like the last two, was a disappointment. The quality of his work had been declining. His most current was late. Without fail, he released a book every nine months, but she'd had to wait longer for this one. With other authors, she figured it came with the territory. They got so popular and the demand so great that they began churning out books faster than they should.

But he mattered. He'd always mattered to her, since she discovered his books when she was only twenty-one. It wasn't just that he was from her hometown. That was great and gave her a lot to blog about, but there seemed to be a special quality about his writing. Even though it was suspense and the plots could border on outrageous, there was a depth to how he wrote, as though the words came out his fingertips straight from his soul. There were treasures buried inside the paragraphs, from page to page. Sometimes you had to hunt for them, but they were there—little nuggets of truth about your life, cleverly intertwined with murder, mayhem, and madness.

Jules sighed and pulled the book closer. Her fingers typed out the title: "*THE LION'S MOUTH* by PATRICK

REAGAN. Reviewed by Jules Belleno." That was the easy part. Now came the—

Knock at her door.

She moaned quietly, cut her eyes to the door. Was it already *that* time?

The knock again, this time a little heavier. If she didn't get there fast, he'd start calling her name.

"Coming!" She forced the singsong in her tone. Opening the door, she widened her smile. "Hi, Daddy."

"I thought you might not be home. I knocked twice."

"You have to give me a chance to get up and walk over here."

He smiled. "Just anxious to see you. I was in the neighborhood. You busy?"

Always a loaded question. There never was a right answer, so today she just went with no.

"Why not? Why aren't you writing?" He stepped in and she closed the door.

"I am writing. I was about to work on my blog."

"Real writing, Juliet. Blogging is for people who can't write professionally. You know how capable you are. You've got real talent."

They went to the kitchen, where she took another mug from the cabinet. She didn't even ask, just poured him coffee. "Dad, I've told you this. There are some really talented bloggers. Very gifted. Have thousands of followers, reaching more people than if they published a book."

"Well, you should get *paid* to write. That's how they did it in my day." He'd gotten a few articles published in a military newsletter, so he was an expert. "People would write and get paid for their thoughts and their words. Now people offer all that stuff up for free. I told you about my dream, didn't I?"

Her dad's memory was getting kind of bad. He'd told her four times. She watched his shaky hands try to get the coffee mug to his lips before he pressed on with the dream.

"The one where I saw your book at a bookstore, for sale? It was at the front where they put all the famous people?"

"Yes, you told me."

"Well, you're not going to be a famous writer if you don't write something."

"I'm not interested in being famous, Dad. I love to write, but it's more for the ability to explore things, think things through, wonder about things."

"Writers can make good money. I know a couple of generals who've written some bestsellers in their retirement."

Her dad was a Marine. It had been expected of Jules to find the *hoorah* in every part of her life. And she had. She'd found Jason.

Jules sighed.

They'd done this so much that her dad had gotten good at retorting himself. "I know I get pushy about this stuff. I just know how talented you are, Juliet. You could make it as a writer if you'd try. You've got to stop moping around this house, you know? Get out, enjoy life again."

She couldn't hate him for it, but she resented it all the same. With his flattop haircut, now gray at the temples, and his angular face that held the bluest sparkling eyes, he would never be able to totally get on her bad side, but he'd given it a good run for many years. He was pushy, opinionated, and completely lacking in self-awareness, but he'd been in three wars, so he always had at least some grace with her.

"I'll get something out there. I've been working on a few things."

"You have? See!" Then he frowned. "Are you just telling me what I want to hear?"

She only smiled.

"I was thinking of taking a little road trip next month, down the coast. What do you think?"

"Nah."

"What could be so bad about a road trip? What else do you have to do?"

She shrugged. "I have things to do."

He chugged his hot coffee the way only a Marine could, then slammed the mug down on the counter with a small smile. "A bit tame. I like mine real black."

"That's why you have your house and I have mine."

"Your way of turning down my offer, again, for you to come live with me?"

"I like it here," she said. "Trust me, I'd get on your nerves very fast. I get on my own nerves."

"Not possible. I want you to give it another thought. Think it through completely, not just your first instinct. Like I told my men, instinct can carry you an awful long way, but full analysis can save your life."

She smiled warmly at him, the kind of smile that lets a dad know his little girl is going to be okay. She'd become good at faking that smile. He looked like he was about to burst at the seams, so she threw him a bone.

"I sort of got a story idea last night while I was—"

"Go with that! Yes! Someplace to start already and it's not even lunchtime. There's a reason Marines rise before sunup. We put more into life before breakfast than most people put into their whole day. You got my blood in you, baby."

"I am fully pepped."

"When you were born," he said, wrapping his arm around her waist as they walked to the door, "I was disappointed. I already told you this story."

"You wanted a boy."

"I wanted a boy. I'm so glad it was you instead."

She patted him on the shoulder. "Dad, don't worry so much about me, okay?"

"I wouldn't if you ever left this house."

"This is a good, safe place for me." And it was. She still felt connected to the world, through a twenty-inch screen.

"I may go fishing tomorrow."

Doubtful. It was starting to get too cold, for one thing. He had good intentions, but they rarely saw the light of day. "Have fun."

"Maybe we can have a fish fry, invite some of these neighbors you refuse to get to know."

"I know all the people I need to know." She gave him a little help out the door. "Off you go."

He gave her a white-flag wave and climbed into his truck. A sadness sank into her soul as she watched him go. That was the best part of his day. It was all downhill from here.

Back at the computer, she took a long, slow sip of her coffee and stared at the blinking cursor. Ugh. It was so hard to say what she needed to say about Patrick Reagan, but at the same time, she knew people read her blog for her honest opinion. And her honest opinion was that he just didn't have what he used to.

She typed the words carefully: *I can't put my finger on it.*

His stories still contain the fast-paced plot, the heroic law enforcement character, and the surprise twist.

But it's like he had magic in his fingers once. And now that magic is gone. He can still type, still use his fingers in remarkable ways, but maybe the curtain has been pulled back a little and we're seeing the wizard as he is for the first time.

What causes writers to lose their magic? Maybe they don't even know. Maybe every writer has only so many genuinely birthed stories, and after that, they're just cranking the levers and using the smoke and mirrors to try to sell us on the idea that we should suspend our disbelief.

I'm his biggest fan. Patrick Reagan is still one of the finest American writers with which we've been gifted. He always will be. But maybe our expectations exceed what he is capable of.

THE LION'S MOUTH had all the right elements. Great premise: a Secret Service agent must determine if a president under whom he once served is corrupt. But at the end of the read, I didn't really care what happened to the character. Any of the characters. And that's the very first thing a reader must do: care.

Everything from the plot to the dialogue seemed to fall flat. I felt like grabbing the book by its jacket cover, shaking it, and saying, "Don't tell me it's terrifying. Terrify me!" And that's where the most problematic issue lies, I believe. He's telling me how I should feel about what he writes. Yet every great storyteller knows it's the fine art of taking me by the hand and showing me that has the most effect on a reader's soul. It's how writers slip it all into us while we're not looking. While we're reading words, they're making magic happen, and when that magic lands right in our hearts, we're theirs forever.

I am in mourning. But I am confident that one day soon, Patrick Reagan will capture me again.

2

IN WISSBERRY, MAINE, the speed of traffic was never a problem. In fact, from a law enforcement perspective, it was one of the best places to work if you weren't a thrill-seeker type.

Today, for Chris Downey, the traffic was unnerving, like the drawl of a slow-talking Southerner you needed fast information from. Chris gripped the steering wheel and clenched his jaw, trying not to lose his temper. This wasn't an emergency call at all. It was barely a call that should be taken seriously. But Chris knew—when this man was involved, it would be no ordinary call.

On Bartleby, he accelerated even though it was a narrow,

graveled road that was going to force him to rinse the dust off his car later.

At the top of the small hill, the house came into view. His stomach turned at the sight of it. His skin instantly dampened and he wiped his forehead with the back of his hand.

On the front porch, Chris saw him—a hulk of a man who filled any doorway he passed through. It was the first day of bitter cold temperatures, and even from a distance, Chris could see the Lt. Colonel's breath freezing in front of his face in rapid bursts.

Chris parked his car and composed himself. Lt. Colonel Franklin was an overbearing brute and Chris needed to be as professional as possible. Emotionally detached. And firm. He took in a deep breath and started to open the car door.

But before Chris could get it all the way open and stand up, the Lt. Colonel was standing so close he could barely climb out. Chris maneuvered to shut the door behind him and then turned, staring up six inches to meet his eyes.

Chris wondered if the man would even remember him. He stood straight and adjusted his jacket, pulling on his winter gloves after taking off his sunglasses.

"Lt. Colonel, Sergeant Chris Downey." He offered his hand and the Lt. Colonel shook it with the force of a man who could probably kill him using his bare hands. Marines were kind of crazy anyway, but this one was known around town to be, at the very least, pushy and peevish. Although the Marines typically called lieutenant colonels simply *Colonel*, Jim Franklin insisted on the full title. And he'd always gotten his way.

Chris stood straight, trying to grow out of his shadow. "We met a couple of years—"

"I remember."

"So tell me what the problem is."

His face turned red. "The problem? My daughter is missing! What are you, some kind of moron? Didn't they tell you that when I called?"

Chris pulled out a notepad. "Okay, let's start from the beginning. When is the last time you saw—?"

"At 0900."

"What day?"

"Yesterday."

Chris kept his expression even because he didn't want to upset the already-upset Lt. Colonel, but Jules had been missing barely over twenty-four hours. There were a billion reasons that could apply.

The Lt. Colonel stepped forward into space that wasn't really there. "Downey, I've got a gut feeling. Analytically, I get that this isn't alarming. But my gut feeling, coupled with intelligent analysis, has saved my life and my men's lives in places that you'll only see in your nightmares." He stopped, took a deep breath, cutting his hand back and forth over his flattop. Then, quieter, he said, "Something is wrong."

"Tell me what makes you think that."

"I visit her often, always at the same time. She's always up, has always made coffee, is always at her computer working on that ridiculous blog she thinks is going to change the world. I told her she needs to publish a book but . . ." He stopped himself, put his hands on his hips. "The point is, she is always here."

"Maybe she's out for coffee or ran to the store?" Chris looked around. "Is her car here?"

"Yes, in the garage."

"Does she usually walk to the store or drive?"

"Both. She prefers to walk, to cut through the woods. But this is when she writes. She would be here."

"Any chance there was some kind of emergency with someone she knows, that she would leave unexpectedly?"

"No."

"No? No possibility?"

"Young man, if you know anything about my daughter, then you know she doesn't leave her house often, and she doesn't have friends."

Chris looked down, trying to hide the guilt he knew would be shining in his eyes. "I do know about her. . . . I mean, not a lot. Not like you. But . . ." He looked away, up to the house. "We used to be friends."

The Lt. Colonel nodded. "I know he was a great loss to you."

Chris tucked his notepad away. "Why don't I step inside."

"It's locked."

"You have a key?"

The Lt. Colonel looked sheepishly at his shoes. "She took that away about a year ago. I guess I was getting on her nerves." But he unexpectedly smiled. "Of course, the absence of a key never stopped me before."

Chris laughed. "Okay, well, technically I shouldn't encourage a break-in, but let's see what we can do here, trusting there will be minimal property damage."

"Nobody will even know we were here. Pay attention," the Lt. Colonel said, walking toward the house. "I learned this in special ops."

Using a splintered matchstick, he had them inside in less than three minutes. The house was quiet, tidy, and smelled like vanilla and some kind of fruit, maybe blackberries. Chris walked around, carefully observing, but nothing seemed out of place. He remembered Jules being very neat, a product of having a military father. Her bed was made. There looked to be no signs of distress anywhere in the house. From what he could tell, she'd taken her wallet, purse, and keys. Adding that to the fact that the front door was locked, he concluded she'd probably walked somewhere, which wasn't unusual for this town. It was awfully cold, and when the cold weather hit, fewer people walked. But no snow yet.

The Lt. Colonel followed him everywhere. "See what I mean? Something is off here."

Chris opened the dishwasher and peered in. The dishes were dirty—but not freshly dirty. Coffee had dripped from the top shelf to the bottom but was dry.

Chris stood and faced the Lt. Colonel, whose arms were crossed above a slightly round belly that Chris was sure had emerged since retirement. "I'll be honest with you, sir. There does not seem to be evidence of foul play of any sort here.

Everything is pointing to the fact that she simply left and will be back. Obviously you've tried her cell phone?"

"She keeps it off most of the time. It went to voice mail, but that's not unusual. She doesn't really like to talk on the phone." He stared at his feet. "She doesn't really like to talk at all."

Chris stepped forward. "Sir, this should be an encouragement. It appears that everything is fine. I'll tell you what. I'll drive around town, keep my eye out for her."

"I'll do that too. No reason to just stand around inside this house."

"Exactly." Chris walked to the door. "I don't suppose you can get this locked again with a matchstick?"

The Lt. Colonel only smiled.

"How long do I give her," he asked at the doorway, "before I should be really worried?"

Chris tried to reel in what was certain to be a pained expression emerging on his face. The department wasn't going to take this thing seriously for at least another forty-eight hours. Even after that, with no evidence of foul play, she could have just as easily gone on a trip, maybe to get some space. But none of those explanations were setting well with him. He didn't admit this out loud, but he knew Jules had become a woman of rigid habits, which were not easily broken.

"Sir, you know the personal connection I have to Jules." Chris pulled out a card, took his pen, and jotted down his cell number. "If she's not back by sunup, go ahead and call me."

The Lt. Colonel regarded the number, then tucked the card in the front pocket of his shirt. "I just have a hunch."

"You're her father. It's your job."

He stepped off the front porch. "Just make sure you do yours."

Chris nodded and walked to his car. As he drove off, he glanced in the rearview mirror. The Lt. Colonel stood on the porch, the door behind him wide-open, drinking from a flask.

3

SHE'D SLEPT WRONG. Already, before she even got out of bed, her back ached, and the fact that both her shoulders felt like they'd been pulled out of their sockets might have been her first indication that she should adopt a new sleeping position. She was on her back now, though, which wasn't how she usually woke up.

Jules hated waking up. Opening her eyes left everything behind. Memories of Jason were fine, but it was in her dreams that she *felt* him. There, she talked with him, and they weren't remembered conversations. It was a new adventure when he showed up. Maybe once a week she'd at least glimpse him in a dream. Sometimes he'd just appear in a doorway and stand there. Sometimes he'd be walking far away in a garden, barely visible to the naked eye. It didn't matter. Even a few seconds was enough to make her feel he was still there. Just to see him. Just to hear his voice.

But then it came time for her to open her eyes. Always at the same time in the morning. And always with deep regret.

She stared upward, expecting to see the ceiling. But the room was pitch-black. Had she awoken in the middle of the night? It happened sometimes, but rarely. Of all things, she tended to be a good sleeper.

Turning her head caused pain to shoot through her right shoulder. Where was her clock? She tried to reach for the lamp she could not see. But her arm stopped and yanked backward.

Jules cried out in pain. Her eyes, wide-open now, could barely make out her room. Nothing was making sense. The window was on her left, not her right. She stared through the darkness, trying to find the doorway, but her eyes weren't adjusting quickly enough. Her gaze cut back to the window. The tiniest sliver of light was slicing through what looked to be heavy curtains. At the very top, where they weren't quite pulled together . . . moonlight.

But she didn't have curtains in her room.

She yelled and tried to sit up. But again, she barely moved. She had a sense that her arms were above her but couldn't feel anything beyond her shoulders. Why couldn't she feel her hands? *Where were her hands?*

"My hands! Jason!" It flew out of her mouth even though

she knew he wasn't around. But maybe this was a bad dream. Maybe he would come.

Jules thrashed her legs, tried to twist her body, but it only caused more pain. She screamed, and this time light filled the room with a loud creak. She looked toward it. A doorway. And in the doorway, a dark figure.

"Help me!" she cried.

The figure walked forward. His footsteps didn't make a sound. "Stay quiet," he said. "And calm."

"Where are my hands?"

He was by her bedside now but still backlit, so she couldn't see any features of his face.

"I told you to stay calm."

"What is happening?"

"Drink some water."

She didn't know why, but she lifted her head to drink. And he put a glass to her lips. The water was barely cold, just the right temperature. She hadn't realized it, but she was thirsty. He took the water away too soon.

"What is happening?" she asked again, trying to remember to stay calm.

"You will know in time." His voice was smooth and low, like a growl or a purr—she couldn't decide which. He reached for something. Suddenly she felt her hands, high above her head, prickly and tingling. But they were there.

She felt warmth and realized his hand was on hers. Then a peaceful drowsiness settled over her, and her body relaxed.

Her shoulders stopped hurting. She did not care at all whether she had hands or not.

Jules turned her gaze to the window again. The white light absorbed part of the darkness, swimming peacefully through the air. Its line waved like water in an ocean and she swore she could hear crashing waves.

She closed her eyes and went to find Jason.

⌐└

"Chris!" Addy's frantic voice cut through the quiet night air. "Chris!"

Chris jerked to a sitting position. He threw off the covers and reached for the gun in his nightstand. He felt a hand on his shoulder and turned to find Addy standing by the other side of the bed.

"What's wrong?"

"Someone is knocking," she said, her voice a terrified whisper. "At the front door."

Chris heard it now. He looked at the clock—3:12 a.m. The pounding continued.

"Stay here." Gun in hand, he hurried out of the bedroom, down the hallway, and into the foyer. As usual, his little sister didn't listen. She was right on his heels. "I'm coming!" he yelled. Then he turned to Addy. "Get on that couch and don't move."

He flipped on the porch light and peered through the peephole. Then groaned. He slid the gun into the drawer of a small entryway table.

Unlocking the dead bolt, he opened the door. "Lt. Colonel."

The man was standing in the middle of the porch, swaying like a tall weed against a moderate breeze. His eyes were bloodshot and angry. He snarled as he regarded Chris. "Why aren't you out there looking for her?"

Chris stepped out and closed the door behind him, catching a whiff of alcohol on his breath. "Sir, it is the middle of the night."

"I know what time it is," he said, waving his hand toward nothing definitive. "Don't you think I've been counting every single second?"

"Lower your voice," Chris said. He didn't have a lot of tolerance for drunks. Especially those who drove. Chris glanced at the Lt. Colonel's pickup truck, lights still glowing through the dark, the driver's side door wide-open.

"Tell me what's going on."

"Didn't mean to interrupt whatever carousing you've got going on in there. Whatever woman. Whatever she's doing in there. Heard her screaming, making all kinds of noise." He swayed again.

"That's my sister. She's staying with me for two weeks."

"I can't find her." The meanness in his eyes faded, replaced by tears. "I've looked for her. I've looked everywhere for her."

Chris took a deep breath. "All right. Give me a second. Just stay right here." He walked inside, shut the door.

Addy was upright on the couch, curled up in a blanket. She hopped to her feet and followed him to his bedroom. "Who was *that*?"

"Jules Belleno's father."

"Jules? You mean, Jason's . . . ?"

"That's right."

"What is he doing here?"

Chris went to his closet to pull on jeans and a shirt. "I saw him earlier today. He couldn't find her, was worried."

Addy walked into the closet, her arms wrapped tightly around herself for warmth. "What are you talking about?"

"I don't know what this is," Chris said, feeling his own aggravation. "He claimed something was wrong, but she'd only been missing for twenty-four hours or so."

"But he's here, in the dead of night?"

Chris glanced at her. "And drunk."

She looked him up and down, like she'd just noticed he was getting dressed. "Where are you going?"

"First of all, I'm driving him home. After that, I don't know." He looked at her. "Addy, this doesn't sound like her, to disappear."

Addy stared at the carpet. "I don't know her that well. I just remember you talking about her, and I met her at the funeral."

"I went through her house. Everything looked fine. Her car's there, but it's not unusual for her to walk to someplace like the store or fish market."

"Maybe she finally had a nervous breakdown. I mean, is it really that unexpected? After Jason . . . you know, she sort of turned into a recluse. She always seemed like such a . . . complicated mess."

Chris rubbed his tired eyes and didn't answer.

"You couldn't force her to let you help," Addy said, resting a hand on his arm. "Don't be so hard on yourself."

He went to the front door, grabbed his gun, tucked it in the waist of his jeans, and said, "Well, you're awake. Get my truck keys and follow me over there so I don't have to take a cab home."

"You look horrible," Maecoat said as they stepped into roll call. "Like there might be a woman involved."

"Funny," Chris said, but if his eyes looked as bad as they felt, he knew he was in for some ribbing today.

"Seriously. You don't get bags like that unless you're talking way into the night about how you feel and how she feels and how you both feel together."

"Only you'd know something like that, Maecoat."

"You're trying to tell me that the whites of your eyes look like rivers of blood because you got a good night's sleep?"

Chris sighed and glanced up to see the captain delayed in a conversation right outside in the hallway. He lowered his voice. "It wasn't a woman."

"I have *got* to get you a life."

"It was the Lt. Colonel."

"Franklin?"

"Yep."

"You know how many times I've had to take that guy home? I once found him in a ditch. No joke, four o'clock in the morning. No car. Nothing but him, passed out."

"Yeah, well, this is a little more complicated."

"Yeah?"

"Juliet Belleno is missing."

"Missing? What does that mean?"

"He hasn't seen her since Tuesday morning."

"So he tried to file a—"

"Yeah. But . . . I mean, there's something to be said for his concern. Jules hardly leaves the house. Ever since Jason . . . you know—she just doesn't leave, except maybe for the store or something like that."

"You get into the house?"

"He had a key." Chris glanced at the ground. He'd never been a very good liar. "Everything checked out. Keys, purse, cell phone gone, but car still there. So a friend could've come by and gotten her. She could've taken the bus somewhere."

"What are you going to do?"

Chris shrugged. "I don't know." He looked again toward Captain Perry, who was finishing up his conversation. "You know how flexible the captain is."

Maecoat smiled. "Yeah, I'm sure you'll really have his ear."

"I should try."

"Worth a shot, I guess. But Perry hates the Lt. Colonel."

"They have their own little war going, don't they?"

"So the rumor goes."

The captain walked in and the morning lineup went as usual. They were briefed on a couple of robberies. Teens gathering too late at the beach.

Maecoat bumped his arm as they were dismissed. "Louie's at noon?"

"Sounds good."

Because Wissberry was a fairly small community—under ten thousand residents—their police force consisted of thirty rotated partners. Some weeks Chris rode by himself; other weeks Maecoat was with him.

Chris stood, trying to decide what to do. He'd left the Lt. Colonel passed out on the couch of his daughter's home to keep watch for her, after promising the man that he'd do what he could today.

"Downey, you just going to stand there all morning?"

"Sorry . . . sir . . ." Chris blinked and regarded the captain, who gave him a small smirk. Well, he seemed to be in a decent mood. "Cap, can I talk to you for a second?"

"What about?"

Chris decided to leave the Lt. Colonel out of it for the moment. "You know Jason's wife, Juliet?"

"Sure."

"Her family is concerned. She's been missing for almost forty-eight hours."

"You know the drill."

"I do," Chris said, stepping closer. "But Jules isn't really the type to just go away without notice. In fact, in the last couple of years, she doesn't really leave the house much."

"That's what I hear."

"So I think there might be some validity to his concerns."

The captain finally looked up from his paperwork, over

the rim of his glasses. "Look, Chris, I can appreciate your personal interest in this. But you know how strapped we are for manpower. I can't put a detective on this for another day, and that's if we're lucky. You see where I'm coming from, don't you?"

"Yeah. Of course." He paused. "Maybe I can take a preliminary look into it. See if I can find something of interest."

The captain took off his glasses, gave Chris a weary look.

"It's not just anybody."

The captain blinked long and hard. "Sorry, Chris. It's got to wait. I can't bend procedure, and you know that."

"Understood." Chris nodded with no intention of complying whatsoever.

4

"YEAH. THIS IS GREAT. Just great," Maecoat moaned as they got out of Chris's squad car. "These crab cakes are no good cold."

"You didn't have to come. You *shouldn't* have come. *I* shouldn't be here at all."

"And my crab cakes are cold. Bad idea all the way around."

"His truck's gone," Chris said.

"And that's the only reason I'm trailing you on this thing. I'd hate to take a big-shot Marine down with a stun gun, but I'd do it just because he thought about opening his mouth."

Chris walked up the front porch steps, hoping that the door wasn't unlocked. Then he could say he tried, it was locked, and his hands were tied. He wasn't sure what time the Lt. Colonel had left, but he probably wasn't in top-notch condition. Chris reached for the door, slowly turned the knob.

It opened. Chris sucked in a breath and glanced at Maecoat.

"Well, what are you waiting for?" Maecoat said.

They walked in, Maecoat stuffing a crab cake into his mouth. "Wow," he said, food bulging from his cheek. "Tidy, huh?"

"Jason used to talk about how much her military-like neatness drove him crazy. And he was no slob. But she put his organizational skills to shame." Chris walked through the house, noticing this time how everything—drawer, cabinet, basket—was labeled. Everything had its place. There was nothing random anywhere in the house.

He walked to a small table near the kitchen, his eyes roaming over the five picture frames of Jason and Jules. Jason had nicknamed her Jules when they first met. Her given name was Juliet, but Jason had insisted he was no Romeo. In his vows at the wedding, though, he'd surprised everyone by proclaiming, "My love for you might just put Romeo to shame." Jules burst into tears because Jason was not a man who openly expressed his emotions much.

Jules fit her better anyway, Chris always thought. She was athletic and pretty in a natural sort of way. Long, wavy brown hair and a grin that set the room ablaze. She was shy, though, and Chris was more used to seeing her laugh at Jason's jokes than tell her own.

A few weeks before Jason and Jules were married, while he and Chris were sitting in their car eating lunch, Jason had said, "Promise me something."

"What?"

"If something ever happens to me, take care of her for me."

"Nothing is going to happen to you. That's why God gave you me. I'm like your guardian angel, except with more muscles. And I'm a good shot."

"Downey?"

Chris blinked. "Yeah?"

"You blanked out for a second," Maecoat said.

"Sorry." Chris realized he was staring at the wedding photo. He picked up the frame and noticed the date engraved on the frame. "Maecoat, come here."

"What?"

"Look at this date."

"Yeah, what about it?"

"That was Tuesday. Tuesday would've been their anniversary."

Maecoat nodded, setting down the Styrofoam box that contained his food. "That's not good. But she could've just gone away, right? Just some time to think?"

"Maybe." Chris set the photo down. "Except *maybe* isn't good enough here. It can't be a coincidence she went missing on the day of her anniversary."

"You're probably right," Maecoat said. "But it is also most likely a sign that she took off to get away."

"Without telling her dad? The one person who consistently

checks up on her? She wouldn't do that. I know Jules. She's too caring of a person."

"Maybe she's finally gotten fed up with the old guy."

Chris turned, scanning the room. "We need to find her calendar."

"That won't be hard. Everything is labeled."

"You get on that. I'm going to check her computer."

"Whoa . . . wait a minute. Chris, we can't . . . I mean, taking a peek is one thing. Getting into her computer? You could get in real trouble. You know that. We're just nosing around a little bit here. Right?"

"You go find that calendar. I'll take the fall for this."

Maecoat sighed and wandered off. Chris sat down at the perfectly neat desk that housed a desktop computer and flat-screen monitor, his hands shaking slightly. He was breaking every protocol and procedure there was, and he took it seriously. But he had to do this for Jason. He'd already failed once and now Jules was missing.

He pulled the chair close and leaned forward, moving the mouse. Like he thought, the computer had been in sleep mode. To him, this meant she had intended to come back. If she knew she'd be gone for a while, it would have been turned off. Especially with all of the eco-friendly, energy-saving devices he'd noticed around the house.

"Found it!" Maecoat called from the kitchen. "In a drawer labeled 'Calendars.'"

"She's making this easy on us," Chris said. The computer

awakened to her Facebook page. Her last post read, *Hoping the rain moves out today!*

Maecoat walked in. "Nothing unusual on her calendar for Tuesday, yesterday, or today. But Tuesday's date is lightly circled in pencil. Nothing written."

"Did the sun come out Tuesday?"

Maecoat stared at him. "You're seriously asking me that?"

"Yes."

"I was busy admiring the grass."

"Humor me."

Maecoat sighed. "I think it did. I was working that accident on the highway and it seemed like it got a little warm. I took off my gloves."

"So maybe she did walk to the store."

"There are a lot of maybes here."

Chris stared at the computer. He was crossing the line here. Big-time. His hand retreated from the mouse and he stood. He had to trust the system. At least partly.

But he also had to eliminate some of the maybes.

5

JULES OPENED HER EYES. She'd been with Jason again. They'd sat on a park bench and she told him that she'd been angry with him. Why couldn't he save her from all this grief? Why couldn't he help her move on? She knew it was "till death do us part," but Jason never believed in death. He said the soul goes on. He believed in a heaven that she never could fully wrap her mind around.

She'd feared death ever since she was a child. It was just as sure as her birth, but that didn't make it any easier to swallow. Death seemed to be the most unnatural thing a human could experience. What was this life for if not loving and living and changing and breathing? What was the point of it all if death took it away?

Her wrists were sore. Why? She briefly closed her eyes again, trying to summon Jason back. She had also had a nightmare, but it was far away now, its sounds swallowed by other memories and thoughts. She remembered nothing but emotion: terror followed by a strange, overwhelming comfort.

Then she noticed them again. The curtains. When did she put up curtains? The light, bright and spraying around their edges, hurt her eyes. It was like she had a hangover. Since when did morning light hurt her eyes?

She turned to look at the bedside clock, which was not there. Her gaze caught something red written on the white ceiling. Her vision was still blurry and a throbbing headache required extra effort to focus.

DON'T TELL ME IT'S TERRIFYING.
TERRIFY ME.

Jules gasped, scrambling back toward the headboard, reading and rereading the large red letters. Those were her words . . . the words she'd written on her blog. She glanced around the room, her mind barely able to translate what she was seeing. There was nothing familiar. This was not her bedroom. She looked down at herself. She was in soft, cotton, button-up pajamas. She didn't own a pair of pajamas like this. She always slept in a T-shirt and shorts.

Her limbs starting to tremble, she stared at the ceiling

again, trying to reason out what was going on. But her mind was so foggy. It felt like every thought had to be pushed through a wall of mud.

Then she heard footsteps at a door she'd hardly noticed. The grain was clearly visible in the wood. It looked sturdy, heavy, thick. Below the door, where more light seeped through, a shadow appeared and the footsteps stopped. She wanted to run to the window, try to escape, but she wasn't sure what she was escaping from. Maybe there had been an accident. Maybe . . . maybe this was all a bad dream. She rubbed her wrists, noticing again that they were sore. Red marks wound around both of them.

"Jason," she whispered. "Jason, I need you."

The knob turned slowly, and then the door opened. A man stood at the threshold for a moment, observing her. The fact that he looked familiar comforted her a little. But she couldn't place him. Balled at the top of the bed, squeezing her knees to her chest, she watched him carefully. He held a tray with a bowl and a glass of water.

"You're awake," he said, so low and deep, like wisdom had just found its voice. He stepped toward her. "I brought you some food. You really must eat. Your stomach is going to feel ill if you don't."

"Am I sick?"

"Not yet. Thus, the food." He set the tray down at the end of the bed. The smell of a cream soup streamed toward her.

She looked at him. His eyes, hazel and heavily hooded, were round and perceptive, stunning against the filtering light. His features seemed chiseled from the finest, smooth-est stone. He had deep creases on either side of his mouth yet didn't seem prone to smiling.

"Do I know you?"

"Not really," he said mildly, opening a packet of crackers for her. "You probably believe you do, but you don't. You simply do not."

"Do you know me?"

Those wise eyes studied something in front of her that she couldn't see. "I shouldn't know as much as I do," he finally said, then focused on opening another packet of crackers.

She glanced up at the ceiling, at those horrible words scribbled in dark red.

"Your words," he said.

"I wrote them on my blog this morning." A deep, heavy pain crushed her chest.

"Not this morning. Tuesday morning. Stay calm." His voice purred the command, his words echoing against all her thoughts.

"I don't understand what is happening." Tears dropped down her cheeks and she wiped each eye with the back of her hand.

"You lack a lot of understanding," he said, pushing the tray closer to her. "That is why you are here. There is an ignorance about you that doesn't become you."

And then, with one blink, Jules knew him. She gasped and covered her mouth. "You're . . ."

He stood abruptly, causing the food tray to tip. Soup

sloshed out the side of the bowl. He seemed bothered by it and stared at it for a long moment. Then looked up at the ceiling as though he was noticing the words for the first time.

"Yes, I am." His tone sounded like the grumbling of a distant thunderstorm. "And I intend to." He lowered his gaze to her. "Don't try to escape. You will die out there," he said, nodding toward the window she couldn't see out. "There is nobody nearby. You will stay here, with me, until we are finished. You have a lot to learn." He stepped toward the door. "Don't scream. I don't like screaming. Nobody is around to hear you but me, and I can't state clearly enough how much revulsion I have for that sound."

He walked out and shut the door behind him. Then there was a slight rattle, like he was locking it.

Jules stared at the soup. She wasn't hungry. Her stomach hurt and was quickly becoming nauseated.

Had she finally lost her mind? Many thought she already had. But as far as she knew, she had a firm grasp on reality. So what was this?

That man at the end of the bed . . . It wasn't. It *couldn't* be. She had to have gone crazy. She was in a mental ward, maybe, and her mind was just not able to process it all, so she was escaping to another place.

Jules got up slowly, stumbling through swirling dizziness. She steadied herself with the help of the end of the bed. She was barefoot and the cold floor stung the bottoms of her toes. She noticed, as she looked down, a pair of leather slippers resting on the floor at the corner of the bed.

They felt like pure pleasure when she slipped them on. The air had a chilling bite to it. With quiet footsteps, she walked to the window and carefully pushed the curtains aside. Light glared into the room and she shaded her eyes.

Outside, the sun sparkled against a dusting of snow. Tall, majestic trees enchanted the birds, who chirped cheerfully, their beaks pointed toward the sky. The clean, crisp smell of pine found its way to her, and it almost felt like she was standing right in the forest. A rabbit hopped into view, its ears board straight, its eyes wide and alert. What was this, some kind of twisted fairy tale?

She blinked . . . and remembered suddenly that this was not their first encounter. She'd seen him at the grocery store. She'd reached for a package of pasta but dropped it. When she stood back up after stooping to retrieve it, there he was.

"You're . . ." She wanted to whisper and shout it at the same time. "You're Patrick Reagan!"

His face lit in a gracious smile. "I am. And you are?"

She'd gushed about what a big fan she was, what an honor it was to meet him in person.

The memory flashed in and out of her mind, and then she was back at the window, cold and helpless.

Slivers of images winked and glinted inside her thoughts, like pieces of metal buried in sand on a sunny day.

She and Patrick walked on the beach, drinking coffee, the foam of the ocean washing toward their feet.

Then they were on a bench, talking. He wore a fedora and sunglasses. She could see her reflection in them.

But like detached passages from a novel, the scenes were useless in trying to figure out how she ended up being held against her will in a remote cabin.

Jules glanced down at her wrists again, still red and bruised. This was no fairy tale. But why had Patrick Reagan come to usher her into a nightmare?

6

THE LT. COLONEL WAS known for his rigid and unbreakable habits, and right now, that was making Chris's job easier. He and Maecoat had worked two traffic accidents, but now they were in town at the only coffeehouse, Perks, a socialization mecca for the retired crowd during the day. The old folks had even managed to run off the younger crowd—which they'd dubbed the Wi-Fis—by literally taking over the place with dominoes and checkers. It was their last claim to stake and they did it robustly, mostly because the fishing industry was hurting. What had been a thriving industry decades ago lacked manpower these days. This generation didn't want their parents' jobs. They liked technology. So the old generation decided to take it away, one hot spot at a time.

As they pulled to the curb near Perks, Maecoat sighed. "I don't have to go in, do I?"

"If you want coffee, you do."

"You're not going to bring me one back?"

"Come on, I could use some help with this guy. We've got a window here. Afternoon drinking hasn't started yet."

"I'm also lying for you. We never stop on break here and you know it."

Chris rolled his eyes. "I get it. I owe you big-time."

"I'm talking Boston Bruins tickets big-time."

"Fine." Chris started to get out.

"And I want Addy's famous clam chowder."

Chris cocked his head. "Seriously."

"I like when your sister comes into town."

"I'm not a fool. I know it's not the clam chowder you dig."

"Just saying." Maecoat shrugged, glancing toward the coffee shop. "I don't work for free."

"Fine. Hockey tickets. Addy's clam chowder. But don't hit on her."

They walked toward Perks, which was bustling with slow-moving seniors. As they entered, the chime rang and the crowd turned to stare them down.

Chris hoped the Lt. Colonel was still in his same routine, even with his daughter missing. He surveyed the room and quickly spotted him in the corner, nursing a shot of caffeine and what looked like a pretty bad hangover. He wasn't sure he'd ever seen a flattop so disheveled.

They approached cautiously. The man never looked up. "Lt. Colonel."

His gaze rose, then his head. "Chris."

"May we sit, sir?"

He glanced at Maecoat, then said, "Just you. Not him."

Maecoat threw his hands up. "No arguments from me. I'm going to get something frothy."

Chris slid into the other side of the half-moon booth. "How are you holding up?" he asked.

The Lt. Colonel didn't answer for a long time. Then he said, "I don't remember much, but I recall I might've paid you a call at an ungodly hour."

"It's fine, sir. You're entitled. It's your daughter."

He ran his finger along the bottom of his nose. "She's kind to me, and she shouldn't be. I've not been the father I should've been." His eyes stayed on his coffee.

"Sir, I just want to help you find Jules."

"When she was young, I was gone a lot. On the other side of the world. Now I'm still gone, just in a different way."

"You check on her every day. That's something."

"She needed more from me when Jason died. I couldn't give it. Never been able to, which is why I'm alone."

Chris wished he had a cup of coffee to wrap his fidgeting fingers around. "Look, I went to Jules's house again and noticed something. The day she disappeared was their anniversary."

The Lt. Colonel looked up. "Their anniversary?"

"I saw the date on a framed picture of them."

He looked pathetically guilty. "I should know these things. But I wasn't invited to the wedding."

"Since it was their anniversary, maybe she did go off to be by herself for a while. Wouldn't that make sense? Maybe went to a place they enjoyed together?"

"No. That doesn't sound like her. Besides, every anniversary they stayed home and Juliet fixed him one of his favorite dishes. That was their tradition, as best I understood it. They'd go walk on the beach before dinner."

"How do you know this?"

"That blog she writes. Puts a lot of personal stuff on it. I don't agree with it. Have told her that. But it has been her passion. She likes to write. Guess people are interested in that stuff. I think she's got some real literary talent myself, but she doesn't listen to me." He lowered his gaze again. "Sometimes I don't know my daughter unless I read all that blog junk. I try, but there's always this wall between us. Guess my drinking doesn't help."

"Does she use Facebook or Twitter a lot?"

"Son, I don't know what any of that means. It's all I could do to figure out how to read her blog. I read it because she's my daughter, not because I like it. I think all this technology is ruining everything about our society. But don't get me started." He sipped his coffee, kept his eyes low. "What's your gut telling you?"

Chris sighed, glanced toward Maecoat, who was hitting

on the barista. "That we don't have enough evidence of foul play. But I don't think there is evidence she took off somewhere either. There didn't seem to be clothes missing from her closet, and her suitcases were still there. Granted, neither of those things are proof. She could've used another bag and just taken a few items. But I'm going to keep looking."

"She's all I got left." His bottom lip quivered.

"I know. I promise I will do everything I can to find her. I . . ." The words caught in his throat. "I made a promise to Jason that I would watch out for her."

The Lt. Colonel crushed the paper coffee cup in his hand. "I guess we've both failed, then."

"The grocery store? Now?" Maecoat said, clawing at his cheek. While flirting with the barista, he'd managed to down four espressos and something with caramel. "I say we drive around and look for those teenagers who've been vandalizing the bridge. Get a good foot chase going."

"This won't take long," Chris said, parking the car. "Stay here if you—"

"Can't. Feel like walking."

"Fine."

"Why are we here again?"

"The Lt. Colonel said she always went to the store on Tuesdays. He also said for their anniversary she always cooked Jason his favorite meal. So I think it stands a chance that she might've come here."

"I am pretty sure the captain would be having a cow right now if he—"

"I need you to give me a break and stop complaining," Chris said, snapping his gaze sideways toward his partner. He liked Maecoat, but the dude could be awfully self-absorbed. Jason would've never whined like this.

"I just don't get the urgency."

"I know you don't. It's personal for me, okay? So let's leave it there."

They walked in and Chris took a photo out of his pocket of Jason and Jules. He talked to a couple of cashiers, but neither of them remembered if Jules had come in. They knew her to be a regular but didn't know when they'd last seen her. Maecoat went to question the guys in produce and the meat department.

After talking to the last cashier and the manager, to no avail, Chris noticed a teenager wearing a black shirt and pants staring at him from the far corner of the store. When Chris put his full attention on him, the kid quickly turned away.

Chris approached him. "What's your name?"

The kid looked up, shoved his hands in his pockets, and swayed back and forth.

"What's your name, son?"

"Seth Steven Moreman."

There was something off about him. Why wasn't he making eye contact? "Am I making you nervous?" Chris asked, stepping closer.

"Everyone makes me nervous." He looked at Chris's gun. "I like your gun. It's a Glock 22."

"You like guns, do you?"

"Yes. I can name every gun made just by seeing a picture. I can also tell you what kind of bullet each uses. The earliest known English breech-loading rifle was made in 1689, and the entire English army was equipped with flintlocks by 1690. The first patent for a single trigger lock was registered by James Templeman. The patent number was 1707."

If Jules were a gun, this kid might be helpful.

"Why are you here?" Seth asked.

Chris pulled out his picture. "I'm looking for this woman."

"She was here on Tuesday at 10:47 a.m."

Chris held the picture closer. "You're sure? Her?"

"Yes. Positive. She comes every Tuesday."

"But I'm concerned only with this last Tuesday."

"She was here."

Now Chris was concerned about why he knew so much about Jules's grocery store habits. "What makes you sure that you're right?"

"I'm right."

"How do I know you haven't mixed up the dates?"

"I never mix up dates." The boy finally made eye contact, looking highly offended.

"Maybe you're remembering wrong."

"I am not," the boy said emphatically.

"What was she wearing?"

"I don't know."

"You know she was here, down to the minute, but don't know what she was wearing?"

"I don't like clothes. Colors bother me. I try not to look at them."

Chris took a deep breath. "Did you talk to her?"

"I don't talk to customers. I only sack their groceries, and we don't offer plastic, so their only choice is paper. I don't have to ask them which they want."

"So she bought groceries?"

"Yes."

"What did she buy?"

"I don't know."

"I'm still having a hard time understanding how you remember this," Chris said pointedly.

"I have a memory of her for two reasons. First, she is nice. She always says hello to me even though I don't say hello back."

"And the second?"

"It was the day that he came in."

"Who?"

"Patrick Reagan."

"The writer?"

"Of course. He's one of the most brilliant writers our country has to offer. He was raised on a farm in Pennsylvania. His mother was a seamstress. His father worked the mines. He's sold over ten million books, though his critics believe he sold out to commercialism. Before that, he won a Pulitzer for fiction when he was only twenty-eight."

"That's grand. I don't read his stuff."

"You should."

"So let me get this straight. You remember that Juliet Belleno came in on Tuesday at 10:47 a.m. because it was the same day that author Patrick Reagan came in."

"The same time, too."

"Okay."

"It was unusual that he was here in the winter. He does not live here in the winter. He has a cabin up in the mountains somewhere."

"Let's get back to Juliet. Do you remember her leaving the store?"

"Yes."

"Did she seem distraught?"

"No."

"Did she talk to anyone while she was here?"

"I don't know. Not while she was checking out."

"Okay. Thank you for your help."

Chris turned to find Maecoat walking toward him, a small sack in his hands.

"What? It's a snack for later. Find out anything useful?"

"Yeah. She was definitely here on Tuesday, according to Seth over there."

"Well, we know they don't have surveillance footage. None of these stores are equipped for it," Maecoat said. And it was true. Much of the town had not caught up to the technology that would greatly help the police department. And liked it that way. Some of the lobster boats weren't even equipped with GPS, much to the frustration of the Coast Guard.

"At least we know she was here. That's where we start trying to figure out what happened."

"Where to next?"

"The beach."

"I was hoping you'd say the speed trap."

IT WAS THE SAME DAY, she assumed, when Jules woke again. By peering out the window, she could tell the approximate time. The sun's light was warmer and softly hued. She'd been sleepy all day, napping on and off as if it were a lazy Sunday and she had a paper to read. But there was nothing to do but lie on the bed and try to figure out her circumstances.

She'd concluded a while back that she was not dreaming. There was something extremely tangible about it all, her dizzy head notwithstanding. More than anything, it was the vivid smells around her that caused her to believe this was all real. The soup was the most fragrant she'd ever smelled, like it had cooked for hours. She could taste the fresh herbs in it.

The cream was divine. Despite her lack of appetite earlier, she'd eaten heartily, crackers and all.

She'd not seen Patrick Reagan again, however. She listened for sound outside her door, but it was very quiet.

Anxiety was starting to overcome her as the dizziness in her head faded. She sat on the edge of the bed and chewed through her fingernails, eyeing the door. She'd already tried the window. It was locked down and the glass looked thick.

As the once-bright sunlight dimmed outside the window, she planted her feet firmly on the ground, without the slippers, and stomped across the cold wood floor. She hadn't checked to see if the door was really locked. She firmly grasped the handle but it didn't budge. She made a fist and began pounding. It felt good. Released some of the aggression she was feeling.

"Hey!" She put her face close to the door. "Hey! You! Let me out of here! Do you understand me? You can't hold me here! You can't do this!" It sounded so ridiculous coming out of her mouth. First of all, he obviously could, or she wouldn't be here. Secondly, she was yelling through a thick wooden door at her favorite author, who had kidnapped her. Between the shouts, she'd take a breath and wonder if she was really losing her mind. Maybe, just maybe, it had fractured.

But along with the smell of the soup, she'd smelled him when he'd delivered it. It wasn't cologne—too light for that. But there was a certain scent that reminded her of a walk in the woods. Or Christmas. Pine, maybe? Musk?

"Heeeeyyyyy!" Her voice had risen to a screeching pitch.

Then, footsteps.

Jules breathed hard. Stepped back a little.

Silence.

"Listen to me! I want you to let me out right now!" She stepped forward again. "Now! Right now! Now!"

Another sound. A key in the door. She took several steps back, put her hands on her hips, waited.

As the door slowly opened, she wished her chest wasn't moving up and down so rapidly. She planned to take a stand or defend herself if he attacked her, and she had enough adrenaline for either, but it was showing itself a bit too early.

Patrick Reagan regarded her for a moment, and she regarded him. His hair, just like in the picture on the back of his books, was soft brown and wavy, flowing back like a tidal wave. He didn't wear a particular expression as he looked at her.

Jules tried to find a few words, but nothing came out. As usual.

He stepped into the room and then looked her up and down. "Why are you still in your nightclothes?"

She glanced down at the luxurious pajamas she'd found herself in when she'd first awoken. "Maybe I should be asking you how *this* happened?" she growled, gesturing wildly at herself.

"You dressed yourself," he said. "I suggest you do it again. I don't serve supper to people in their pajamas."

Suddenly she felt improper, as though she were a houseguest who'd rudely overslept. But that thought was so *weird*.

She folded her arms, tried to speak slowly. "Dress code aside, what is going on here?"

"All in due time." He gestured toward a closet. "You'll find something suitable in there."

I'm not interested in this bizarre bed-and-breakfast you're running, she thought, wishing she could speak as harshly as it sounded in her head. "I want to go home."

He coolly put his hands in his pockets. He wasn't overly tall, probably not even six feet, but he seemed to tower over her with his presence. "Do you really, Juliet? You really want to go home? It's that fulfilling, all by yourself, peering at a computer screen?"

"Don't act like you know me."

"But I do."

"How is that? We've never met before this."

"You're a fan, are you not?"

Was. Less so by the second.

"You're quieter than I imagined you to be. You don't come across that way on paper." He gave a small smile.

Jules whispered, "You spied on me?"

He laughed. "I don't have to spy on you. You bare your soul every day, don't you? For all the world to see?"

Jules glanced at the ceiling. "You read my blog?"

"Isn't that the point? That people read it? Don't you hope they get to know you?"

"But . . ." *Him?*

"You've been disappointed by my last three books."

Jules took a deep breath. That was what this was about?

Her mind scrambled to remember the words she'd used to show her discontentment with his latest work. They didn't seem harsh at the time, but as she stood in front of him now, her review did seem . . . regrettable. "It's not personal," she mumbled.

"It's not personal for whom?" he asked. "You? Or me?"

Neither. She'd critiqued it as a piece of literature. She put her trembling hands behind her. "I didn't mean for the review to hurt you."

"If you'd known I'd be reading it, you would have perhaps chosen your words more carefully?"

Jules's nostrils flared at the insanity of the entire situation. She found herself growing bold. "I actually chose my words quite carefully. I always do."

"So you meant every word?"

How was she to play this? She studied his eyes. There was a gentle, wise veil to them. "Yes. I meant every word." She pressed her lips together and kept eye contact. "And if you must know, I am not a fair-weather fan. I am still as loyal as ever."

He blinked as if he was not expecting that answer. Then he turned. "Get yourself presentable. Dinner will be ready in twenty minutes."

He closed the door and did not lock it. Jules let out a breath and a cry, covering her mouth as she rewound the conversation in her head.

"Jason . . ." Tears filled her eyes and spilled over. "You're not going to believe what is happening to me."

Near the window was a closet with a sliding wooden door. Inside, she found an array of nice winter clothing, ranging from sweaters and shawls to slacks. No jeans or sweats. The shoes she'd worn to the grocery store were neatly placed on the floor next to some other shoes she didn't recognize.

She changed in the bathroom—a cold, overly tiled, suffocating room. Inside the medicine cabinet were a new toothbrush, toothpaste, mouthwash. But on the counter she found another toothbrush that appeared to have been used and half a tube of toothpaste. Next to it was a hairbrush, hair tangled around it. She picked it up and for the first time noticed herself in the mirror. Her eyes were bloodshot and she looked pale and drawn. It reminded her of how she'd looked the morning after she learned Jason had been shot to death. She remembered waking up after maybe thirty minutes of sleep and staring in the mirror. She didn't even recognize the woman who stared back at her.

But something told her that she'd better look the part of a pulled-together woman, because the man holding her had to be unraveling in some way. If she seemed composed, maybe she could talk some sense into him. Or better yet, run for her life.

She set the brush down. One thought kept scrolling through her head: Patrick Reagan read her blog. It never occurred to her that he might. Would she have said things differently? Had she been unintentionally cruel?

She washed her face and then noticed, on a small vanity near the tub, a beautiful silver watch set out as if on display.

She picked it up and marveled at all the diamonds. If she wanted to be on time for dinner, maybe she should wear it. But the time had stopped, at twelve o'clock on the dot. It seemed odd to her that she didn't even know what time it was.

Turning toward the door of the bedroom, she walked with weak knees. Somehow she was going to have to gather the strength to face what was on the other side. Because the writing on the wall made her fairly sure his intentions were to truly terrify her.

⌐ ∟

His shift had ended two hours earlier, with a lecture from Maecoat about how he needed to let things rest for a couple of days. Jules would probably return.

"You're right," Chris had said with an assuring smile as they walked out of headquarters, all the while making plans to head straight back to Jason's house.

The sun was setting earlier, and by the time he grabbed something to eat, it was almost entirely dark. He drove his pickup over to the Belleno home. He doubted the house would be locked, and he planned to use this to his advantage.

But standing on the porch, he found that the door was locked, much to his dismay. Had the Lt. Colonel gotten it locked again? With a matchstick? Or did someone else have a key?

He rattled the door again, but it was definitely dead-bolted.

So now what? He knew how to pick a lock. But should he? What if the captain found out? All these thoughts were swirling around in his mind when the dead bolt turned and the door opened.

"Lt. Colonel," Chris said, trying not to sound bewildered.

"Chriiii . . ." He opened his arms. "Come in, on in." He stumbled backward while maintaining a sloppy smile. "She's not back, if you were wandering . . . wondering."

"Where is your truck?"

"I'm not sure."

Chris followed him in and shut the door. "I came by because I wanted to look at her computer," he said, watching the Lt. Colonel lurch toward the couch, where he plopped down.

"You got some way to track her with it?" He picked up a bottle of bourbon from the table.

"I have some new information," Chris said, sitting down at the desk near the couches. "She was at the grocery store Tuesday. Midmorning."

The Lt. Colonel leaned forward. "You sure?"

"A kid there remembered her, a sacker."

"So what does that mean?"

"It means she was in her regular routine."

"What does the computer have to do with any of it?" He was now settling back into the cushions, listing slightly to the right.

"I want to look at her Facebook page and her blog, see if that offers any clues." Chris cleared his throat. "This needs to

RENE GUTTERIDGE

stay between us, sir. Technically, there is no official investigation and I shouldn't be doing this."

"Well then, get to looking," he said; then his gaze wandered to the ceiling like there might be something of interest going on up there. "I'm no fan of your procedures anyway."

By the time Chris had Jules's computer out of sleep mode, the Lt. Colonel's head had tipped backward and he was snoring. Chris counted that as a blessing.

He was hoping her Facebook page was still logged in. When he woke the computer, her page pulled right up. This time he checked her statuses over the last week. Some were generic, but others offered more clues about the fact that her anniversary with Jason was coming up.

He read carefully, including the day she disappeared. The day before she was supposedly seen at the store, her status read, *Making pasta from scratch tomorrow.* That offered no clue that she was going to the store or at what time. But as he trailed backward through her posts, there was an obvious pattern—enough to know that she was in a routine. Someone could easily garner enough information to know what she was up to. The problem was, she had nearly two thousand Facebook friends. How could he know which one had intentions of harming her, if she was harmed at all?

The Lt. Colonel groaned and rolled to the side, his head awkwardly turned in to one of the cushions, his mouth hanging open like he was in midsentence.

Chris returned his attention to the computer. He spent an hour reading through her blogs. She was passionate about her hometown, about Maine, about all that her state had to offer, and about . . . Patrick Reagan. Her last post had been about his latest book, *The Lion's Mouth*. The review wasn't favorable.

Chris sat back in his chair, mumbling through thoughts, wondering if there was a connection in the fact that Patrick Reagan was at the grocery store at the same time.

"Ridiculous, Downey." He got up from the desk as his mind nagged at him to reconsider the possibility. It was clear that Jules had an affectionate admiration for the author. But most of this town did.

Chris, like everyone, knew where the author lived. It was a sprawling estate a mile from the coast. The house was impressive. Built in 1842, it had belonged to a host of famous personalities through the ages. He thought Reagan had lived there about three decades. Whatever the case, it kept the department busy whenever a book released—always a traffic problem as tourists drove by, attempting to get a glimpse of the king of suspense. But Seth was right—as far as he knew, Reagan spent the winters elsewhere.

Later that evening, Chris was still pondering it all at his kitchen table when Addy arrived home following dinner out with the girlfriends she liked to visit when she came into town.

Addy eyed him coming in, got a carton of ice cream out of the freezer, and grabbed two spoons, joining him at the table. "Whatever this is, it requires ice cream," she said, sliding a spoon toward him.

"Wish I had an appetite," he said.

"No one needs an appetite when it comes to ice cream. Come on, eat up. Sugar helps you think."

Chris obeyed. "By the way, please don't give Maecoat the time of day."

"Greg?"

"Call him Maecoat, please. *Greg* sounds like you're friends, and I really don't want you to be friends with him."

"I thought you liked him."

"He's fine. I do. But he's really girl crazy."

Addy smiled. "Thanks, but I can handle myself."

"The problem is that he can't. You see what I'm saying?"

"Thanks for the heads-up."

"Also, I told him you'd fix him your famous clam chowder."

"He owes you for something."

Chris sighed. "Yeah."

She twirled the spoon in her mouth. "I guess Jules hasn't shown up?"

"No. Last seen at the grocery store as far as I can tell."

"Still nothing unusual coming up?"

"No, not really." Chris set his spoon down after only a couple of bites. "Tell me what you know about Patrick Reagan."

"The author?"

"Yeah."

Addy shrugged. "I'm not a fan. Too commercial for my taste. I mean, I know he lives here—I know which house. But that's about it."

"He's supposedly a recluse, right?"

"That's what I hear."

"Tell me I'm crazy, okay? But Jules wrote an unfavorable review of his book on her blog the morning she disappeared. Then this kid at the grocery store tells me that Patrick Reagan was there at the same time Jules was."

Addy considered it for a moment. "Well, okay. Could be a coincidence."

"Kid also said he doesn't spend the winters here. He's always at some cabin in the woods."

"Sounds mysterious."

"Yeah. But is it wacked out to think there could be a connection?"

"So you're saying that Reagan takes Jules because she wrote a bad review of his book?"

"Crazy, right?"

"Yeah. A little bit." She scooped more ice cream. "I mean, first of all, how would he know her? And how would he know she would be at the grocery store at that exact time?"

Chris nodded. "Exactly. Except . . ."

"Except?"

"I got on her Facebook page and her blog. If someone was following her posts, they could pretty easily figure out a pattern. And she is definitely a pattern girl."

"So she always goes to the store at the same time, on that same day?"

"Yes, according to her father."

Addy nodded. "Well, then I guess it's not that far-fetched, is it?"

"Isn't it, though?" Chris put his head in his hands. "It's ludicrous. Authors don't kidnap fans because of bad reviews. The dude has written a ton of books. Surely this is not the first bad review he's received. Aren't they supposed to have thick skins and all that?"

"I knew many writers in college. One was a close friend. He was a sensitive dude. Wrote romance. But I figured you have to be in touch with a lot of feelings to be able to write well."

"Yes, well, this guy writes about murder and mayhem. What kind of feelings is he in touch with?"

Addy put the lid back on the ice cream. "You're not going to let this go, I'm assuming?"

"How can I? She's Jason's wife. Widow . . ."

"Then I think you better go find Patrick Reagan."

ALL SHE HEARD WAS a room full of people laughing. Then a single voice. Then more laughter, like they all were in the presence of the funniest person alive. Patrick Reagan didn't strike her as even the tiniest bit humorous.

Unsure what to do, Jules stood for a moment at the bedroom door, trying to process yet another bizarre moment in her day.

As she listened more carefully, she realized she was hearing a TV. Along with being humorless, he didn't strike her as being a TV watcher either. For some reason she pictured him sitting near a fire in a dark turtleneck, smoking a pipe with Spanish tobacco in it, reading James Joyce for pleasure.

The man had graduated with honors from Yale, though he'd been outspoken about his dislike for the school ever since. His mother had been a seamstress, his father a coal miner who'd died tragically in a car accident in New York when Patrick was just fifteen.

He'd implied over the years, in the few interviews he gave, that his mother never accepted his career in literature and that she felt he had a mind meant more for science. Whatever the case, Jules thought he was suited perfectly for what he did. From what she'd read, he was always a bit embarrassed by the widespread success of his novels and their commercial appeal. But to her, it didn't in any way diminish his talent. He had such a command of the English language and used words in a way that made her want to read and reread everything he wrote.

Blinking her way back to the fact that she was still standing by the door, she heard the voices again and realized it was, indeed, the canned laughter of a sitcom.

Jules opened the door and stepped lightly into the hall. As she rounded the corner, she saw a warm, comfortable-looking living room with leather chairs and couches and bookshelves on every wall, each running as high as the ceiling.

Patrick sat with his back to her, leaning forward, engaged in what he was watching. The TV was small, but a modern flat-screen. She held her breath, taking in as much as she could. The room had a fireplace, but no fire. Off to the right looked to be a kitchen, painted dark red, with a dinner table in a very small dining area off the kitchen. Another hallway was just opposite where she stood, but she couldn't tell where it led. There were two doors on either side of the cabin. Both looked like front doors.

Patrick chuckled suddenly, right along with the laugh track. Jules didn't know which show he was watching; she didn't watch TV very much herself. But it looked like maybe *Mary Tyler Moore*.

Her hand slowly made it to her mouth as she began to realize where she might be. The cabin? The famous cabin? Nobody knew where the rumor came from that there was a hidden mountain cabin somewhere in Maine or one of the New England states. Some even speculated it was in Canada. But it was legendary among his fans as the place Patrick Reagan retreated to every winter to write his books.

Was she really here? Could it be?

Outside, it was almost completely dark. But it all made sense. She'd peeked out the window earlier and seen trees, like she was in the middle of the forest.

"You're early."

She gasped, not realizing he'd even turned to notice her. "I'm . . . I'm sorry."

"You've interrupted my show," he grumbled, picking up the remote and shutting the TV off.

"I'm sorry. Please, don't mind me. . . ." The words sounded ridiculous as they spilled out. But she always sounded ridiculous when she spoke. "I just didn't want to be late."

"Hm." He eyed her, then went to the table, pulling out a chair for her.

Jules sat and he gently scooted her forward. On the table were shiny brown ceramic bowls, with a silver spoon to the right of each one, a napkin neatly folded over the bowl, and water glasses already filled with ice.

He took her bowl, went to the stove, and dipped something into it from a large, cast-iron pot. When he returned, the bowl was steaming and smelled amazing. It looked to be stew. Maybe lamb stew. He brought to the table a loaf of Italian bread, already sliced, on a cutting board.

She waited patiently, her hands trembling underneath the table.

Patrick joined her shortly, his own bowl filled. He sat down and stared at her for a long moment. She was hungry again, though her stomach churned with uneasiness that hid the hunger from time to time.

"I am going to give you this warning one more time," he said. He looked toward the door to her left, where a rack held several coats and two pairs of boots sat underneath. "Do not try to escape. It is too treacherous out there. More snow is expected tonight, and we are in a very remote place. You'll die on this mountain if you try to get away."

"Are you going to harm me?"

"Why would you ask such a thing?"

Jules glared. *Why would I ask such a thing? I don't know—I'm locked away in a room, with words scrawled across the ceiling—*

"Did you intend to harm *me*?" he asked.

"What?"

"When you wrote those words? Those are your words on the ceiling."

She sighed and stared at the steam rising from her bowl. "So this is what it's all about. I hurt your feelings." She looked up to gauge his reaction. He seemed calm enough, but there was something raging in those eyes.

"I'm only doing what you asked," he said. "You asked me to terrify you, so here we are. Boo."

A lump formed in her throat and she picked up her spoon. "I'm hungry. If you don't mind, I'd like to bless the food and eat."

"Do what you must." He picked up his own spoon and began to eat.

Jules closed her eyes, too scared to really pray, but it was a habit that Jason had introduced her to when they met, and she couldn't recall a single meal she'd eaten since that was not blessed in this way.

Help me, Jason.

She opened her eyes to find Patrick watching her from across the table. Jules took a bite of the stew—delicious. She gobbled down more. The bread was soft on the inside, chewy on the outside. She tried to focus on it for a little while.

"So your complaint," he said between bites, "is that I didn't scare you enough in the book."

Jules looked up, trying to decide if he really wanted an answer. As she engaged his eyes, it seemed to her he was a man acquainted with deep sorrow.

She stirred her spoon around in her bowl. "How did I get here?"

"A question for a question."

"My husband asked a lot of questions, and he was good at his job, so I guess it rubbed off on me." She tried to think about the last thing she remembered. "I was at the store, buying things to make dinner, and as I walked to the parking lot . . ." That's where things got fuzzy for her. Had she bumped into him there? She remembered a conversation but couldn't pull any of the details.

"Not just any dinner."

"Excuse me?"

"You weren't buying groceries for just any dinner, were you?"

"How do you know that?"

"As you look out of that little window every day, do you wonder where all your words go?"

"I didn't say anything about Jason or our . . ." Her words trailed off as she tried to hold back tears.

He gestured toward her bowl with his spoon. "Eat up."

She did, silently, for the rest of the meal. She hated how much he thought he knew about her from her blog or whatever else he was reading. He wasn't on her Facebook page. She would've remembered friending Patrick Reagan.

"Do you feel a lot of guilt?" he asked suddenly, as he finished his own bowl.

"About what?"

"About Jason's death remaining unavenged."

"I don't know what you're talking about,"

"They never caught the men who shot him, did they?" He wiped his mouth. "It was in the newspapers for a while. Then it went away. Everyone sort of forgot, didn't they? Life goes on all around you, but you can't seem to go on."

"You don't know anything about me." She threw her napkin on the table and scooted her chair back.

"I know more than you think."

"Good for you." Tears dripped down her face. "So if you've set out to freak me out of my everlasting mind, you . . . well, congratulations." His face filled with an expression that seemed to indicate not surprise at her tirade, but something else. "What do you want from me?"

"You've got it all wrong, Juliet. It's what you want from me." His voice would have been soothing and calming in any other circumstance.

"What I want is home. To go there. Now."

He nodded. "Of course you do. That's where you believe your life is. Don't you think I understand that?"

She noticed the fingers of his right hand twisting the wedding band he wore. His wife had died three years ago, according to the papers.

"You don't think people will be looking for me?"

"People? Who would that be? With whom do you still associate?"

"My father." She sniffled away the rest of her emotion. "He will look for me."

"Is he the one who drinks so heavily?" He paused, smiled mildly. "I'm good at reading between the lines."

Jules sighed a loud exasperation. "So you have me. Now what are you going to do with me?"

"That is the trouble with this younger generation. No patience."

"No. The trouble here is that you've kidnapped me. Against my will."

"This is what you want. Trust me."

"Did you read that between the lines too? Somewhere in the middle of my post about the history of our lighthouses?"

He regarded her a moment, then stood and carried his bowl to the sink. Normally she would do the same, even as a guest, but she refused and let her bowl just sit there. He rinsed his and washed it thoroughly by hand. As he dried it, he turned to face her. "You can't be that ignorant, to believe that there are not layers to what you write, what we all write. I remember you wrote on your blog about all the meanings one single scene had for you in . . . *Die Gently*, I believe."

Jules threw her hands up. "Awesome. Maybe later we can gather the two of us and have a book club."

"You're not as well-spoken as I'd imagined."

Now more angry than scared, she glared at him. "The fact that you've been imagining me at all is creepy."

Suddenly he looked wounded. Or confused. Something flickered across his face but she couldn't capture it fast enough. "I see."

She bit her lip. If she was going to get out of here, she needed to think—and speak—more wisely.

"Sorry," she offered. "I guess I'm just kind of wound up at the sheer . . . weirdness of it all. I mean, not everyone can say they've been kidnapped by their favorite author."

"You don't have to placate me."

"I'm not. I've read everything you've ever written, even your short stories from your early years. I wait all year long for your next book. You're a terrific writer. One of the best. But you already know how I feel."

"Hmm."

"I just don't know what I'm doing here." Tears stung her eyes again. As normal as she wanted to sound, none of this was normal.

He blinked slowly, as if he were sleepy or bored or following distant thoughts.

"Why don't you pick a book." He pointed to his collection.

Jules gazed at the walls. There had to be thousands of books there.

She didn't really feel like picking a book, but his mood had shifted and she was starting to feel less bold and more scared again. She pretended to gaze at the selection, though her mind was reeling about how she might alert someone she was here. She had yet to see a phone or a computer. Just a TV.

She scanned the shelf in front of her. A lot of classics: Tolstoy, Dostoyevsky, Faulkner, Hemingway. The list went on. She pulled *If on a Winter's Night a Traveler* by Italo Calvino from the shelf.

Patrick smirked as he noticed and gave her a small "how clever" smile. He then busied himself with cleaning her bowl and didn't seem to care or notice much more. With his back still turned, he finally said, "Off to your room."

"I don't really want to stay in there. It's cold and . . . and I'm alone."

He set the bowl down and turned to her. "You are right that you are alone." He paused. "I have never brought a visitor here, so respect the privilege."

Clutching the book, Jules walked back to her room and closed the door. After a few moments, she heard the door lock.

Crawling onto the bed, she pulled the quilt that was neatly folded at the end over her legs. She curled up into a ball and cried. Then she prayed to Jason, that he would hear her and rescue her like he had so many years before.

Outside her room, she heard the canned, carnivalish laughter of another sitcom.

9

CHRIS STOOD ON THE PORCH, hands deep in his pockets, hoping that 9:30 p.m. was not too late. By the long pause that followed his ringing of the doorbell, it seemed it might be. He'd been to the captain's house only one other time, for a Christmas party right before Jason died.

Finally a shadow moved across the small window to the left of the door. Then he heard locks being unlocked.

The door opened and Captain Perry stood in sweats and a Boston Red Sox T-shirt. "Downey?"

"Sir, I wanted to see if I could talk with you for a little bit."

The captain widened the door and stepped aside. "I'm glad you're here, actually. I've been wanting to talk to you."

That didn't sound good, but Chris walked in, following the captain into a small sitting room, with a floral decor that looked like the wife had been 100 percent involved. The captain turned on a couple of lamps, and they took seats opposite one another.

The captain had aged pretty drastically over the past couple of years, ever since Jason's death. His hair was almost completely white and deep wrinkles were etching their way into both cheeks.

"Sir, I've been investigating Juliet Belleno's disappearance." Chris waited, watching for the captain's reaction to his insubordination.

The captain sighed and rubbed his forehead with a thumb and forefinger, like he was trying to pull the wrinkles off. "I know."

"You do?" Chris cleared his throat. "It's just that . . . it's Jason."

"I know," the captain said again, his expression softening. "The Lt. Colonel giving you fits?"

"Yeah, a little," Chris said. "But he's doing okay. Very worried, as you can imagine."

"So what have you turned up?"

"Well, there's no sign of forced entry, and everything seems to be in place. I probably would've left it at that, except . . ."

"Yeah?"

"This is going to sound crazy. But I talked to this kid at the grocery store, and he said he was certain Jules had been in on Tuesday morning. He distinctly remembered it because he said that Patrick Reagan was also in that morning."

"Patrick Reagan was at the grocery store?"

"Yes. And the kid said it was significant because Reagan doesn't stay here in the winter. He apparently has some mountain cabin he goes to."

"That's the rumor. But he's sure he saw Patrick Reagan?"

"He was more than sure. I guess he's a fan. So here's the weird part. I was going over Jules's last blog to see if there were any clues about what's going on. Her last post was a review of Reagan's latest book, and it wasn't flattering. I know it's so far-fetched, but I can't help wondering if it was a coincidence that Reagan was at the grocery store at the same time as Jules."

"How would he know that? You think he followed her?"

"Maybe. She inadvertently gives a lot of clues to her whereabouts on Facebook, as most people do. But he doesn't seem to be a friend on her page. I don't know," Chris said, running his fingers over the top of his head. "I know this sounds implausible and all that. But I don't feel like I can just look the other way, let it work itself out. She's Jason's wife, you know?"

"You keep reminding me of that, but that's no good reason for going behind my back, Downey." The captain seemed deep in thought. "I know you want to do all you can to help her."

Chris stared at the carpet. "That's the thing. I haven't, really. I told Jason before he died that I'd take care of her if anything happened, but Jules didn't want to be around anybody and I didn't push back. I just let her be."

"You can't help someone who doesn't want to be helped." Captain Perry leaned back and stared at Chris for a moment. "How are you doing with Jason's death?"

Chris shrugged. "You just go on."

"I really wish we'd gotten those guys. I wish with everything in me, you know?" The captain traced the armrest of the couch with a thumb. "You're sleeping okay at night, all of that?"

"All of that," Chris said plaintively. After Jason died, he'd been given a piece of paper with a list of things to watch out for, symptoms that he might be sliding into depression. He'd tossed it before he even left the police station. It wasn't what he wanted to hear.

Yeah, he'd had sleepless nights. So what. Shouldn't he? How could he rest peacefully knowing the guys who murdered his partner were still roaming around out there?

"Anyway," Chris said, "I think the Reagan angle is worth checking out. I'd like to get a search warrant and take a look around his home here."

"That's going to get dicey."

"I know."

"Rumor is, nobody can get ahold of Reagan during his 'writing season.'"

"I get it. Probable cause is going to be a factor."

The captain looked irritated but focused. He stared hard at Chris. "He was your partner, so I suspect you're not going to be able to let this go."

"No, sir. It seems it's the least I can do."

The captain sighed. "The DA owes me a favor or ten. I'll see what I can do about getting us a search warrant. It's going to be a complicated mess. We may move more slowly than you'd like. But I'll officially open an investigation."

"I'll take what I can get."

"Do you think you can keep the Lt. Colonel in line?"

"If I can show him we're making some progress, I guess I can."

"That guy gets on my nerves. He's radical and crazy in the head, you know?"

"If we can show him Jules is okay, I think he'll be grateful, maybe give us less of a hard time."

"We can only hope."

Chris smiled and stood to shake the captain's hand. "Sir, thanks for the time. Sorry to disturb you at this late hour."

"No problem. Get some rest, okay?"

They walked to the door.

"You know," the captain said, "I met Patrick Reagan a couple of years ago."

"I remember he came to the station a lot for a while, but I was on shift mostly, didn't run into him."

"Yeah. The governor called the DA asking for this special favor. Reagan was researching a book, wanted access to the police department and all that. Interviews. Wanted to look through random evidence and files, just for a feel of how it all worked."

"How was he?"

"Didn't really see him much. He came in at weird hours, didn't converse, except I remember he wanted to interview one of the detectives, Walker. Walker agreed. That was about it. He was around for maybe two weeks, then disappeared, except to send like five hundred cookies from France to the department as a thank-you. I hear he's a brilliant guy, but the man is quirky to say the least." The captain yawned. "Old men like me have to get to bed early. You take care of yourself, Chris. I'll keep you updated on the progress we're making on the search warrant."

Chris stepped out into the cold, feeling a little more assured that at least the captain believed there was something to look into. And it was nice not to sneak around anymore. He was afraid his theory that Reagan might be involved was going to get him laughed out of the state. It felt as kooky as it sounded coming off his tongue.

He took out his phone and called the Lt. Colonel. Calling him at night seemed like the best time. He'd most likely be passed out and Chris could just leave him a message. He didn't want to give him too much information, especially about Reagan. The last thing he needed was the Lt. Colonel hounding their most famous resident.

He left a short message about the opening of an official investigation and tried to leave out as much detail as possible.

Then he drove twelve miles to the cemetery where they'd buried Jason. It was over a hundred years old, with tall pines clustered on the five acres. Jason was buried in the northeast corner with the rest of his family, including great-grandparents. With no siblings and his parents dead, Jason had been the last living member of his immediate family.

Chris shrugged under his heavy leather jacket, trying to stay warm. A brisk wind snapped and jumped through the trees and over the hills, lifting his hair and stinging his skin. Winter had arrived far too early this year.

Above, the stars twinkled brightly away from the town's lights, and a gentle light glowed down onto the grave site. Chris walked the unpaved path to the far side of the cemetery and easily found Jason's headstone, shorter and squarer than the rest.

He knelt beside it, reading the inscriptions about Jason: a loving husband, loyal friend, faithful officer. The grass was withering against the early cold, but it was thick and had grown in well.

From his back pocket, Chris pulled a bent and worn picture out of his wallet. It was of Jules and Jason, their engagement photo. Chris had given him a hard time when he was handing them out, teasing that he'd been domesticated in the worst sort of way . . . downsized to a wallet picture.

Jason took it all in stride. He laughed so much at himself that it was hard to give him a good ribbing because it seemed nothing really insulted him.

Chris had taken the picture, vowing to do something with it, like a practical joke. But it ended up staying in his wallet, the only picture he carried there.

He held it up a little to get a good look at it in the dim light. They were so happy; their eyes had an extra, magical sparkle to them. But as far as Chris was concerned, Jules always had that look. The first time Jason brought her to O'Malley's to meet the guys, Chris had found himself unable to stop staring at her. She was naturally beautiful and Chris wasn't sure she was wearing any makeup. And her smile was wide but gentle, like she knew everything about you instantly and still liked you.

She was quiet most of the time but had begun coming out of her shell the more comfortable she became with Jason's friends, and Chris found she actually had a pretty good sense of humor when she wasn't too shy to use it.

He'd guarded himself from liking her too much, out of respect for Jason, but she became the woman that all other women were judged against in Chris's book. And unfortunately for those women, they had a high standard to reach. None had, so far.

Chris set the photo against the headstone and moved a nearby rock to hold it in place.

"I'm going to bring her back," Chris said as he stood. "I'm going to bring her home safely. If it's the last thing I do."

10

WHEN JULES AWOKE, the curtains were wide-open. The light filled the room so dramatically that she held her hand up to her eyes as if she were out at the beach with the sun glaring off the sand.

She sat up. She was certain she'd closed the curtains last night. Then she noticed the door to her bedroom was open. She hurried over and shut it. There was no lock on her side of the door, but she leaned against it, breathing hard. She'd hoped as she wept herself to sleep last night that she'd wake up in the morning and be back home.

Or maybe that she wouldn't wake up at all.

She walked as quietly as possible to the bathroom and

shut the door. It didn't have a lock either. She washed her face and brushed her teeth. In the closet, she picked an outfit—a warm sweater and matching slacks. She slid on her shoes. The wrong style for what she was wearing, but that was the least of her concerns.

Her heart pounded wildly as she geared herself up for walking out of the room. She'd thought last night about how she might get herself out of this predicament. She knew Jason would want her to think, to keep her wits, to stay strong and aware and astute. Every time he worked some tragedy, he'd come home with tips. A woman drove her car into the water, so Jason showed Jules how to escape a car if she were underwater. A teenager was kidnapped a few years back, so Jason gave her ideas of how she might handle the situation, pretending to go along until there was a moment she could get away. He'd even cautioned her about her Facebook page and her blog, not to tell everyone she was going out to the store or that they were leaving on vacation. He was such a cautious man, and she loved him for it. But the truth was, he'd always made her feel safe and she never feared anything when he was around. When he was gone, she began to fear everything. Yet even with all the irrational fears she dealt with, she could've never seen this coming.

So, Jules, what are you going to do here?

She heard his voice like they were practicing some safety maneuver. First, she decided, she had to understand the man she was dealing with as best as possible. Most of what she knew about him was from his books. And the question was, could anyone really know a writer from just his books? How much of himself did he put into his writings? Was it all just make-believe, or were there elements of truth hidden behind each passage, clues about what made the writer tick?

She knew the answer to that. And he had actually come out and said it, with his quip about reading between the lines.

It occurred to her that Patrick really liked the female characters he wrote. There was at least one strong female character in each book, witty and discerning, cleverly working her way in or out of a crime, deftly escaping even her wisest foe.

So. Maybe she should be one of those characters. If she didn't show her hand but wisely worked her way around and through and into him, then maybe she had a chance to, at the very least, talk some sense into him. Even to escape.

Be a character. She tried to think through some of her favorites. Alise Domingo, the street-savvy detective who barely topped five feet but had a martial arts background. That wasn't going to work. The most Jules knew to do was get out of a choke hold. *"And if all else fails,"* Jason had told her, *"bite the living daylights out of them."*

There was Sabrina Farmer, the burned-out detective from Queens who'd gotten hooked on meth. When her boyfriend, a firefighter, died on 9/11, she tried to clean up her act. But she'd inadvertently gotten tied to a Mexican drug cartel, and the only way to save herself and her young daughter was to go undercover . . . as a drug addict.

Nancy Montgomery was a fun character. An ATF agent

whose only asset was the fact that she seemed to be able to read people's minds. Other than that, she was a terrible agent. But when she started reading clues that one of her partners was contemplating murder, she had to get out of her comfort zone and figure out how to stop him without showing her hand.

Yeah, maybe Nancy. She could do Nancy.

A loud sigh escaped. Who was she kidding? She couldn't even do Juliet well.

"There's no use stalling anymore," she said, hooking her thumbs through her belt loops like an old Western showdown was about to take place.

She walked into the living area. Patrick was at the table where they'd eaten the night before, an old-looking typewriter in front of him. He was clacking away at it, briefly observing her before going back to his work.

On the other end of the table were a bowl, a cup of orange juice, and a spoon.

Jules waited for him to say something, but he didn't, so she sat down and began to eat.

"Ugh . . ." It was just the first response to what looked to be an appetizing breakfast. But it was stone cold.

He looked up at her, one of his eyebrows raised. "Breakfast was served three hours ago."

"I don't know what time it is."

"Any person with a decent amount of self-discipline has an internal clock that awakens her. It's 11 a.m. Is that when you normally rise?"

She regarded the bowl and continued to eat. "It's not bad cold." Trying to sell it, she took a few more bites. "So what should I call you?"

"Brilliant."

She forced a smile at his joke. "Mr. Reagan? Your Highness? The Grim Reaper? What?"

He lifted an eyebrow at her again. "You may call me Patrick."

"Fine. You may call me Jules."

"I think Juliet fits you better."

"Then you don't know me very well."

He went back to typing for a long while. She silently ate her cold oatmeal and drank her warm orange juice, watching as he pecked away with two fingers, fairly fast but not as fast as she typed. His focus was on the keys, not what he was writing, and his eyes were distant as he typed, like he was not really present in the room.

Here she was, in Patrick Reagan's cabin, watching him write. She was pretty sure she'd imagined this once or twice. She decided to make the most of it, take in all the details. If she got out of this alive, she'd have blog material for years.

The paper rolled as he continued to type. When he reached the bottom, he pulled the sheet out, turned it over, and set it atop what looked to be a thin stack of papers. He looked at her. "You're eating breakfast and I'm about to fix myself lunch. I guess you won't be needing lunch." He stood. "Haven't you heard, the early bird catches the worm? I work more before noon than most of your generation works in a week—unless, of course, you consider FarmVille work."

She laughed. It seemed to surprise him. But it was funny, especially to someone who equally hated all those Facebook games. "You know what they say. Writing is 5 percent work, 95 percent staying off the Internet."

"You won't find anything of the sort here."

"Well then, I don't have anything to work on. Maybe you have a chore or two I could do around the cabin? And you've been rude not to give me the full tour."

He smirked. "You seem chipper for a woman who was so distraught last night."

"It's amazing what a good, long night's sleep will do." This was good. Nancy was kind of coming through.

He stood and took the bowl away from her. She was somewhat thankful but had only eaten half. Then he slid the papers toward her, still upside down.

"I'd like your opinion."

"On?"

"These few pages. Give me your first impression of them."

Jules swallowed. How was she supposed to be fair and unbiased?

"Maybe that's not such a good idea," she said, sliding the papers back his way. "The last time I read one of your books, it ended up . . . messy."

"Don't you know who I am? What I can offer you by letting you read these pages?" His voice had a booming quality about it. Maybe it was because he was standing over her. "Do you know how many writers would kill for a chance to read just three pages of my unedited manuscript?"

She tried to keep her voice steady. "Of course. It's an easily recognizable honor."

He snorted. "You're just saying what you think I want to hear. Your generation, you're a bunch of self-absorbed snobs, unwilling to be mentored or taught or shown a way other than the easy way." He pointed toward the pages. "This—what's on this page—takes decades to master. Do you understand that? Do you understand it's called a craft because it must be shaped and molded? You cannot read a textbook and understand the nuances and commandments of this process."

Jules generously nodded. "I respect the process. I know it's difficult."

"Do you know because you have *any* idea of what it's like to pour your blood onto the page?"

Jules took a deep breath, placed her hand on the pages, and slowly pulled them toward her. "I'd be honored to read them."

He was breathing hard, but then his breathing slowed as he watched her turn the papers over. "This is raw, right out of the typewriter. *Raw*, Juliet. It's mad and insane. It's forbidden and foreboding—all those risks that a writer takes to get to the truth. Do you understand what I'm saying to you?"

Jules nudged out a nod.

"Then read." He walked to the sink and she felt her body tremble. Nancy slid down the drain of despair. Weak, vulnerable Jules had returned.

But now she had to concentrate. She had to read this and absorb it. Certainly there would be a quiz.

Her eyes focused on the first line and she gasped, her hand covering her mouth.

His body, riddled with bullets, lay in a pool of blood, beside the white sailboat named *Greed*.

She looked up through the tears welling in her eyes. Patrick was at the counter, fixing something for lunch, his back turned.

With the exception of the name of the boat, he'd described exactly how Jason died.

11

THIS IS A TERRIBLE MOVE.

Chris nodded. He knew that was what Jason would say if he were sitting in the seat next to him. But then again, Chris argued in his head, this was his wife they were talking about. Jason had been fiercely protective of Jules. One time, at a Christmas party, some of the guys had made harmless remarks about Jules's "hotness." Chris watched helplessly as Jason rose, walked the length of the room in long strides, and in a tone so cool and measured it sounded rehearsed, let the four detectives know where they could shove it.

It definitely kept Chris on guard. It was a side of Jason he'd never seen. In fact, he would've described Jason as wholly placid before that night. Nothing rattled the guy. Once, a rare earthquake hit the coast. They'd been eating breakfast at the diner when the entire place shook. Chris had hopped up in a lame attempt to do something, like save his own life, and was seconds away from diving under a table when the shaking stopped. Jason just smiled and sipped his coffee, most of which had actually sloshed from his cup.

As the morning café crowd buzzed with excitement, Chris had found his seat. He raised an eyebrow. "You were awfully calm."

"Spent a couple of years in California as a kid." Jason grinned. "We mostly just wonder where the epicenter is."

"What if it was right here?" Chris asked.

"Then you're probably not going to be asking any more questions." They'd laughed for days about it and Chris had to endure some good ribbing as Jason reenacted his reaction for the guys.

Chris gulped his coffee, trying to chase away the memory and grogginess. He hadn't been sleeping.

Through the night, he wrestled with the conversation he'd had with the captain. The captain had said all the right things, but there was something to his tone. Something placating. The idea that they could get a search warrant without Patrick Reagan around was ludicrous. Chris knew he'd failed to establish probable cause. He hadn't even established that a crime had been committed. Unless the DA owed the captain his life, there wasn't going to be a search warrant coming.

And Chris wasn't willing to wait three days for the captain to call and say it wasn't going to happen.

So he'd continued poking around this morning, questioning neighbors. Had they seen Reagan? They all said no and that he never came around in the winter. Chris asked the closest neighbor if he'd seen any activity.

"None, except the cleaning lady who comes twice a week, on Tuesday and Friday."

"She comes even in the winter?"

"Faithfully, all year-round."

"What time?" Chris had asked.

"Around noon."

So here he sat, waiting for her. Drinking coffee as his eyelids fluttered. He never would've been good on a stakeout.

Suddenly the iron gate swung open and a small, dark sedan pulled into the drive. He started his car and pulled in a few feet behind the cleaning lady. The gate didn't close after him. And she didn't seem to notice. She parked her car around back and out of sight. Chris pulled into the front, circular drive.

He waited a few minutes, then rang the doorbell. He wasn't on duty, but he was in his uniform, breaking every code and law he knew.

The cleaning lady greeted him with wide eyes and broken English. "What is matter?"

"Probably nothing, ma'am. But I need to ask you a few questions. May I come in?"

"ID?"

He showed his badge. She nodded slowly and let him in, looking nervous. "The sir no like anyone here."

"Well, I'm not anyone. I am the police." Not on duty nor with permission, but that information didn't need to be discussed. "There is probably no reason to worry, but we were asked to check in on Mr. Reagan by a close friend." Another lie. Wow. This seemed to be coming a little too easily for him because lying wasn't his talent.

He glanced around at the large marble foyer. The chandelier could kill a colony if it fell.

"A close friend? He no have close friends."

"Editor."

"Ah. Okay. Yes."

"I understand that he does not live here in the winter. Have you seen him?"

"No, no. He has no been here at all."

"But you've been getting paid? Everything is going normally?"

"Yes, yes. He very good about paying right time."

"Nothing unusual or out of the ordinary going on that you know of?"

She shook her head.

"I am going to have to take a look around."

"Of course. Just do not touch. No touch. You understand?"

"I know you've got a job to do, so I'll let myself out. This will just take a couple of minutes."

She nodded and carried her cleaning supplies upstairs.

Chris turned and took in the enormous house. Stately and rich with historic detail, it looked as if it had been restored, since it was built over 150 years ago. He could see a spiral staircase, a massive kitchen and formal dining area, and plenty of space between several sitting rooms. He walked carefully, studying the details. It was a house, but not a home. There seemed to be no warmth.

At the far end of the house, next to a back door that led to gardens and maybe a pool, was a study. The doors to the room were iron. Inside, bookshelves lined two walls, filled to capacity. A shiny wooden desk sat in the dead center on an expensive-looking Oriental rug. The walls that did not house books were filled with large, framed pictures of Reagan's book covers. Award plaques filled in the empty spaces.

Chris glanced around at the covers and the titles. All seemed to be pretty grim. He was more of a lighthearted guy himself. Never understood the appeal of horror or the like.

But these things didn't keep his attention for long. Instead, it was drawn to the white paper strewn across the entire room, as if hundreds of pages had been tossed into the air and allowed to float haplessly to the ground. Some pages were crumpled. Others torn.

"Maybe he wasn't happy with his latest book either," Chris said with a smile to himself. He tried to get a feel for what he was looking at. Words filled every page he could see. He picked one up and read a few sentences. It was definitely part of a novel.

He carefully picked through each piece, trying to find a

cover page or some indication of who wrote this and what it was. Each page had a number at the bottom, but no author name.

It took about ten minutes, but he finally found the first page, wadded up in a corner of the room. Very simply, in type barely bigger than the rest of the manuscript's and centered on the page, it read, *The Daring Life of Enoch Mandon by Blake Timble.*

"Not a fan, I guess," Chris said as he turned and peered around the room again. Something had set Reagan off, and most likely, Chris was holding the crumpled culprit in his hand.

Chris's cell phone rang. "Yeah?"

"Chris, it's the captain."

"Hi . . ." Chris dropped the page he was holding as if Captain Perry could see him.

"Listen, it's going to be a no go on that search warrant. I'm sorry, but you knew it was a long shot."

"Sure. Thanks for trying."

"I was thinking . . . I might send you with Detective Walker to New York, see if we can get any information from Reagan's editor or agent."

Chris clutched the phone. "Really?" It was unusual to be sent in person, but every good detective liked to look people in the eye.

"I know you and Jason were close. I get how personal this is to you. I mean, the chances are that we won't find anything. But I think it's worth a try."

"I'd appreciate that, sir."

"Good. Walker's on the phone with them now and is going to try to get you both on a flight up there this afternoon. If you've got important plans, drop 'em."

"Very good. Thank you."

"I'm only doing this for Jason."

"Yes, sir. Thank you."

Chris slid his phone back into his pocket and walked out of the office, quietly closing the doors behind him, but not before glimpsing one more time the sea of white madness that covered what in all other respects seemed to be a very tidy study. Maybe this wasn't a clue to what happened to Jules, but it certainly pointed to the man's state of mind. And whoever Blake Timble was, he ought to watch out.

⌐ ⌐

"What are you doing?" Jules looked up at Patrick as he stood over her. "Is this supposed to be some kind of joke?"

"It's called *The Living End.*"

"I don't care what it's called. It's cruel."

"It's necessary." He peered sharply at her.

"I don't want to read a scene about how my husband . . ."

"You think this is about your husband?"

"I don't think it's a coincidence, no." She glared at him. "Did you have something to do with his death? Is that what this is all about?"

He walked away from the table for a moment, pacing

a bit and seemingly distracted from the tense conversation they were engaged in. He was rubbing his brow furiously and mumbling to himself.

"Speak up," Jules growled. "I can't hear you."

He stopped and turned to her. "That's because you are not listening. You believe you know, but you don't. You don't know anything!"

"Then why don't you explain it to me?"

"Because you're obtuse! All of your generation is obtuse! Unwilling to scrape at the bottom to find deeply buried truths. You want to scratch the surface of everything you write about. You want to merely play, tickle a feather across the parched and cracked land and call it observation."

Jules wiped her eyes, vaguely aware that there were still tears in them. His nonsense was beginning to terrify her.

"And they call you brilliant. Brilliant! All of you."

"I don't know what you mean." Jules clutched the edge of the table.

"Do you not think that I understand what they're trying to tell me? They send me a manuscript, ask for my blessing. 'It's won this award and that award,' they declare. They want an endorsement, but what they are really trying to impart to me is the idea that I've become irrelevant. But truth is never irrelevant. And these new, celebrated young writers who break all the rules and write with some perceived wizardry or magic undertones are celebrated. Celebrated! They're hacks. Blake Timble is a hack!"

Jules froze as the words spewed out of his mouth. His

face turned red and his eyes narrowed, slicing back and forth between each breath he took.

"This is the fluff that the publishing world wants now?" he continued. "This is asking a lot of questions and solving nothing. This is pretending to be relevant when in reality, it's only smoke and mirrors. Blake Timble cannot go where he needs to go to make his book what it needs to be." Then, as though he'd suddenly been bathed in some kind of sedative, Patrick seemed to realize he was ranting. He glanced at her as if he'd forgotten she was there. His hand ran across his chest like he was making sure he still had a heartbeat. The other hand pulled at an earlobe, what appeared to be a nervous habit. But he seemed to have resolved inside of himself that he should calm down.

He cleared his throat. "You will take those pages, and you will read them in your room. You may come out when you are finished, and we shall discuss them like two civilized human beings. Understood?"

Jules stared at the stark paper on the table. "This hurts," she said. "You're hurting me. Do you get that?"

Patrick nodded. "You have a lot to learn, Juliet. And learning is painful. Pain is the greatest teacher. We learn that the first time we reach our little hands up to touch a hot stove. You cannot come to any real conclusions without suffering. I truly believe that. It's just that many people are not strong enough to endure. But you're strong enough."

Jules was trying to decide whether she was hearing a compliment or a threat.

"I see brilliance in you," he said as tenderly as if she were a baby rabbit sitting in his cupped hands. "And you must believe me when I say this is for your own good." He waved his finger in the air. "I sense talent in you. I see heart. I feel your soul but, right now, only its edge."

Jules clutched the pages. "I don't want to read these."

"I will call you when dinner is ready." He nodded toward the bedroom. "Don't go in there and pout and feel sorry for yourself. Learn, Juliet. Learn the power of the gift. We will discuss it all over dinner, more matter-of-factly than now, as I understand you're still in shock." He shooed her with his hands. "You will find a red pen in the drawer next to the bed. Use it wisely. Find my weak points, but more importantly, find yours."

Long hours passed and shadows shifted across the room. Jules guessed it had been five hours but was not sure. Outside her room, she could hear him in the kitchen.

She knew she looked a wreck. But it had been grueling hours of reading and rereading, trying to figure out what he wanted from her. Surely he wasn't just after a critique partner.

At first she'd circled a thing or two with the red pen, written some rudimentary notes, but her heart wasn't in it. She'd lain on the bed, her arms and legs stretched out like she was in the middle of a jumping jack, staring at the message on the ceiling that had fulfilled its promise. She loathed the day she wrote those words.

After a short nap and another crying session, she decided

to try to tackle the pages without being emotionally tied to the scene. It involved a police officer named Kurt who was shot multiple times as he was investigating some kind of theft ring. His partner, Jake, had tried to save his life that night by administering CPR. The scene was written in vivid detail, with Kurt gurgling blood as Jake tried to listen to his last request, Jake begging him to hold on while trying to protect them both from an enemy that was hiding in the dark, perhaps poised to strike again.

It was vintage Patrick Reagan, but so much of it mirrored what happened to Jason that she was having a hard time concentrating on the task at hand. And truthfully, she didn't really know what the task at hand was.

Was he trying to tell her he wanted an honest review, that he had a thick enough skin? That was hard to believe, considering his rants. He seemed to be telling her that he wanted her to know something, but like a good suspense novel, he kept only small clues coming. What did Patrick Reagan know?

He spoke in weird riddles. He wanted her to find her weak spots? She was clutching it in her hands. Jason's death would forever be a weak spot, a place where she could easily be broken time and time again. But she suspected the author in the other room already knew that.

"Dinner is served," she heard him say formally from outside her door. The shadows from the day were long gone and darkness had settled outside. And inside as well.

12

"ADDY, YOU ARE out of this world," Maecoat moaned as he leaned over his soup bowl.

"You mean the *soup* is out of this world?" Chris asked from the other side of the dining table. In the kitchen, Addy smiled.

"What did I say?" Maecoat asked.

"Whatever's on your mind," Chris growled.

Maecoat flashed a grin at Addy. "You really are a spectacular cook."

"Thank you, Greg," she said, bringing her bowl to the table and joining them.

Maecoat pointed his spoon toward Chris. "Is he always such great company at dinner?"

Addy cocked an eyebrow at Chris. "Usually a little livelier. Something on your mind, Brother?"

"Just . . . trying to figure out this Jules case. There're so many unanswered questions."

"The good thing," Addy said, "is that there is no sign that harm has come to her. That's good, right? In the police world?"

"An optimist. I like that," Maecoat said.

"Since when?" Chris said.

"Since riding with you, grumpy."

Chris sighed. "I know. Sorry. I've just got a lot on my mind." Even Addy's world-famous chowder didn't sound appetizing. He looked up at them. "The captain is sending me to New York tomorrow. With Detective Walker. We tried to get it set up for this afternoon, but they had to schedule it for Saturday."

Maecoat sat up straighter. "Seriously? Why?"

"I presented him with this idea about Reagan. He seemed at least somewhat intrigued."

"That's surprising. The captain doesn't seem intrigued with much these days, except making our ticket quota and budget."

"Honestly, I was surprised at how seriously he took me. I mean, he asked the usual question—how was I doing and all that—but as far-fetched as the theory sounded, he actually seemed to think I was onto something."

"What's in New York?" Addy asked.

"Reagan's editor and agent."

Maecoat asked, "So what's going to happen? You're going to go in and ask his editor if he's involved in some disappearance of a lady they've never heard of?"

"I guess. I'll let Walker take the lead." Chris set his spoon down and leaned back. "I just can't believe that he was spotted in town, which never happens in the winter, on the same day Jules wrote a bad review of his book. That can't be a coincidence, can it? The same grocery store? At the same time?"

"Weirder things have happened, like how this soup magically disappeared in this bowl here. Seconds, Addy?" Maecoat held up his bowl.

Addy smiled graciously. "Sure." She rose and went to the stove. "I read her blog last night. I wanted to get a feel for what you were talking about."

"And?" Chris asked.

"And I think that she's a very sad woman. You have to kind of read below the surface, but she's crying out in her loneliness. She's heartbroken in every way."

"How'd you come up with that?"

"I guess you have to be a woman—"

"—which you are," Maecoat inserted cheerfully.

"Shut it, Maecoat," Chris said. "Go on, Addy. What do you mean?"

"I mean that she's trying to reach out to the world while keeping herself fully protected inside her home. She doesn't know where to turn to help her anguish."

"You gleaned all that from lighthouses and the history of that famous poet?"

"Sure. The poem she quoted from Freezan was about whether the perils of life are worth the risk of love. And the lighthouses. It was obvious how she paralleled their existence to her own—a single light shining against a dark harbor."

Maecoat looked impressed. "What were you? A genius major?"

"You're getting pathetic now," Chris said.

"Hey, it's getting me more soup. I'll go real pathetic for chowder."

"I was an English minor." Addy shrugged. "So maybe that's how I read. Maybe I see metaphors in everything."

"You read any of Patrick Reagan's stuff?" Maecoat asked.

"Not lately. I did a few years ago. I'm not into the genre, though."

"When you were reading Jules's blog, do you remember her ever mentioning a writer named Blake Timble?"

"No. Who is that?"

"Nobody," Chris sighed. "Just another random clue that is leading nowhere."

"Maybe you'll find something tomorrow, right?"

"Yeah."

"So," Maecoat said as Addy returned to the table with his bowl, "who is up for a nice warm fire and long conversations into the night?"

Chris hunched over his soup bowl and ate in silence.

Dinner first, Patrick had insisted. Then they could talk. The food was nice. A seared chicken breast and roasted winter vegetables under generous amounts of gouda, all between sourdough. It was simple and elegant and under any other circumstance would've been delightful.

They chatted mildly, mostly about him. He talked about the places he'd been to research his novels, the famous people—including two presidents—that he'd met over the years. It was as if he was trying to impress her, which seemed ridiculous. She'd already been impressed with him over the years. He had to know that if he'd read anything other than the last two, maybe three, reviews of his books.

There was a candle lit between them, a short, fat one that made it seem like they'd stepped back into the nineteenth century. The warmth and flickering of the candle set Jules at ease. For the moment, she was pretty sure Patrick wasn't going to murder her. The glowing amber light washed over his face, softening his features. But something kept telling her to stay on guard. Maybe it was Jason.

As dinner wound down, she decided to make herself useful. She went to the kitchen to start cleaning the dishes.

"Your notes? Written on the page?" Patrick pointed to the white paper waiting on the table near where she'd sat.

"Yes," Jules said, barely above a whisper.

"Hm."

She turned her back to him, thankful for the distraction

of washing the dishes. She didn't think she could bear watching him read her notes. She'd tried to think like an editor would and been glad for a few typos, just for something to circle. He'd given her only one scene, so it was hard to understand the whole context. And it was still hard to understand why he'd written something similar to her husband's murder.

After a few minutes Patrick simply said, "Good thoughts."

Then he came to the sink and dried while she washed. She wanted to watch him, figure out what was making him tick. But instead she dutifully washed and he dutifully dried, like they were some old married couple in a routine they both knew.

After he finished drying the last dish, he grabbed a bottle of wine that sat on the counter. "Care for any?"

"No. Thanks."

"Suit yourself. Good for the heart, though." He took a glass, held it between two fingers, and poured gently. "In more ways than one." He walked to the living area, sitting himself down and staring into the fireless fireplace.

There was nothing left to do in the kitchen, but Jules wasn't sure she wanted to be near him. She still had no concept of time. What she wouldn't give for a clock or a watch with a working battery!

She decided to join him in the living room. It was cozy, with afghans and plush pillows. Architecture magazines were neatly spread across a coffee table that was formed out of a large tree stump. A few logs sat next to the fireplace. The room smelled like pine. But with the sun set, the cabin was even colder. She took one of the afghans and spread it over her legs as she sat down.

"It's awfully cold in here," she said. "Why not light a fire? That's such a lovely stone fireplace."

"It was. Yes, it was," he said quietly.

A few minutes passed. He'd sip his wine, swallow it slowly, stare into the air.

"Patrick," Jules finally said. "How long do you intend to keep me here?"

"As long as it takes."

"But I don't want to be here."

"It's because you don't yet understand." He sighed and set his wineglass down, turning his attention to her. "Do you think I am in the sagging middle?"

"I don't understand."

He just stared at her.

"What is the 'sagging middle'?"

"I thought you would know such a thing," he said, looking away and returning to his wine.

"Obviously you have a lot to teach me," Jules offered with a small smile.

He seemed to want to oblige. "The sagging middle usually happens around chapter 17. Somewhere within the second act. It is the most difficult area for the writer to wade through. The beginning is easy. Your task is to set everything up. To introduce all the characters. The end can pose challenges, most especially if you've written your character into a corner, but that makes it that much more fun to try to resolve. But the sagging middle . . . that's where your sub-plot runs out and your characters have shown all their cards. Where you must rise up out of the ashes or you will lose your reader."

Jules nodded. "I see now."

"No. Not everything. Not yet." He leaned back more comfortably in his chair. "There are some who say I'm in the sagging middle of my career. My own personal chapter 17. What do you say?"

Jules kind of wished for that glass of wine now. "The last thing I said got me into a lot of trouble, so maybe I'd do well to keep my mouth shut."

He smiled at her. Not the warmest of smiles, but an acknowledgment of her wit, she guessed. "You're here now, with me, so you might as well get it all off your chest."

"This conversation lends itself to a nice fire."

"It stays unlit," he said tersely.

"Fine. But your 'guest' is freezing cold, so you should at least acknowledge that. To get back to the subject at hand, you know that I am a big fan of yours, if you've read anything I've written at all."

He nodded slightly while gazing at the fireplace.

"True, I haven't cared for your last three books. The last two in particular. So what? Plenty of people have liked them. Obviously. You remain on the bestseller list. What does my opinion matter to you?"

"I suppose it matters because I believe you have great insight into my work. You always have. I've appreciated that, you know," he said, glancing slightly at her. "With the invention of the Internet, any hack can type out his opinion, with no thought to what he's doing or saying. Sometimes I wonder if they've read the book at all. They cheapen our world, our offerings, by their ignorance. An opinion not steeped in wisdom and intelligence is worthless. But you . . . were different."

Jules swallowed, hoping not to say the wrong thing. She'd once read that he never read his reviews. But here he was, confessing to it. "Thank you. It was easy because you always drew me in deeply to your stories."

"I'd say you're just trying to flatter me, except I know it's true. You've said so for years."

Jules nodded and smiled at him. Something about him made her want to make him feel okay. For years, she'd imagined him as a man completely in control of his world. A man who rose above everything and everyone else. But now, as he sat in his chair with his glass of wine and his empty fireplace, she was sensing something much different about him.

"Patrick, why am I here? Why am I really here?"

He didn't answer.

"You can trust me, Patrick. You know that."

"You can't trust anybody, Juliet. Because you don't know that, you're here. And because you don't believe me, you're going to have to be here awhile, until I can prove it to you."

"Maybe I understand more than you think."

"I am certain you don't." He looked at her. "I can see it in your eyes."

"What, exactly, do you see in my eyes? You're not a mind reader."

"But I am an observer. It's what makes me able to do what I do. You are an observer too. That's what makes me look away—I know you can see. It is why you can hold my gaze for mere seconds."

Jules held her breath as she watched him. He was back to staring at the fireplace.

"It would be much more gazeworthy if there were fire in there," she said with a small smile.

He rose and she thought she might've convinced him, but he left the room momentarily. She glanced at the door. How easily she could run! But like he said, she had no idea where she was. And it was snowing. She didn't even have a coat. But his hung by the door. Still, as far as she could tell, she wasn't in immediate danger.

Patrick returned with a stack of paper in his hands. He set it down beside her, then picked up his wineglass but took no more sips. He stared toward the curtainless window, though it was dark outside. The only thing visible was the light from the porch and the snowflakes that fell through it.

"What if I'm not in chapter 17? What if I'm actually at the end, ready to reveal everything? Wouldn't they be surprised? Wouldn't they wish they'd not chosen their words so carelessly?"

"Who is 'they'?"

He blinked as if he'd forgotten she was there. "Go away now," he said. "Into your room. You have reading to do."

Jules stood, throwing off the afghan. "Fine."

"Don't be childish. This is important work."

She glared at him as she picked up the pages. "No. *This* is childish. Your toying with me. Your speaking in riddles."

"I'm doing this for your own good."

"Doesn't feel like it."

"Pain can be a good teacher."

"I don't need to be taught."

"Then already," he said smoothly, "I see that you are in desperate need of truth."

⌐ ∟

"Who was that?" Addy stepped out onto the porch, where Chris stood with his jacket zipped high as it would go.

"It's cold out here. You should get a coat."

"I'm fine," she said, wrapping her arms around herself. She leaned against the other post. "The Lt. Colonel?"

"Yes. Drunk out of his mind. Confused. He thought I'd left a voice mail saying that I'd found Jules."

Addy reached out and squeezed his shoulder. "You're taking this so hard."

Chris couldn't deny it. He stared into the patchy groupings of trees that surrounded his house. "The last time I saw Jules was on the front porch of her home. We . . . She was upset. With me. Not really, I guess. But she said some things and I should've been strong. I should've understood where that pain was coming from."

"What did she say?"

"She blamed me for Jason's death. Said I should've had his back. Which is true, Addy. Of course I should've had his back. I just . . . I never saw it coming."

"You couldn't have. Chris, you can't continue to blame yourself—for Jason's death or for Jules."

"But I've failed Jason twice now. I couldn't protect him, and then when things got rocky, I stopped checking in on his wife." Chris stared at the grass. "I should've kept checking on her, even if she didn't think she needed it. Now she's gone to who knows where. And I'm no closer to finding her than when I started."

Addy stepped closer, put her arm around him. "Maybe you'll get something big tomorrow in New York. This Walker guy pretty good?"

"Yeah, I guess. That's what they say. Kind of egotistical, but who isn't around that department, you know? I just appreciate the captain letting me stay on the case. It's a nice gesture." His fingers were freezing and he dipped them deep into his pockets. "He was acting strangely."

"Who?"

"Jason. A couple of weeks before he died. He was withdrawn, not really himself. He was always such a funny guy, and he just looked so burdened. I thought he and Jules were having problems, but he didn't want to talk about it. He said he would, but he didn't want to yet. I gave him his space. That's what he seemed to need. Just some space."

"Well, I'm not giving you any space," Addy said. "I'm staying here with you until you find Jules."

"Sis, you don't have to—"

"I know I don't have to do anything. But you need me."

"Please tell me you're not hanging around because of Greg Maecoat."

"Sweetie, I promise, he's not on my radar. I'm nice to him because he's your friend."

"I'd trust that guy with my life, but not with my sister. You know what I mean?"

Addy laughed. "I know what you mean. Now, you stay out here and ruminate for a bit longer. I'm going to make us some hot chocolate. And then you're going to get some rest so you'll be ready for tomorrow."

"Yes, ma'am."

Addy went inside and Chris tried to get his thoughts in order. But he couldn't piece together one coherent thought without flashing back to Jules on that porch, tears streaming from her eyes. She'd yelled at him, told him never to come by again. He knew it even then—she was engulfed in grief—but he was dealing with his own grief and couldn't put it aside long enough to go back to her.

But he'd still felt this sense of needing to protect her. From then on, he kept an eye on her from a distance. It got harder, the more reclusive she became. He figured, though, she was safe enough in her house. Maybe one day that grief would lift and she'd be able to live again.

"Jules, where are you?" he whispered. But his words disappeared into the dark like his frozen breath.

THEY WERE AT THE AIRPORT at 6 a.m. and arrived in Manhattan still in the early morning. Jeff Walker seemed like a decent guy. He'd been with their police department for about seven years, but Chris still didn't know him well. Turned out he'd worked in New York for ten years before that but wanted a slower pace and to get his kids out of the city.

Once in New York, they'd hailed a cab and were now standing on the sidewalk below one of many shiny, flashy skyscrapers that towered to the heavens. Like flowing river water, people moved effortlessly around them, as though they were a couple of immovable logs.

"We're going to go in pretty casual," Walker said, gazing

upward while stroking his reddish-brown mustache. His head was shaved like the rest of his face.

"Yeah. I'm just following your lead. Bet the guy's ticked he had to come in on a Saturday."

"It's a she. And she didn't seem like it was going to be a problem."

Through revolving doors, they walked into the lobby, a sparkling assault of gold letters, shiny tile, and sculptures that looked to be from another planet.

They found the directory and went to the elevator. Once inside, Walker hit *18*.

"What's your gut tell you about this?" Chris asked.

Walker shrugged. "I don't know. Captain seemed to think it was worth looking into."

"It sounds crazy, doesn't it?"

"A little. But he knows what Jason meant to you."

"Think he's just placating me?"

Walker smiled. "Maybe. But we might as well have fun with the intellectual crowd while we're here, right?"

"Hope I can keep up," Chris laughed.

"Follow my lead. I'm a professional. It's all about throwing multisyllable words into the conversation with ease."

"You've lost me already. I'm a one- to two-syllable word guy."

"Me too, me too. Where I come from, a three-syllable word can get you punched in the gut and thrown out of the bar."

Chris grinned. "Glad we're on the same page."

"And trust me, we'll all be on the same page when we're done in there. I spent three years in New York doing hostage negotiations. We're just going to find our common ground."

"Good luck with that. I haven't picked up a book in years."

"Well, when all else falls short, flash 'em the badge, right?"

The doors opened into a large waiting area complete with a towering white marble desk, behind which sat a receptionist, stick thin except for lips the size of buffalo wings.

"They have a receptionist even on a Saturday?" Chris asked. The office was buzzing with a weird energy like it was a Monday morning or something.

Walker stepped up and put his badge on the desk. "I'm Detective Walker. This is Sergeant Downey. We're with the Wissberry, Maine, police department here to see Clarice Rembrandt. She's expecting us."

The poor girl looked startled—not because they were there, but just in general. Maybe it was her sprouted, spidery eyelashes. "You're with . . . ?"

"The Wissberry police department in Maine." Walker flashed a wide, friendly grin that said, *We're asking all nice, but we don't have to.* It seemed a little ridiculous since the editor knew they were coming, but Chris figured Walker was just having some fun with her.

She rose, her bones protruding through her black dress. Her elbows looked as sharp as the stilettos she marched away in.

Walker glanced back at Chris and shrugged. "What's with all the excitement around here?"

They heard a door slam.

"Maybe that's what happened to Little Bit," Chris said, nodding to the desk. "She got slammed in one too many doors."

Walker shook his head. "Why do women want to look that way?"

The receptionist returned, the clacking of her heels arriving a few seconds before herself. "Right this way," she said.

The receptionist led them down a long hallway. They emerged in a large room with windowed offices on both sides and the open spaces filled with cubicles. Chris took in the atmosphere. People were milling about like it was a newsroom and a story just broke.

At the end of the room were double doors, already open to a small reception area with a desk and a computer, but the secretary wasn't there. They followed Little Bit into another, larger office. She didn't walk all the way in but quietly gestured toward the two leather chairs in front of the desk.

The woman behind it had a stick-straight bob, cut at the nose rather than the chin. She wore big square glasses that completely consumed her face. Her hair was jet-black, her skin as pale as the white foam of the shoreline. Chris thought she looked like a cartoon character.

In front of her, a tall stack of white papers rose from the shiny waxed desk. She carefully set the papers aside before making eye contact with them. She stood right before they sat and offered her hand in a way that made Chris feel like she might want them to kiss it.

"I'm Detective Walker. This is Sergeant Downey," Walker said, pitching a thumb toward Chris. Chris shook her hand carefully, afraid he might break it off. Her fingers were ice-cold. She really had no color on her at all, except the tip of her nose, which was bright red like she was nursing an illness or had just stepped out of a meat locker.

"Gentlemen, please, have a seat." With her severe features, her soft-spoken voice came as a surprise. "I am Clarice Rembrandt, Patrick's longtime editor."

"Thank you for coming in to see us on a Saturday," Walker said.

"I was here already," Clarice said, relaxing in her chair. She folded her hands slowly and deliberately over her lap. "We're pushing a book out four weeks early. It's a major undertaking."

"Well, thank you, then, for your time, ma'am," Walker said, pulling out his notepad. "We just wanted to ask you a few questions that would pertain to an investigation we're conducting."

"An investigation of Mr. Reagan?"

"No. Not yet."

"So you would like me to answer questions about our most famous author without knowing why. And these answers might incriminate him?"

"Most likely not," Walker said coolly. "But they might help us find a missing woman."

"He writes mysteries, Detective. He doesn't typically create them."

"We just think he might have seen something in Wissberry. We would like to question him about whether or not he saw a woman at a grocery store, but we can't seem to locate him."

Suddenly her very small face opened up into a gigantic smile, revealing teeth that looked like they'd seen their share of coffee. She tossed her head back and chuckled reservedly, the way Chris suspected the uppity crowd liked to do at their uppity parties. Nobody *howled* in this circle, he bet.

Chris and Walker exchanged glances.

"Something funny?" Walker asked.

"Sorry. So sorry," she said, blotting the corner of each eye with long fingers. "I just feel bad that you flew all the way here to ask that question."

"Why is that?"

"Because everyone knows that Patrick Reagan never emerges in the winter. *Everyone* knows that. I would think, since he is a resident of your town, you would know that too."

"We are aware of his . . . habitation schedule. . . ." Walker winced at his apparent attempt to use a big word that sounded more like they were talking about zoo animals. "That is why we found it unusual."

"Whoever thought they saw him is mistaken. I've known Patrick for twenty-five years. He does not come into town in the winter. He simply wouldn't do it."

"We beg to differ," Walker said.

"Did anyone see him again?"

"Not that we know of."

"How many people saw him?"

"So far, just one."

She shook her head and combed long fingernails through her short hair. "Trust me, he wasn't there."

"Humor me," Walker said with a tight smile. "Let's pretend he was. If I wanted to get in touch with him, how would I do that?"

"I'm sorry—I can't give that information out."

Chris suddenly leaned forward. "You don't know how to get ahold of him, do you?"

Her eyes shifted to Chris as if she'd just noticed he was sitting there.

"Well?" Walker asked.

Clarice paused longer, her eyelashes fluttering with thought. "Well, he likes to be left alone in the winter. That's when he writes."

"So how do you contact him when you need to?"

"We don't need to," she said with a short smile. "Ever. We want him writing, obviously."

"Is Sergeant Downey right? You don't know how to get ahold of him?"

She sighed loudly. "It's just how we work. The way we've worked for years. We leave him be for the winter months, and when spring comes, he usually reemerges with a perfectly polished manuscript."

Walker started to ask a question, but Chris piped in. "Except the last couple—last three—weren't that perfectly polished, were they?"

"That's subjective."

"His sales have been down. His critics haven't been kind. It's not been a good couple of years, has it?"

Clarice looked irritated, but weirdly, not at Chris. "The quality of his work—and his promptness—has slipped a little," she said. "But that is to be expected. Patrick lost his beloved wife, Amelia. It's been . . . difficult for him."

"Is there anything you want to tell us about Mr. Reagan's behavior lately?" Walker asked. "Has he been acting unusual?"

Clarice might be highly intelligent, Chris observed, but she apparently was not gifted with a poker face.

"Look," Chris said. "We know how to be discreet. We just need information that might help us find Mr. Reagan so we can ask him some questions. A woman is missing and we really need to find her."

She threw her hands up. "There's no other way to say this. Patrick is late."

"Late?"

"On his manuscript. That is not like Patrick. He's always been prompt on his deadlines. But not anymore."

"But he released a book this fall. *The Lion's Mouth.*"

"That's correct. But that book was supposed to release in the summer. He was months late on turning in the manuscript. And now he's late on the next one, which means once again moving his release date and all the financial commitments that go with it. It's just been a big mess." Her voice warbled with emotion.

"Has he told you why he is not finished?"

"No. He keeps saying he needs more time. That's all. He

needs more time." She shrugged. "He's Patrick Reagan. We don't have the luxury of doing anything but waiting."

"So you've talked to him lately?"

"No. I'm sorry."

"But you're his longtime editor."

"I've only gotten mail from him."

"E-mails?"

"No. Snail mail. Updates periodically. He's quite a kind man. He tells me not to worry, that this book is going to blow my mind. But we live and die by the deadline in publishing, so I've not been able to heed his advice."

"Perhaps his agent will be able to give us some information? We've got an appointment with him too."

Clarice smiled broadly. "Good luck with that."

"Don't tell me he winters down as well," Walker groaned.

"No. Not at all. He'll be there."

They thanked the editor and rose to leave, but Chris stopped and turned. "One more thing."

"I'm extremely busy."

"Understood. I'll make it quick. Have you ever heard of a writer named Blake Timble?"

Clarice's eyes widened as though Chris had made an indecent gesture. Walker noticed and looked back and forth between the two.

"How do you know that name?"

"Can't reveal that, ma'am, but obviously you know who I'm talking about."

Clarice sank back into her chair, rubbing her temples. "Why am I not surprised? Of course it was leaked. Of course!"

"Who is he?"

"A new writer we've acquired through a contest we ran. We had 940 entries, Sergeant. This writer won the contest and we're publishing the manuscript next spring. But we're keeping the winner's identity a secret."

"Why?"

"From our angle, it's great PR, to build up the suspense. But the author also wished to remain anonymous in a sense, choosing to use a pen name."

"Was Patrick Reagan involved in choosing the winner?"

"No. The winner was chosen by our editorial board."

"Would there be any reason Mr. Reagan would be upset by this manuscript?"

Clarice looked curious. "I don't believe so. I mean . . ." She paused and both Chris and Walker stepped closer, hanging on her next word. She sighed as if this was going to require a long explanation. "We did actually send him the manuscript. We don't typically do that. Mr. Reagan's publishing stature gives him the right to refuse endorsements of his work and refuse to give out endorsements of other people's work. He's quite critical, so long ago we decided to stop sending him anything to endorse because he was rejecting everything. But . . . this manuscript, it was special. I've been in the publishing industry for thirty years and it's some of the best literary writing I've ever seen. We thought that we might have a chance of getting his endorsement, which would be the equivalent of striking gold."

"Did he give you that endorsement?"

"We haven't heard from him. We sent it a couple of months ago to his house in Maine, unsure of whether he would read it or even see it before the spring, but we thought we'd try."

"What's the book about?"

Clarice smiled mildly. "For that information, you're going to need a search warrant."

It had been a cold Tuesday in November when Chris Downey came to her door at 11 p.m. with the captain, Don Perry. And as Jules opened the door and looked at their faces, she'd known they'd not come to rush her to the hospital. He was already gone.

Chris held her upright as she listened to the captain's brief explanation of what had happened to Jason. ". . . shot multiple times down by the shore at Hennessey dock. Chris tried to . . . but he didn't—he just . . . before the ambulance could get there . . ."

She was collapsed into Chris, staring at the blood on one of his hands as it held her at the waist. She had no recollection of how she got into the house or who was there, until her father arrived. When he sat down on the couch, she literally crawled into his lap and buried her head in his neck.

He went with her to identify Jason at the morgue. The police department said it wasn't necessary, but Jules had to know that he was gone. The room was sterile and brightly lit. There were three tables, all cold and metal. Jason was on the third, the farthest from the door. The mortician gently pulled the sheet away from his face. He was light gray, like smoke from their chimney. His lips were purple and there were dark shadows down his cheeks and around his eyes. Her father kept his arm steady around her shoulder as she simultaneously pressed into and pulled against him. She wanted to touch Jason, to hold him, but instead she stayed still, staring at him like he was some sort of lab specimen.

After that day, she always regretted not touching him. She knew it was pointless, but she wanted to be stronger for him. Since then, she hadn't been strong a single day.

"You're wallowing. . . ."

Jules sat up in the chair. Had she dozed off? She glanced around. Patrick sat across from her in the living area, immersed in the pages she'd returned to him.

"What?" she asked.

"That's what you said here. That I'm wallowing in unremarkable details."

Jules held her breath, tried not to look scared. "Just an opinion."

Patrick raised an eyebrow. "Observant."

"Thank you." She rubbed her eyes. "What time is it?"

He didn't answer, just continued reading. She was becoming weary of the lack of schedule, the lack of purpose here.

She had nothing to do but critique a man who was obviously sensitive to critique. Her stomach hurt most of the time.

The fogginess of the sleep she'd slipped into faded, along with the sounds of her own cries that she replayed so often from that night. It was apparently only midmorning, judging from the sun, but she was exhausted. She hadn't slept well last night. Or any night.

Suddenly Patrick set down the pages on the coffee table and looked directly at her. "Tell me about your father."

Jules shifted. "Why do you want to know about my father?"

"What else is there to do to pass the time but get to know one another? I suppose we both feel we know each other in some sense. You, from my books. Me, from your Internet writings. But we don't really know one another, do we, Juliet?"

"I suppose not," she said. She picked up the hot tea he'd served her a while ago. It was now cold. "And maybe we should throw out first impressions."

"I realize you think I'm a madman."

"Worthy to be cast in one of your novels."

He laughed at that and she laughed too. She didn't know why, really, because she felt in no way amused by any of it.

"So—" he gestured to her—"your father."

"My father. Lt. Colonel Jim Franklin, a career Marine. Worked his way to the top. Served in three wars."

"A good man?"

"A very good man."

"But not perfect."

"Who is?"

"Go on."

"He retired about ten years ago. Shortly before that, my mother died. She'd battled cancer on and off for most of my childhood."

"I'm sorry to hear that."

"My father took it hard. Plus he saw some gruesome action in Afghanistan. He struggles with the bottle."

"I see."

"But he loves me. I love him. We have a great relationship before noon."

"Interesting."

"After that, I let him be." She gazed out the window. The light was brightening the room in small increments. "I know he's worried sick about me. I can't even imagine what he's going through right now."

Patrick leaned forward, took off his reading glasses. "Juliet, you will not guilt me into anything. You're here for a reason. You must trust me."

"I can't. I'm sorry. This is too weird. If you wanted my editorial opinion, we could've met over coffee."

"So it is quite obvious you're here for other reasons."

"I can't imagine a good reason to kidnap someone and hold them hostage."

"That surprises me. I took you for having a good imagination."

"I wish I were imagining this."

"You don't find my company enjoyable? From all the writing you've done about me, I would think this would be an opportunity of a lifetime—you and I sitting across from one another, shooting the breeze." *Shooting the breeze* came out awkwardly, like he'd never used the phrase before.

"Why am I reading your book? And why a random scene here and there? It would make much more sense to read it in order."

"I will share a secret about myself with you, Juliet. Nobody knows this."

She leaned in, noticing his eyes sparkled like a little boy's. "I'm most useful in my writing when my thoughts are chaotic. The systematic reordering comes later. But the helter-skelter of words and thoughts and scenes—that's where my imagination likes to dwell. When my scene is complete, if it is strong and readable out of context, then I know for certain it will stand with the rest of the book. I guess I am fond of chaos. I've never been able to stand well in an ordered world."

"That is fascinating." She was just the opposite, functioning only in a well-ordered environment. Chaos terrified her in more ways than one.

His eyes dimmed a bit. "This book has been different, though." His words trailed off and he stared into the air for a moment, then returned his attention to her. "So give me your impression of the scene you just read for me."

"I thought it was good. The tension was there."

"You liked the dialogue between the two police officers?"

"Yes. I liked how there seemed to be this seething anger between them, simmering just below the surface."

"Good, good. You got that even though you had no context for it."

"And I like the main character. Kurt."

"He's a good man."

"I can tell. He . . ."

"Reminds you of someone?"

Tears welled in her eyes. "Jason."

Patrick nodded understandingly. He put his elbows on his knees, clasped his hands together, and in the most tender voice she'd heard him use, said, "Juliet, I want you to listen to me."

"Okay."

"I am going to terrify you. But in the end, you will see that, like your husband, I am a good man."

14

"LISTEN, I'M ALL FOR LITERACY, but I'm just saying, the publishing world is filled with quirky people," Walker said as they turned the corner from Broadway onto West Fifty-Seventh Street. "I'll read a Grisham book. All day long. He's in the airports. Real mainstream. And I've seen him on TV. He looks like a guy you'd want to talk to in a bar. But some of them, with their pale skin . . . I mean, come out of the cave. Get some sunlight."

"So did Reagan strike you as weird when he was hanging around the precinct?" Chris asked. "He's in all the airports."

"He was all right. A little stuffy for my taste. When you talked to him, he was there but kind of wasn't there, like things were ticking inside his head and he was distracted by it. And there's got to be some kind of brilliance rolling around up there to write a novel. But you don't have to be kooky. That's all I'm saying. Take Stephen King. The guy's books could scare the swastika right off of Charles Manson's forehead, but he's not walking around with crazy, bloodbath eyes, you know?"

Chris shrugged. "I guess."

"And judging from Miss Priss back there, the editors are a whole other kind of kooky. Now we've got to go see the agent." He groaned. "Just give me your regular thief, you know?"

"I guarantee the agent's going to be normal. I mean, these guys are about striking the deal, right? It's a business venture."

"Maybe you're right. I just hope he speaks our language."

"Let's hope."

Walker stopped and sniffed the air. "You smell that? Coneys."

"Our reward for a long day's work?"

"You got it. But ten bucks, or a coney, says this agent is a wack job."

"You're on."

They found the building and rode the elevator to the twenty-fourth floor. The receptionist, not quite as skeletal as the last one, politely guided them to a conference room, where she asked them to have a seat. Coffee and water were waiting. It seemed quiet, as an office should be on a Saturday.

"Fancy," Walker said, examining the coffee cup. "Real china."

"Hope it's real coffee," Chris said, pouring a cup. "I'm exhausted."

Within a few minutes, the door opened and in walked an early-thirtysomething man dressed in a pink sweater with a plaid button-up shirt underneath, hanging out at the bottom. He wore a blue bow tie and, of course, chunky square glasses. His hair was gelled in several different directions—the quintessential artsy look that seemed like it took way too much effort.

"Hi," the agent said, looking a little frazzled. He was glancing at a message on his cell phone as he shook their hands. "Bentley Marrow."

"Detective Walker. This is Sergeant Downey."

"Look," he said, dropping into the chair across from them, "I can explain. Well, not really. I mean, the guy's a mess. But I'm just asking that you keep this on the down low, okay? I'd so appreciate it. We're really trying to get him into an anger management program, and we've not been that successful. *Obviously* he shouldn't have been drinking and driving, and there's absolutely no excuse for him hitting on that female officer like he did. But that was the alcohol. And *obviously* we don't approve of this at all, but you understand what this would do to his career? Right?"

Sweat popped up in beads on his forehead.

"When was Mr. Reagan pulled over for a DUI?" Walker asked.

Bentley's eyes widened. "Patrick Reagan?"

"Yes."

"Oh . . . oh . . ." He cursed with relief and held out his hands like he wished he could rewind what he just said. "I am so sorry. I thought you were talking about another author." He chuckled nervously. "You're not here about . . . Fredrick Sebastian?"

"No. Patrick Reagan."

Bentley took in a deep breath. "Stellar. Okay. Sorry for the miscommunication. My secretary had just said two officers, and I assumed—we've been dealing with this since last night. . . ." His hands were doing most of the talking. "Okay, about Patrick. Yes. I remember. You two are from Maine. What is going on?"

"We need to ask you a few questions pertaining to an ongoing investigation in Wissberry, Maine," Walker said.

"What does this have to do with Patrick?"

"He may have been one of the last people to see a missing woman, but we can't seem to locate him. Being his agent, we're assuming you would know how to get ahold of him for, say, an emergency."

Bentley pushed his glasses up his nose. "Well, um . . ."

"Let me guess. He disappears for the winter to some mysterious cabin in the mountains and you have no idea how to reach him."

"Um, yeah."

Walker threw his hands up. "Seriously. How can anybody

just disappear for a few months? Not that I wouldn't love it, but doesn't this guy have any responsibilities?"

"To finish his book," Bentley said.

"It's just hard to believe," Walker continued, "that you can't find someone. What if there was an emergency? Doesn't this guy have any family that might need him?"

"His wife, Amelia, went with him to the cabin before she passed away. They had no children or other family that I'm aware of, except one distant cousin who tried to claim part of his fortune about ten years ago. It was dismissed in court."

"How did he take the passing of his wife?"

"I wouldn't really know," Bentley said, glancing away. "The truth is that we don't speak much. Hardly ever, in fact."

"But you're his agent. Aren't writers and agents tight?"

"Usually, but I'm not really his agent," Bentley said. "On paper I am. I look over contracts and that sort of thing, but that connection you're talking about . . . well, he had that with Ike."

"Who is Ike?" Walker asked, taking notes.

"You don't know who Ike Patterson is?" Bentley looked genuinely baffled.

Chris glanced at Walker, then said, "We're more up on the seedy underground crime scene, so you might have to enlighten us."

"Sorry. It's just that the guy is a legend. He was probably the most well-known literary agent in New York and maybe the world. He died about five years ago at the age of ninety-two, down the hall in his office that overlooks Manhattan. Right at his desk. Fell face forward onto a manuscript. The dude did what we all want to do, right? Die doing what we love?"

Chris bit his lip. *Not everybody wants to die on the job.* But he kept listening.

"He was the greatest, smart as a whip, never missed a beat, even at his age. He didn't even start using a cane until he was ninety. Never wore glasses. Dressed in a suit every single day."

"So Mr. Reagan and Mr. Patterson were good friends?"

"Very good friends. Patrick trusted him with his life, and Ike made sure Patrick was taken care of in every single way."

"So did Ike know where this mysterious cabin is?"

"If he did, he took the secret to his grave. Ike always claimed he had no idea, but I think otherwise. I don't know that Ike ever went there, but I believe he knew where it was."

"So Ike died a few years ago. How did Patrick take that death?"

Bentley's pained expression said enough. "You have to understand their relationship. Ike . . . shielded—yes, that's a good word—shielded Patrick from the more . . . unpleasant sides of this business."

"Such as?"

"Really anything negative. Everything that went to Patrick went through Ike first. Ike was able to communicate with him in a way that made Patrick feel secure. Even if there was something uncomfortable that needed to be discussed, Ike did it in a way that worked."

"Pardon me for saying it," Walker said, "but Patrick sounds like he might need some thicker skin."

Bentley smiled condescendingly. "Like you, maybe? Tough and manly?"

"Well, thank you for that, but no," Walker said. "I just mean that every profession has its positives and negatives. Why was Mr. Reagan so sensitive?"

"It's not necessarily sensitivity, but more like . . . balance. In order to do what Patrick does so brilliantly, he's got to be able to go deeper and farther than most of us are capable of. Ike understood there was a balance needed to maintain that level of creativity."

"So we're talking the ecosystem of the imagination."

"Something like that," Bentley said. He laced his fingers. "So what is this about a girl missing?"

Chris said, "A woman. The last place she was seen was at a grocery store, and we have a witness who said Patrick Reagan was there at the same time. We wondered if he'd seen anything."

"Your witness is mistaken. He never emerges until spring."

"So we hear," Chris said. "After Ike's death, what happened to Patrick?"

"Ike mentored me since I was eighteen, so I assumed responsibility for all his clients. I'm actually Ike's nephew."

"I see."

"I'm a highly qualified agent, but Patrick . . . he just wanted Ike. He didn't want to deal with anyone but Ike."

Chris looked at Walker. "It sounds like Mr. Reagan doesn't have a full grasp on the ups and downs of life."

"I don't think that's a fair statement," Bentley said. "His wife died two years after Ike and I think he just hit a rough patch."

"Can you explain what that means?" Walker asked. "Rough patch?"

"The ecosystem got polluted."

"Ah." Walker jotted that down. "So he didn't want to deal with the young, hotshot agent that took Ike's place."

"He didn't want to deal with anybody, including his editor."

"She told us," Chris said, "that he's late on his current project."

"That is true, but he said he needed more time to research and that when it was finished, it was going to be mind-blowing."

"That's *stellar* in literary terms," Walker quipped.

Chris laughed but Bentley wasn't amused. "As you can imagine, I'm very busy, so are there any more questions?"

"One more," Chris said as they all stood. "How does Patrick take negative reviews of his work?"

"Patrick does not read reviews of his work. It's counter-productive. And of course, the reviews and critiques are subjective. Many writers don't read them."

"Sorry—just one more question," Chris said. "Is Mr. Reagan Internet savvy?"

"We got him hooked up to e-mail in 2004, if that's what you're asking."

"What about social networking?"

Bentley laughed. "No. You're talking about Facebook and

Twitter? Absolutely not. He has a website that is maintained by his publisher. Patrick has nothing to do with it. The man doesn't even own a cell phone."

"Okay. Well, thanks for your time," Chris said as they walked out of the conference room.

"Yeah," Walker said. "Thanks. Oh, and your shirttail is hanging out." He winked and gestured to it.

Bentley just stood there with an odd expression as they headed to the elevator. Once inside, Walker cracked up. "Did you see that look on his face?"

"I know. We probably should've mentioned his hair was out of place."

Walker died laughing. "Honestly, I don't blame Patrick for not wanting to turn over his life to a guy named Bentley who wears bow ties and oversize glasses. His name might be Bentley, but he drives more like an Isuzu."

Chris laughed but then turned his thoughts to the information they'd gathered. "I'm seeing a pattern here. Reagan had to deal with a lot of loss in a short period of time."

"I can't believe nobody knows where this cabin is." They stepped off the elevator. "You think your witness can be trusted with his account that Reagan was at the grocery store? Maybe he was mistaken."

"The kid seemed pretty perceptive." *Maybe too perceptive,* Chris thought.

They were about to exit the lobby when Walker's phone rang.

"Walker. . . . Yeah. . . . No kidding. . . ." He looked at his watch. "Yeah, we can catch the one thirty. . . . Okay, bye."

"What?"

Walker groaned as he continued to walk. "No coneys. We gotta get back. Reagan's house was broken into and ran-sacked."

15

"PLEASE . . . *PLEASE!*" Jules was backed into the corner. Her legs shook so much she couldn't hold herself up. She slid down to a squatting position, her arms wrapped around herself. "Please . . . just . . . just stop it!"

Patrick turned to her, his face an enraged mess of bulging veins and splotchy redness. He was breathing hard, like a bull about to charge.

Jules tried to control her fear, to patiently wait this out, whatever it was, and not get herself killed. She glanced to the front door. Did she dare brave it? She had no idea what he was capable of. Moments before, they'd been discussing literature. Now . . . was she going to have to beg for her life?

"I'm sorry . . . ," she whispered. "I've offended you. I didn't mean to."

"Offended me?" A wicked resentment flashed through his eyes. "You think you've offended me?"

"I don't know," Jules cried, as earnestly as possible, trying to reach into him for that other man she'd known a few minutes before.

Patrick studied her, like he'd just noticed she was terrified. He blinked and blinked again, as if shaking an unseen image out of his mind's eye. Jules stayed perfectly still, replaying in her own mind what she'd said that had caused him to rage.

She'd mentioned her fondness for his fourth book, *Crashing Tide*, and how the characters were portrayed, the difficult decisions that had to be made. She remarked about how much she loved the hero's journey in each of his books. Something led to something else, and Jules asked about his wife . . .

Was that it? She couldn't recall the exact moment. He'd stood as if stretching his legs. Maybe she just assumed he was stretching his legs. But it didn't seem threatening right away. She'd looked up, midsentence, to find him glaring at her, fists balled at his sides. She'd asked him what was the matter. And then it was a blur. He'd been yelling things that didn't make sense; she'd gotten up but he told her to sit down, except she didn't, and now here she was, cornered like a frightened animal.

Patrick's face slowly returned to a normal color as he scraped his hands through his hair. He seemed unable to look at her. Jules rose slowly, afraid, but not wanting to seem as vulnerable as she looked.

He finally met her eyes, remorse in his own. "I . . . I shouldn't have done that."

"You're right," she said sternly.

"But you're naive, Juliet. Horribly naive. Is everything so black-and-white for you?"

"You're going to have to be more specific."

"You believe it is wrong to murder someone."

"Yes." Her heart pounded in her chest at the word *murder*.

"I do too." He stared at the ground. "But sometimes it's merciful. Does mercy ever trump your black-and-white world?"

"I believe you're a merciful man."

"Then you don't know me very well."

"I'm seeing a few different sides to you."

He looked at her. "I am not sure if there is any decency inside of me."

"Of course there is."

"I always imagined that I would know right from wrong. It might be blurred for other people but not for me."

There was a long pause and Jules studied every inch of his face. His eyes dimmed and wandered.

"In your books," she said quietly, testing the waters, "the protagonists and antagonists are clearly drawn."

He cut his eyes sideways to her. She waited, but he didn't speak, so she continued. "There is always a pursuit of justice."

He turned, folded his arms, looked up at the ceiling as if

searching for answers. "I set out to do the right thing, and I am not sure if I can now." He looked at her. "You're just so . . ." He didn't finish his sentence. His hands dropped to his sides. "Maybe I should send you home. Maybe everything should go back to how it was."

Jules stepped closer to him. She realized in that moment that she had not seen a single picture of his wife in the cabin. From what she'd read in the very few interviews he'd given over the years, Amelia was everything to him. She liked having pictures of Jason around her, but maybe they grieved differently. "Patrick, I am sorry your wife died."

His eyes lit for a moment, but the fury washed away like tidewater.

"I need you to be immersed," he said, his tone changing ever so slightly. She sensed the danger was gone, and something else had arrived. "You've got to be pulled into the story. You've got to see deep into it and work your way through it all, snake your way through. Do you see? You can't just rest on the surface. You can't be a boat, gliding over the top, barely slicing the water open. You've got to be drowning, under the water, under the surface, looking up at the light."

Jules nodded though not really understanding what story he was referring to or why.

"Nothing but that red pen, do you hear me? Only notes in red."

"Why?" She put her hands on her hips, locking eyes with him.

He turned to face her completely. "Because it will remind you of the blood that I poured out onto the page and the blood that's going to be required from you, too."

She felt hysteria bubble to the surface of her emotions. Her chest rose and fell faster and faster, even though she wanted to remain calm. "You just talk in all these riddles and say things that don't make sense."

"Because you're not cooperating very well."

"I've done everything you've asked."

"Not well enough."

"You're crazy, aren't you?" Jules asked as she swiped tears from her face. "You've lost your mind and now you're pulling me into your nightmare."

"Let me be clear," Patrick said. "It's your nightmare. And you're the only one who can get yourself out of it."

Jules buried her face in her hands. "I just want Jason."

A hand touched her shoulder and she stepped back and batted it away. "Don't touch me, you crazy freak!"

She ran to her room and slammed the door. Within a few seconds, she heard it lock. She lay on the bed, crying for what seemed like hours. The light in the window was all but gone.

She'd fallen asleep at some point and then awoke to a noise at the door. She sat up. Sliding under the door toward her were pages from the manuscript.

If she wanted to get out of this alive, she was going to have to unravel the mystery of the man who was drifting like the snow outside, leaving reality, it seemed, one word at a time.

Two delays at the airport caused them to get back to Maine in the early evening. They went straight to Patrick Reagan's house, where a couple of squad cars were parked and the captain's vehicle too. It had not been snowing in New York, but up the coast, the cold Canadian air was filling in, and large, blissful snowflakes caressed Chris's cheeks as he walked from the car.

The front door was open and the captain stood in the middle of the large living area taking notes. Chris couldn't believe what he saw. Books were pulled off the shelves, tables overturned, drawers and cabinets opened, cushions upended.

Walker and Chris looked at each other with disbelief.

"It's a mess, isn't it?" Captain Perry said.

"Anything taken?" Chris asked.

"We're still trying to assess the situation. We talked to his housekeeper, who was very freaked out and was having a hard time concentrating on our questions. But after two hours of looking around, she didn't think anything was missing." The captain closed his notebook. "And of course, we can't figure out how to get ahold of the man to tell him his house has been destroyed. You two have any luck in New York?"

"Not really. We're still trying to dust the quirk off ourselves," Walker said.

"We learned his agent and wife died within a couple years of each other and that he's been distraught about it. His editor said he's late on a book and that's unusual for him." Chris took in the scene around him. "Somebody was looking for something here, weren't they?"

"You don't suppose it was his publishing house, hoping to find an early draft of his book?" Walker cracked up.

As the captain and Walker continued to talk, Chris made his way toward the office. More than the rest of the house, this room was a gigantic mess. Folders from every drawer were pulled open and thrown here and there. But Chris was interested in one thing: was the manuscript that had been scattered all over the place still here?

It was hard to spot because there were papers everywhere, but as he sifted through, he found manuscript pages in the debris.

The captain walked in and shook his head. "This thing is getting crazier by the minute."

"What time do we think this occurred?"

"Nobody knows. The housekeeper returned, she said, because she forgot some of her cleaning aids the last time she was here."

The captain looked at Walker, who had trailed behind him. "Hey, go talk to Beals. See what they found concerning the outside of the house."

Walker nodded and left, and the captain stepped farther into the office. He closed the door. "Chris, did you come by in uniform yesterday to question the housekeeper?"

Chris looked down and nodded, pressing his lips together to keep from saying something he shouldn't. He'd been busted, thanks to this break-in.

Captain Perry sighed loudly. "I told you to do this by the book. To be patient."

"I know. I'm just so worried about her. Something tells me she's in danger."

"Nothing points to that."

"Is this all a coincidence, then?"

"We don't know what this is yet. Maybe it is. We just don't know." The captain lowered his voice. "I know this is personal for you, Chris, but I'm not going to tolerate insubordination. I threw you a bone. I sent you to New York."

"I know."

"So we're clear. You don't make a move without my approval."

"We're clear."

"What did you find out when you were here, anyway? The maid said you came in and looked around."

Chris took a deep breath. The captain, who was known to have a temper, didn't seem as rattled as Chris expected. "I did."

"You find anything of significance?"

Chris fought the urge to swallow. "Looked like a house that hadn't been lived in. Too tidy, you know?"

The captain sighed and now appeared angry. "We're going to find this guy. I'll tell you that. He can't just drop off the face of the earth."

"What can I do?" Chris asked.

"Go write up your report tonight. I'm going to put you back on patrol tomorrow, but listen, Chris, I'm not going to shut you out of this deal. As soon as we have some leads, we're going to follow them. But I want to be clear: we're going to be following protocol. If this thing is connected and we've got criminal activity going on, then we don't want to mess this up for the DA. I'll kick you off if you screw up."

"I know. I . . . shouldn't have come here. I know that."

Perry put a hand on Chris's shoulder. "It's going to be okay, son."

The captain left the room and Chris wandered out, surveying the mess. Another detective gave him a sideways glance as he strolled by. But Chris was just thankful the captain hadn't blown up. Maybe the guy was mellowing out a little. Maybe he knew how much this case meant to Chris. Whatever the reason, he'd escaped unscathed, which was a minor miracle.

He wished he could slip back into the office and grab some pages of the manuscript, but he couldn't risk it.

If they weren't looking for that manuscript, then what were they looking for?

It wasn't a robbery. There would've been valuables taken. They wanted something else. Something more valuable than gold.

Chris tossed and turned erratically in the short amount of time he actually slept. He found himself jolting awake, gasping for air, his voice echoing distantly as he yelled for Jules, somewhere deep in his dreams.

Addy was up early and had fixed him breakfast. She set

a large mug of coffee in front of him at the breakfast table. "You look terrible."

"Thanks."

"How did New York go?" Addy had been gone visiting friends all day and late into the night. They hadn't had a chance to talk yet.

"I can't shake the feeling this is connected to Reagan. His house was ransacked sometime yesterday while we were in New York. But nothing was taken."

She sat back in her seat. "Bizarre."

"Nobody knows where he goes in the winter. He literally disappears."

"What are you going to do?"

"I'm going to keep looking for her. I can't stop. I can't give up."

She nodded and patted his arm. "I know. But you can't let it consume you to the point where you're no good to anybody, especially Jules. Promise me you'll take care of yourself."

"I promise." But there was no one to be any good for. Addy could take care of herself. Nobody depended on him.

He finished his coffee quickly. "I've got to go."

"You don't go in until the afternoon, do you?"

He wiped his mouth and grabbed his things. "You going to see Heather today?"

"Yeah. Can't wait." She grinned. "You want to join us for lunch? Heather's single again."

Chris laughed. "No thank you. Cute girl, but runs through men like a drunk driver plows through orange hazard cones."

"That's not fair," Addy said. "She's just had a string of bad . . . choices. You would be a great choice. You would treat her right, which is what she needs."

"Thanks, but no thanks."

She pouted. "You're going to stay single your whole life? I kind of had visions of being an aunt someday."

"Ooookay, cart way before the horse."

Addy followed him to the door. "I just think you'd be happier settled down, with a family to come home to."

"You don't think I'm happy now?" Chris asked.

"I think you could be happier and could make someone very happy, too. You're a good man, and there aren't many of you left these days."

He gave her a quick hug and scruffed up her hair. "Thanks, Sis."

"That's another 'thanks, but no thanks,' I guess."

"You're so good at pouting."

"I know. It usually works on you."

"Say hello to Heather for me."

Chris left, headed straight to the place he knew he shouldn't go.

16

"WHAT ARE YOU DOING HERE?" The Lt. Colonel stumbled through the front door like the house had just jolted forward and tossed him out. His eyes, bloodshot and glowing mean, seemed unable to focus on anything in particular. His clawlike grip on his whiskey bottle released suddenly, and the bottle fell to the porch, shattering. This led to a string of cusswords blistering through the morning quiet.

"Okay, Lt. Colonel, let's come in—"

"Don't call me that! Stop calling me that!"

"Fine. Jim, get into the house." Chris took his arm. The Lt. Colonel resisted at first but wasn't functioning well enough to do much about it. He made his way forward, tripping over the edges of rugs and running into the ends of tables. Chris hoped he wouldn't fall and get hurt, making Chris have to call an ambulance and explain why he was at Jules's house in the first place.

The Lt. Colonel made it to the couch, crashed onto it, then started bawling.

Chris sat on the chair opposite the couch and tried to figure out what to do with the man. His face was wet and sticky with tears when it emerged from his hands. He wiped his eyes with shaky hands. "She left, Chris."

"Jules?"

"Of course Jules. She left. Why wouldn't she? What does she have here? Me. That's it. And what a treat I am."

"Do you know she left?"

"Doesn't it make sense? Look at me and tell me that doesn't make sense."

Chris clasped his hands together and leaned forward, his elbows on his knees. "Sir, you're being hard on yourself." He almost winced as he said it because the man could obviously see what a wreck he was.

The Lt. Colonel seemed to be getting a grip. "You religious, Chris?"

"Nah."

"You know Jason was religious."

Chris nodded. He knew well.

"The rest of the family had all but given up on me. But not Jason. He never did. He invited me to family gatherings, always came by to see me. He told me he'd help me kick the bottle."

"He was that kind of guy."

"He was a little preachy, I'll say that. Carried that Bible around with him all the time. That was a pathetic-looking thing, worn-out, half the pages falling out."

Chris laughed. "Yeah. He inherited it from his grandfather."

"I told him I'd buy him a new one, but he never wanted a new one." The Lt. Colonel's eyes filled with tears again. "The truth is that I couldn't be there much for Juliet because when Jason died, I lost . . ." His voice quivered. "I lost the only friend I had."

Chris stood, his own throat swelling with emotion, and sat down next to the Lt. Colonel. "Me, too," he whispered. He patted the other man awkwardly on the back.

"He was a good man," the Lt. Colonel continued. "What every father dreams of for their daughters. He was like a son to me."

Chris nodded, smiling at a memory. "Jason was like the brother I never had. My sister, Addy, is terrific, but she likes to mother me too much. Thinks I need a wife, like, yesterday."

The Lt. Colonel grabbed Chris's sleeve. "Don't take family for granted."

"Yes, sir."

"Jason told me once that I should pray. That God was not surprised by the condition of my soul. That He would hear my prayers. I never believed him," he said, wiping his mouth with the back of his hand. "I never said that prayer I promised him I would. But last night I said a prayer for Juliet, prayed she'd come back. Prayed she'd be okay. As bad of a man as I am, maybe God would take into consideration that something good came from me."

"You're not a bad man," Chris said. "You've just . . . lost your way."

The Lt. Colonel pondered this for a moment, then rose and walked to the kitchen. He filled a cup with water. "Jason called Him *Father*."

"Who?"

"God. And I wondered if . . . if Juliet considered God to be more of a father to her than me."

Chris didn't know what to say. He'd always appreciated Jason's faith but could never grasp it like Jason did. He believed in God, believed in heaven, but beyond that, there was nothing there for him. He was not a man who had a great deal of faith in anything.

The Lt. Colonel gulped the water. It ran down his chin. He tossed the cup in the sink. "Chris, you have to find her. She's all I have left."

Chris stood. "I will. I'll find her. I am going to need to go through this house again, sir. Go through everything. Try to find any small clue that will help me."

The Lt. Colonel pointed to the computer on the small desk. "Then you should go through that. That's where she lived her life, in that little box." He groaned and held his head as he walked back to the couch.

"I've looked there. It's possible that someone might've used her Facebook posts to begin to understand a pattern of behavior, to know where she might go." He couldn't get into Patrick Reagan with him at this point.

"Then look again!" His voice boomed as he fell into the cushions. "Look again, for the love of pete . . ." His head tilted back, he closed his eyes and began snoring loudly before Chris could explain that the Lt. Colonel needed to keep his visit discreet.

But it was a gift. He could get a lot more done with the man unconscious.

Chris began to roam the house, giving everything he saw second consideration. In their bedroom, he turned on the ceiling fan because even with the cold, it felt stuffy. He looked again at the closet and in the drawers. He searched for anything buried underneath clothes, hidden under the bed. Nothing appeared out of order.

He opened the drawers of Jason's nightstand. His gun. Still there, exactly where Chris kept his own. He wondered if Jules even knew that it was in there, or if she kept it there in case she ever needed it. He picked up the framed picture of Jules sitting atop the nightstand by the lamp. It was a black-and-white photo of her at the ocean, splashing in the waves, laughing wildly at something. Her long hair was blown back by the breeze, and the light from a cloudy day illuminated every inch of her face. It was a gorgeous photo, one that he was sure had been Jason's favorite.

He remembered the day that Jason told him he'd met someone at a backyard cookout. He was enamored with her and talked the entire time they were on duty that day. "If

I never hear the name Juliet again," Chris joked, "I'll be a happy camper."

Jason had smiled. "Then you're going to be very unhappy because I'm pretty sure you're going to hear it for the rest of my life."

"How can you know after one day at a barbecue?" Chris asked.

"You have no idea, man. You're not open to that kind of love."

"I'm open. I'm just way more of a skeptic."

Jason laughed. "Yes. I know. That's why I can't get you to come to church with me."

"If you marry this girl, I guess I'm going to have to come to church, then."

"I guess you will."

Jason's voice echoed through his mind as Chris picked up the Bible that rested on the nightstand. It was the one that the Lt. Colonel had referred to, the one that Jason carried with him constantly, even in the patrol car.

The book was heavier than he expected, its leather cover cracked and worn, like a great bomber jacket. He opened it, and the pages, wispy light, fluttered against the ceiling fan's soft wind. The thing was marked up like a college exam paper. Highlights. Red ink. Dates. Circles. Words.

At the front, there was a place to write a dedication. He assumed the name was that of Jason's grandfather. The Bible had been passed down to Jason upon the old man's death. The heritage this thing held . . . What Chris wouldn't give to know the verses that had guided his own grandparents, whom he pretty much regarded as saints. They'd been religious too, but his own father, who'd served in the Vietnam War, never spoke of God to Chris. His mother sent him to a local VBS every summer, but he figured it was just so she could get some free time from him and his sister.

Chris closed the Bible and set it back on the table carefully, exactly how it had been. Everywhere he looked in the room, he was reminded of Jason. The walls felt like they were closing around him, so he walked out.

The Lt. Colonel was now slumped sideways on the couch, one arm protruding outward, his hand dangling over the back of the couch. His snores seemed to vibrate the pictures on the nearby table.

Chris wandered from room to room, trying to escape the memories of Jason. He kept pushing them out of his mind and tried to think more logically. Yet nothing was getting him any closer to finding Jules.

He made it out to the detached garage, which he hadn't yet searched. Even with the sunlight shining in, it was hard to see, but Chris found the lever on the garage door and lifted it up. Light spilled onto a mess of boxes and junk, piled everywhere that the car wasn't. It smelled musty, like the door hadn't been opened in a long while.

Chris closed his eyes, trying not to feel the regret that was causing his emotions to slip and slide. He should've been here for Jules. He should've come over, helped her go through all this stuff. He could've knocked this out in a day. Maybe she had needed help deciding what to keep of Jason's. Maybe she needed someone to tell her it was okay to throw something away.

He started near the garage door, looking through boxes. Many of them were simply marked *Jason*. One held his police department softball jersey and gear. Another had his college diploma and his police academy documents.

About twenty-five minutes into it, Chris couldn't hold it in any longer. Everywhere he looked, Jason was there, yet absent, and it was no use trying to find clues about Jules. If there were any here, they'd been buried deep inside a dark box somewhere.

Chris slid to the floor and hid his face in his hands. He could really use a drink right now. He knew where to find it, too.

As he turned, headed for the Lt. Colonel's truck, something caught his eye. It was basked in shadows in the back corner of the garage, but one sliver of daylight glinted off it and shone like a small prism.

Chris carefully stepped around the clutter. He removed boxes around the object to get a better view.

He moved closer. It was a piece of the hull of a boat.

Jason didn't own a boat.

17

IT HAD BOTHERED Jules before that she didn't know the time in the cabin. She'd wondered if Patrick did that on purpose, so when he came here to write, time was never depended upon or restrictive—he could choose whether to acknowledge it or not.

Now she didn't care. She'd been lying in bed, on her side, staring out the window, since she awoke. Two hours had passed. Maybe more. She'd watched how the light rose through the window, became clear and bright. But she couldn't make herself get out of bed.

It was the same feeling as when Jason died. Despair. A lack of will to do anything but hide within herself. She couldn't

even cry anymore. It felt like the death of her soul. The fact
was that if Patrick was going to kill her, she wanted him to
go ahead and put her out of her misery. And his. What was
the point of this life anyway? The people you loved ended up
dead, drunk, or in Patrick's case, insane.

She'd adored him from afar for so long. She'd respected his
gift for writing and his need for privacy. He was not known
to be involved in literary circles or VIP parties. He loved his
craft and loved his books and loved his home state.

But with him, a picture did not speak a thousand words,
because if all the pictures she'd seen of him had shared even
half of what he was like, maybe she wouldn't have been so
caught off guard. Instead, his pictures exuded warmth. In
his official author pictures, he stood by a fireplace or a staircase; there were always books in the picture somewhere. He
dressed nicely, in a turtleneck or a suit jacket. He always
screamed classy.

Not crazy.

Jules wondered if her father would even know she was
missing. It depended on how deeply and often he was bing-
ing. He could very well be passed out somewhere for days.

Who was going to save her?

The sound of footsteps caused her to sit up in bed. The
door flew open and Patrick Reagan walked into her room,
sat down quietly in the corner armchair. He stared at her for
a moment. She pulled the sheet toward her even though she
was in cotton, button-up pajamas that completely covered
her from head to toe.

He didn't say anything for a long time.

"What do you want?" she finally asked. It came out as genuine as she needed it to.

"I want to help you, Juliet," he said. "That is all that I've wanted to do."

"Help me with what?"

"To see."

"What? See what?"

He stood, put his hands in his pockets, paced the room as he spoke. "My wife's name was Amelia. She came down with cancer at sixty. It was very fast. The doctor said that it had taken over her entire body. He told us intense radiation and chemo would prolong her life, but Amelia wouldn't hear of it. She wanted to die with dignity and didn't want to be a burden. That was my Amelia. She never wanted to bother anybody or be anything but helpful."

Jules sat quietly. Watched. Listened.

"She wanted to die here." He pointed. "She died right in that bed."

Chills ran over her body.

"And I was with her every day. I watched as the cancer consumed her." His words trailed off and he gathered his emotions.

"I'm so sorry," Jules whispered.

"There was so much grief," he said so quietly that Jules had to strain to hear him. "And when you're immersed, you can't think clearly. You can't see anything objectively. All you can see, hear, or feel is your grief." His gaze found her. "It's all that you know."

Jules nodded, surprised by the emotion she was feeling. In a weird way, she found herself connecting to him. Just hours earlier, she hadn't understood a thing about what he was doing. But now it felt like they had something together. Death had taken their most precious gifts.

He continued, "I've read between the lines, Juliet. I've felt the weight of your words. You're lost, like me. And you can't find peace because there is no peace without truth."

"What truth am I missing?" she asked.

"I am going to show you. But you have to trust me."

She looked at the ceiling, at the words scrawled above her. "I don't know if I can."

Patrick walked toward her and her heart stopped. But he sat on the edge of the bed, at the end, his full attention on her.

"They don't believe I can write anymore," he said. "And maybe it's true. Maybe I can't. Amelia, she was the glue that held me together. She was the straight line through the chaos of my mind." He tapped his temple. "All this has been unraveling for quite some time."

Jules sat perfectly still.

"But inside here, I know a secret. And I have to tell it to you. But you're not ready."

"How do I get ready?"

He studied her for a moment before speaking again. "Do you know what the sagging middle is, Juliet?"

Jules didn't know if she should nod or not. She didn't know if he remembered that he'd asked her this before.

"It is what undoes so many novels." He glanced at her. "And novelists." He stared out the window for a moment, the light shining against his ruminating eyes. "It usually happens around chapter 17 of a book. It is the place where the entire story can fall apart. The depths of the second act. The first act has been a dance between the building of the story and the introduction of the characters. The second act comes and we must build up the conflict and set the stage for a climactic ending. But so often, the writer fails at this point, and the story drags. The words are repetitive. They are weighty and sluggish and sometimes simply a bridge to get to the third act, offering nothing but empty content."

Jules nodded, feeling hysteria building.

"A lot of the critics believe that I am in the chapter 17 of my life. Don't you?"

"No. You're wrong. I've never believed you've lost your touch."

"My last three books have been disastrous, have they not?"

"Why is that surprising? I don't believe any writer is going to hit the mark every time."

"You're not alone," he said, standing again. "Critics everywhere believe my time has come to step down off the *New York Times* list. To go hide in my cave or die in my cabin or bury myself in a hole."

"I don't believe that," Jules said. "And you shouldn't either. Writers don't listen to their critics, do they?"

Patrick blinked slowly at her. "Sometimes they do. When they really respect the critic."

"I . . . You have to know how much I respect you," she stammered. "I've admired you for a long time. That admiration never went away."

Patrick smiled slightly. "Thank you, Juliet. I appreciate your kind words." He took a deep breath. "My dear, it is time for you to get dressed."

Jules slumped. "I'm not up for much. I just want to go home."

"Get up and make yourself presentable. You can't sleep the whole day away."

She ripped the covers off and stood. "I can't sleep, Patrick. Don't you get that? I can't pretend this is a normal situation. You're holding me against my will. You're promising to terrify me. I'm not cozy and warm and fuzzy here. I'm scared."

He nodded understandingly. "To be expected."

"And you're acting kind of crazy," she said, walking to the bathroom. "You're yelling at me and saying things I don't understand."

He looked pathetically apologetic. "I . . . I know. I sometimes . . . break."

She paused at the bathroom door. "We need to get this taken care of. We need to get to the bottom of this, Patrick. Do you understand what I mean? You can't hold me here forever."

"I enjoy your company."

She tried not to look repulsed.

"You have a gift, you know," he said gently.

"No. You have the gift, Patrick. You have to believe in yourself again."

"I'm tired," he said, moving toward the bedroom door. "I'm worn-out."

"Me too. I wake up every day wondering if I'll hurt any less."

"It is time to work," he said and left the room.

Jules closed the bathroom door and put her back against it, catching her breath. There was something about being in his presence that was awe inspiring and terrifying all at the same time. As dazzling as his caramel-colored eyes were, they hinted at deep sorrow. They reflected the heaviness of her own soul. She wanted to know more of him and run away from him simultaneously.

"What secret, Patrick?" She spoke into the bathroom mirror. If she was going to get out of this, then she was going to have to face it.

"God . . . ," she whispered to the Presence with whom Jason was so well acquainted. "Why? What is this?"

A weird sense of purpose stirred in her soul. She couldn't directly identify it, but something told her maybe it wasn't a mistake that she was here after all. Patrick was hurting deeply. But could she offer any comfort? Any wisdom? She was as wounded and weary as he was.

And the truth was, she was terrified of the secret he held.

Jules started to brush her hair.

"Juliet! Hurry it up!" Patrick called, his voice barely audible through the closed bathroom door.

It jolted her. *"Hurry it up."* Like they were getting ready to do something pleasurable or exciting.

She leaned close to herself in the mirror. "Pull it together. If you are going to get out of this, you have to think. Be smart. Don't overreact. Don't underreact. Just do what you have to do to survive and get home." Jules surprised herself, because only moments before, she'd had no will whatsoever to survive even a day.

18

AFTER MOVING SEVERAL MORE BOXES, Chris managed to get a good look at the piece of hull leaned up against the wall. It was dirty white, with the hull number embedded in the fiberglass. Sitting right below the fragment was a cardboard file box, unlabeled, the lid slightly askew. Crouching, Chris took the lid off and peered inside. There seemed to be files and photographs, but the light in the back of the garage wasn't bright enough for him to get a good look. He picked up the box and went inside the house. At the kitchen table, he got a better look at what was inside.

Files. Lots of them. Copied. Photographs of boats and,

more specifically, their hulls, where the numbers were embedded the same way as on the piece in the garage.

Chris quickly flipped through the files. They held police documents on stolen boats in the area. "What is this? Hey, Jim—"

The Lt. Colonel mumbled something and snorted, then returned to unconsciousness.

Chris walked to the couch and shook the man's shoulder until he aroused. "Jim, wake up. I need to ask you something."

The Lt. Colonel's eyes slowly pried open, and he raised his arm to shield them like there was some grand light showering him. "What is it?" he mumbled.

"Sir, I need to ask you something."

"Stop shouting."

"I'm not shouting. Are you awake?"

He sat up a little, his eyes widening. "You find something about Juliet?"

"No. But . . . I found something."

"What is it?"

"Do you know if Jason ever said anything to you about stolen boats?"

"Boats?"

"Yes. Did he ever mention anything about stolen boats to you?"

He wiped a dribble of slobber off his mouth. "I don't recall anything about boats."

"Think hard. Maybe in casual conversation?"

The Lt. Colonel's face turned red. "I said no! I don't remember anything! What's this about?"

Chris walked away from him. "It doesn't matter."

The Lt. Colonel stood, swayed, and almost tipped over. "Is it going to help us find Juliet?"

"No. Never mind. It's nothing." Chris closed the box, picked it up, and went to the door.

"Where are you going?"

"Home."

"What about Juliet?"

Chris opened the door and stepped out, balancing the box with one arm. "Sir, you need to get yourself out of this . . . cycle you're in. If we're going to find her, I need your help. You can't do it like this."

He waved a hand at Chris. "What good is an old man like me going to do you?"

"I don't know yet, but you need to be on standby." Chris walked to his truck and checked the time. He had to get into work. He'd have to look at the files later.

"You're late," Maecoat said as Chris slipped into lineup. The captain noticed, giving him a long, sideways glance.

"Sorry. Just running some errands."

The captain let them go and Chris and Maecoat went to their car. About an hour into an easygoing patrol day, Chris said, "Do you remember anything about boat theft in the community?"

Maecoat thought for a moment.

"A couple years back," Chris added.

Maecoat slowly nodded. "Sure. Big theft ring. Seems like the sheriff's department had to get involved and all that."

"Jason and I were responding to a call on a stolen boat the night he was shot."

Maecoat nodded again. "That's right."

As Maecoat drove on, down into the town square, Chris remembered something. "There had been a string of calls on thefts and attempted thefts, but not in our jurisdiction. Remember that? Nothing was stolen from Wissberry."

Maecoat grinned. "That's because we're the best."

"But then one night, we get that call, and that's when Jason was shot." Chris leaned back in his seat, staring out the window, trying to collect his thoughts. "I never connected that incident to the other boat thefts. Jason's death always seemed so random to me, like we were in the wrong place at the wrong time. I wondered if the shooting had anything to do with the boat theft we were going out to investigate, but not to the others. And of course nobody could connect it to anything at the end of the day."

"They ended up believing Jason's murder to be random, not attached to the boat incident, right?"

"Yeah. They thought it might be gang related. We'd gotten intel that gang activity was on the rise in our area. But nobody knew for sure. Nobody even knew how many men there were."

"Why are you thinking about those boat thefts?"

Chris shrugged. "With Jules missing, maybe I'm thinking a lot about Jason. I always do, I guess."

"Reagan's home being ransacked—was that the craziest thing ever?"

"It's connected somehow. I just don't know how. I don't know how to prove it."

"You got the captain backing you. And Walker on it, right?"

Chris nodded. Maecoat kept talking, changing subjects multiple times like he always did when he got behind the wheel. There was something about driving that got Maecoat talking. Chris responded in all the right places, laughed at all his jokes, but the entire time he was plotting how to get out of the second half of his patrol. He had to get to that box. He had to read through it.

After they stopped to eat, Chris seized the moment as they walked to the parking lot. "Dude, I don't feel good."

Maecoat looked back as Chris stopped and held his stomach. "You okay?"

"No . . ."

Maecoat sighed. "I told you not to get that fish."

"I know."

"Come on. Let's get you back to the station."

⌐ ⌐

Jules walked down the hallway, fully dressed and presentable, with nowhere to go.

As she turned the corner toward the living room, Patrick came from the other end of the house, carrying a large cardboard box. He set it on the coffee table and stretched out his hand to her. "Come. I have something to show you."

She looked at his hand, wondering if she should take it. The thought sickened her for a moment. But if she wanted out of this alive, she was going to have to earn his trust and make him believe she had the same affection for him she had before, when she hardly knew him but thought she did.

When she reached out to him, he took her hand in his. It was warm and strong, but her stomach flipped and flopped as he guided her toward one of two doors she'd noticed the first evening, the one that opened off the kitchen. There were windows, too, but the drapes were drawn. She assumed the windows overlooked much of the same as her room: trees with pathless views.

Patrick turned to her right before he opened the door. "You should brace yourself."

Jules's throat tightened with fear, but a dazzling sense of awe shone through his eyes rather than a threat of harm. He opened the door and guided her out.

Jules gasped, letting go of his hand. Patrick smiled delightedly. Jules stepped forward, a cold gust of wind snapping through her stunned thoughts.

Before her was the most spectacular view she'd ever seen. The mountains rose out of the earth right before her. The clouds rested on invisible shelves, slightly lower than the peaks. The sun spread its light through them, moving shadows across the valley below. A few feet in front of her was a wrought-iron railing, taller than waist high. She was standing on a wood deck, but there was nothing below her that she could see. It was like they were floating.

Patrick joined her at the rail. "The cabin is built into the side of the mountain."

"What is underneath us?"

"Stable support," he said with an assuring smile. "But it gives the feeling that we're stepping into the air, doesn't it?"

Jules turned her attention back to the view, smelling the fragrant pine that swirled on the cold wind. It made her feel like she was on top of the world and, at the very same time, that she was only one tree on a mountainous planet. "No wonder you come here," she said. "I wouldn't ever want to leave."

He stared out at the scene before them too. "It is no mistake, Juliet, that I come here in the winter. The dead of winter. Everything dies in winter, doesn't it?"

"I suppose so."

"But it doesn't die. Not really. It is dormant, inside the earth, protected by the very thing that has buried it alive."

Jules's heart raced.

"So it is no coincidence that I come here in winter, and it is no coincidence I leave rebirthed in the spring."

"I don't know what that means."

"It is too cold for you to stay out here any longer, unprotected." He opened the door. Jules didn't want to leave, but she was getting very cold. She took one more long look at the scenery before her, then stepped inside, warming her hands by rubbing them together. She really wished there were a fire in the fireplace. Patrick went to the living room, and she followed him there. He opened the box, lifted it, and then dumped it.

Hundreds of pages—notes, folders, documents—spilled out onto the large coffee table and the surrounding floor.

"What are you doing?" Jules asked, gawking at the enormous mess that had just been made.

"You can't stay on the surface any longer, Juliet." He gestured toward the mountain of papers. "It's time that you drowned."

It seemed easy enough to drown in the sea of papers in front of her. She knelt beside the table, trying to take it in.

"I will fix you something warm to drink. You begin. This is going to take quite some time."

Jules slipped off her shoes. She longed to be back out on that porch, but instead, she was suffocating behind the dark walls of gloom. And she had no idea where to begin. Or what she was supposed to be doing.

Patrick stood nearby, his fist pressed against his chin, watching her as if with bated breath. As if something dynamic were about to happen. All she saw were random, mismatched documents, notes, pictures of numbers. She pulled one out in particular. Looking at it carefully, she realized it was a picture of a boat's hull. She found another picture of an actual motorboat. She didn't know what kind, but it was a common make and model around their part of the coast. A sporting boat or fishing boat.

Again, a boat. What was she supposed to be figuring out here, other than having a constant reminder of where Jason was killed? She looked up at Patrick. He seemed fixated by her every move, the hot drink forgotten. She tried to ignore him and began digging through what looked to be police reports from towns around Wissberry, reports on boat thefts. She sorted through some handwritten notes on yellow legal paper. She divided out everything that looked similar and began making piles.

After a while, Patrick went to the kitchen. He returned with apple cider and said, "So this is how you work? In compartments like this?"

Jules didn't look at him. "Now you're going to dog how I sort through what is basically a gigantic mess?"

Patrick sat down on one of the couches. "It's not a mess. That's what you're not seeing."

"Maybe this is how I see better."

"Writing *absorbs* confusion and chaos, you see."

She glanced up at him. "No, I don't see. But that's the point you've been trying to make all along, right?"

"You can't box it up nice and neatly. You can't follow a formula. It's like a wildfire. It scorches whatever is dry and dying. Not even water can stop a wildfire. The fire consumes until it reaches something that has already been consumed."

"I'm supposed to make sense out of all this? Scrap pieces of paper? Police reports? Notes?"

He knelt beside her and took a piece of paper off the table. "Look."

Jules peered at it. It was a handwritten police report on a boat stolen in nearby Belfast. She tried to concentrate on the details but couldn't seem to focus with him breathing down her neck.

"Okay, so I read it."

"But you didn't see it."

Jules felt like bursting into tears. "I don't know what you want from me. You're going to make me sit and sift through all this, finding some needle in a literary haystack?"

"Writing is about finding truth. But you can't find the truth if you don't see everything."

"I see. I see!"

"No. You're reading. See. Smell. Feel. Use all your senses."

There was obviously no getting out of this, short of running to the suspended deck and flinging herself off the edge. So she tried to "see."

The cop had responded to a call. The Dershires reported their boat stolen from their cabin. No witnesses. Jules closed her eyes and tried to imagine the scene.

"Good. Good."

She wasn't sure what good this did, but she might as well play the part he wanted her to. She didn't want him throwing a fit again.

After a little bit, she looked up. Patrick had sat down on the couch again.

"I'm going to need some coffee."

He grinned. "Spoken like a true writer."

"You don't have to do this," Captain Perry said.

But he did. He knew he did. He'd taken off the shirt of his police uniform to try to stop the bleeding. Now he just wore a white T-shirt. It was cold outside, but he was completely numb.

He walked the sidewalk up to her house. The door opened before he got there. He stopped short of the porch. Behind him, the captain had begun following. He could hear his footsteps stop too.

He locked eyes with her. Hers were wide, filled with dread and disbelief. Her gaze fell to his T-shirt and then to his pants. He glanced down. There, smeared at his thigh, was a dark, shiny patch of blood.

"No . . . no . . ." She started to step back, tipping like there wasn't any ground for her foot to land on. Chris raced up to hold her. "No! Nooo!"

"Chris! *Chris!*"

Chris jolted awake, gasping for breath. It was dark and his skull cracked with pain. He jumped as he looked up to see someone hovering over him. A hand clasped his shoulder.

"Chris, it's me. Addy. You were . . . having a nightmare."

Chris looked around. He was at the kitchen table. He must've fallen asleep here. The paperwork he'd been going through was strewn across the tabletop.

Addy sat in the chair next to him. "Are you okay?"

Chris rubbed his eyes. "I'm fine."

"You were saying Jules's name."

"I was dreaming . . ." Chris looked down. "That night, when I had to tell her Jason died."

"You've never told me about that night," Addy said softly.

Her scream. He couldn't explain it. He'd never heard a

human being scream like that. It sounded like . . . He shook his head. There were almost no words. But maybe it sounded like a soul trying to escape a body.

"I have worried about you so much ever since Jason died. You watched your best friend die in your arms. And then you had to tell his wife."

"I didn't have to. The captain was going to do it. But I felt I should. I think she's hated me for it ever since. Or maybe she just hates me because I didn't save Jason's life."

"She doesn't hate you, Chris. She hates life. She hates that Jason is gone."

"Now she's gone too."

Addy rubbed his arm and looked over the clutter on the table. "What's all this?"

"Some files I found in Jason's garage. There was a piece of the hull there too, hidden behind some boxes." He pointed to the box. "Look what's written here. 'Trophies.'"

"Trophies. Okay."

"But there aren't trophies in here."

"No, but people put stuff in different boxes all the time, right?"

"Not Jason and Jules. Everything is always precisely labeled with them. He mislabeled it on purpose."

"What's in here?"

"A lot of police reports on stolen boats. A couple of years ago, there was this big string of thefts just outside of Wissberry. It never hit us, but then we got the call to go check out a possible stolen boat . . ."

Addy leaned in. "And?"

Chris's attention locked onto a small piece of paper peeking out from underneath all the others. He pulled it out. It was scrap, torn around the edges, with a faded name and number on it. The name simply read *Roy*.

Chris jumped from the table and hurried to get his keys.

"Where are you going?"

"I've got to go up to the station. I need to pull Jason's phone records."

19

IT WAS LATE in the evening when Jules finally finished sorting through the paperwork and notes. Patrick's handwriting was terrible, so it took a while to decipher any notes he'd written. Mostly about what he wanted to put in the story—ideas, plotlines, character details, all written down randomly.

He'd fed her dinner: roasted chicken with mashed potatoes. Now they sat quietly together as they both finished decaffeinated coffee. Her brain was mush. She'd gathered from the information that he intended to write a book centered around boats or boat theft.

Jason had been gunned down by thugs after he'd received a call about a boat being stolen. That's what Chris Downey had told her. She couldn't make out what Patrick Reagan was trying to do, though. There was nothing specifically about Jason in all the paperwork she'd gone through.

"Tomorrow you will continue reading what I've written on *The Living End.*"

"Okay." Under any other circumstance, the prospect of reading his unpublished work would be beyond thrilling. Tonight it was just one more thing to try to unravel.

There was another stretch of silence. She liked that Patrick was comfortable with it, as though it was essential to his routine. She'd feared silence ever since Jason died. If she wasn't working on her computer, she had the TV on. Its drone made her feel less lonely. Jason used to hum softly—usually something he'd been listening to in the car—sometimes for well over an hour. It would kind of get on her nerves then, especially if she was trying to concentrate, but now she would give anything to hear it again.

Patrick set his coffee cup down and laced his fingers together. "When did you throw away his toothbrush?"

"What?" Jules blinked back into the moment.

"Jason's toothbrush. When did you throw it away?"

Jules couldn't answer.

"I haven't thrown Amelia's away," he said, staring blankly into the center of the room. "I don't know when you're supposed to do that. How many months? How many years?"

Jules didn't look at him. "I don't want to talk about this."

More silence. Jules wanted desperately to go to her room, to sleep. She wasn't sleepy, though.

"She asked me to kill her, you know."

Jules's weary gaze snapped sideways toward him. "What do you mean?"

"She didn't want to suffer through the living decay."

"So she asked you to assist in her suicide?"

"No. She didn't believe in suicide. That was the point."

Jules processed his words.

"*Murder* is too strong a word. Ending someone's suffering isn't like taking a hacksaw to the streets and slaughtering every person in sight," he said. "It seems inhumane that we should decay before we die, doesn't it? Jason was lucky in that way. His decay came after death."

Jules didn't bother wiping the tears that welled in her eyes. She was starting to really hate this man. Once again, he'd broken her.

Her tone was terse. "Jason wasn't lucky in any sense of the word."

"I suppose not."

"So you killed your wife. Is that what you're saying?"

Patrick's expression turned cautious. "You can't judge me. You've no idea."

"Did you kill her to end her suffering or yours?" Jules threw her hands up when Patrick's eyes turned angry. "I'm sorry. Am I offending you? Maybe I'm mistaken, but I believe it was you who wanted me to drown in deep thoughts, so I'm jumping in feetfirst here. Toothpicking my way straight to the heart of the matter." Jules leaned forward, engaging his eyes. "Because you and I both know, Patrick, that the dead one gets all the peace."

His demeanor began to change. He stiffened. He stopped blinking. His sights were set on her. "Did Jason suffer?"

"I'm not going to tell you. I can't imagine what kind of sick mind would want to know that. What am I? Some bizarre research project for your book? Is that it?"

"I believed," he said quietly, "we could understand each other."

"How can I understand this?" Jules said, gesturing wildly at random points in the room. "How does any of this make sense?"

He stood, walked to the table where the documents were piled. "If you work hard enough, Juliet, you will find some answers."

"Maybe I don't want answers." She swiped at her tears. "Maybe I just want to be left alone, to live my life however I want."

"You're too wonderful to be left alone."

The room spun when Jules tried to stand. Her ears burned as her blood pressure shot up. She stared him down as she walked to the door that led out the front of the house, the opposite of the deck. She grabbed the knob, turned it, wondered if it would be locked. But it wasn't. The door came open.

"What are you doing?" His eyes narrowed.

"I'm leaving you."

"It's nighttime. Where do you think you'll go?"

"I don't know."

"It's below freezing. It's been snowing." Patrick stepped forward, and she backed up, one step out the door. "You'll die out there."

"Then I'll be the lucky one too."

"Don't be stupid, Juliet."

"Don't you get it?" she said, taking another step onto the small porch. "I'm unfixable. I'm broken, and the piece I need to be fixed is permanently gone."

"Get back in here." His voice boomed the demand.

With one swift pull, she slammed the door, turned, and ran. Her feet, shod only with thin leather shoes, plunged into the snow, the cold jabbing into her ankles like spikes. With each step, it felt like shards of glass were cutting into the tops of her feet.

No moon or stars were out. A whisper-thin blanket of clouds seemed to hold the darkness captive against the mountain. She stumbled, tripping over rocks, then small trees. But she ran frantically, sure she heard him close behind, running after her.

Suddenly her bare hands plunged into the snow. She fell hard, and her face also hit the earth, the snow folding around her cheek, then up her nose. She coughed and wheezed, trying to scramble to her feet. But they slipped underneath her, unable to gain traction.

She stopped and listened. Footsteps? Or the wind? Rising to all fours, she was able to stand slowly. Her wrist had scraped against a piece of wood, and the blood gushed down her arm, pooling and sticky at her elbow and against her sleeve.

Run. He's going to kill you.

She took off, straight into a dense population of trees.

Her lungs resisted the cold air. And the altitude didn't make it easier. Before long, Jules was out of breath, slumped against a tree, shivering uncontrollably. She fell to her knees, tucked her hands under her arms. She wanted to cry, but she shook so violently that it was like all her emotions were being jackknifed out of her.

She knelt there for a while, so cold she couldn't move. Her feet were numb, except for the occasional slicing pain at her ankles.

Her eyes began to adjust better. The forest around her became clearer. She could see the bark. The twigs. A haunting, whistling sound was distant as if the wind were playing with ghosts in the valley below.

Jules slumped to a sitting position, leaning against the tree behind her. Every part of her body was numbingly cold. But thoughts, as haunting as the wind, drove her attention inward.

Had he really killed his wife?

What was this man capable of?

It didn't matter anymore. She closed her eyes and begged for death to come quickly. She prayed to Jesus because that was what Jason would've wanted her to do. She believed in heaven, more for Jason than she did for herself. But sometimes that made it harder, knowing he was alive but unreachable. That his life continued on without her, and that he hadn't managed to send even a single message back that he loved her. He was just gone, into a life somewhere else.

Jesus, take me to him.

Jules no longer felt her feet or her hands. The sharp pain was gone. A moment of alarm blew through her. Maybe she should try to run back to the cabin. But she knew she was unable to walk. She'd sealed her fate the moment she ran out the door. Her mind whisked through thoughts and feelings even as her body froze. Her hand tingled with warmth as she saw Patrick reach for it in the cabin. Jason's lips brushed against hers as she saw their wedding day. She tasted the sweet buttercream frosting of the cake. The bubbly champagne burned her throat.

A sense of regret shook the delight away as she remembered having to tell her daddy he wasn't invited to the wedding. He would come drunk, she knew, and embarrass her and everyone there. It was as if he knew. He didn't resist, but she'd never seen sadder eyes in her whole life.

She walked herself down the aisle. It wasn't as hard as she thought because she knew she was walking into the arms of the man who would take care of her for the rest of her life.

Jesus, take me.

She waited for death to come.

Instead, her eyes slowly opened. Far above her, tree limbs cracked and swayed in a cold wind that she was not shielded from. She heard an owl. The clouds parted, and a shimmering moon peeked through, bathing her in cold light.

Maybe Jesus was coming to get her, parting the sky, reaching down. *Jesus.* She repeated His name over and over, hoping to be taken, hoping to really believe.

Her teeth chattered and her eyes closed against her will.

Time had passed, she knew, when she opened them again. The moonlight was gone and the forest was inky black. She couldn't move and everything was blurry. Her jaw seemed cemented shut.

Then she heard hasty footsteps and her name being called.

"Jason!" Her voice was unmanageable. Hoarse. "Jason, I'm here!" She knew her mouth moved, but whether she was saying anything audible, she wasn't sure.

Her eyelids were becoming heavy again. The shadows all around her swelled in size, like she was viewing them through the glass of a marble. But out of the swells of darkness he appeared, running toward her, swiping at the limbs that got in his way.

"Jason . . ."

"I'm right here," he said, stooping. His strong arms lifted her. Her head fell back. She couldn't hold it upright anymore.

But she smiled, feeling as if she were floating. "It was nice of Jesus to send you to take me to heaven. What's it like? I bet it's like snow, but warm. Warm snow." She giggled, sounding like herself at nine years old. "How long does it take to get to heaven?"

He didn't answer. He didn't have to. She was with him again, and that was all that mattered anymore.

⌐└

"You get it, right? I mean, this number was the last call he received before he was killed." Chris jumped up and smacked the table. Addy sat with him, sipping coffee, glowering at the time.

"It's also going to be the same number tomorrow at, say, 8 a.m. But what's important about the number? Who made the call?"

"I don't know. It was a burner phone—a phone that is untraceable, unregistered."

"So what does it tell you?"

"It tells me that whoever this Roy guy is, he knows something." Chris scratched his head, his eyes heavy with the burden of sleepiness. The adrenaline was fading. "They missed it."

"Missed what? Who?"

"In the police report. There is nothing about this number in the police report. It could've easily been found if they'd pulled his phone records." Chris sighed. "But with the theory we were all going on, nobody probably thought to pull them." He glanced at his sister. "Addy, go to bed. Please."

"I can't leave you here by yourself. You're too wound up. And bad things happen when you're wound up. Remember the time you jumped off the roof at Mom and Dad's, onto the trampoline?"

He sat down at the table.

It wasn't much to go on, but it was something. "So a guy named Roy called Jason right before he was killed."

Addy nodded, trying to understand. "On an untraceable phone. That's got to suggest some illegal activity, right?"

"What are you saying? Jason was into something illegal?" Chris shook his head. "There is no way."

"I know you love Jason," Addy said, "but to be objective, don't you at least have to consider the possibility?"

"There's no way. The guy was a saint. He didn't even cuss. He never drank. He wouldn't gossip about the most gossip-worthy cops at the precinct."

"Sounds a little too good to be true."

Chris sighed and finally looked at her. "It's just not possible."

"Chris, he was 'randomly' gunned down. But you're a cop. You know that there is hardly a random act of violence. Right? Most often there's a reason behind a crime."

"And this guy knows the answer," Chris said, waving the little piece of paper in the air.

"That's not much to go on."

Chris looked at the papers on the table. "No. But it's all pointing toward the idea that Jason was concerned about something. He has part of a boat hull in his garage. He has police reports on stolen boats from other counties and towns. There's something to this."

"I agree," Addy said. "But how do you find out who Roy is? Look up every person with the first name of Roy in Maine?"

Chris sat back, still absentmindedly waving the scrap of paper. *Narrow it down to Wissberry. The county. Maybe the next counties over.*

He looked at Addy, who was deep in thought with the rim of her coffee mug hovering at her lips. Maybe he could look to see who'd been incarcerated in the last couple of years. It wouldn't hurt. He knew beyond a shadow of a doubt that Jason Belleno was above reproach. And it felt like a betrayal to think otherwise. But he also knew this Roy had answers, and he was going to do everything in his power to track this man down.

20

HEAVEN WAS A COCOON. Every part of her was wrapped in warmth. She felt herself sleeping, which was an odd sensation and aggravating, too. She didn't want to sleep. She wanted to see heaven. She wanted to see *Jason*.

Wake up, she told herself over and over. But the warmth that enveloped her made it difficult to leave her present state. Once, she barely opened her eyes. Just a crack. She saw nothing but glowing light.

She smiled and returned to sleep. Jason had told her that heaven was full of light, that there was no darkness, no tears.

Later—she didn't know how much later, as there was no sense of time in heaven—she began to feel herself awaken. At first she felt perfectly comfortable. But that comfort seeped out of her like hot steam. Then she felt pain, like she was being pricked. The sensation that ants were crawling over her hands and feet caused her to breathe heavily.

She wasn't supposed to feel pain in heaven.

Her eyes flew open. "Jason!"

"Shhh. Shhh," she heard.

"Jason?"

"Just rest."

"Why am I in pain?"

There was no answer. And her eyes wouldn't focus. She saw light and dark and a shadow that looked like a man's nearby.

Jules felt her head being lifted and water brought to her lips. Water. Yes. That was life-giving. Warm. That should be in heaven. But soon the pain returned, gnawing, agonizing.

Then it left. Floated away like a butterfly ascending onto the wind. If her eyes were open, she believed she would've seen it go.

She tried to rest, but something kept her from the perfect peace she'd known just a while before. It was the strangest sensation, like her soul was moving inside her body.

Maybe she wasn't in heaven yet. Maybe she was still traveling there.

Then why was it so black?

So empty?

Jules wanted to scream, but instead she floated again, until she remembered nothing.

Before lineup, Chris asked Captain Perry for a moment in his office.

The captain shut his door, looking as weary as Chris felt. He cocked an eyebrow as he sat down behind the desk and gestured for Chris to take a seat. "You okay, son? You don't look too good."

Chris had only gotten three hours of sleep—and hadn't slept much at all since Jules had disappeared. "That's what I wanted to talk to you about."

The captain smirked. "Cream for those bags? You'll have to talk to my wife."

Chris smiled, trying to appreciate the captain for his sense of humor even though his own had seemed to disappear overnight.

"Sorry," the captain said with a shrug. "You're probably not here to listen to my bad jokes."

"No, it's not that. I just . . ." Chris stared at the ground. "I think I need to take some time off."

"Time off?"

"Jules's disappearance is hitting me hard."

The captain leaned back in his chair. "That's understandable. You know we're doing what we can. I've got Walker on this, and he's the best I have."

"I know."

The captain leaned forward, putting his elbows on his desk. "Chris, time off is fine. I get that you need it. But I don't want you mavericking around, investigating this thing on your own. Jeff's a great detective. We've got to follow protocol. If it turns out that we've got a criminal case going, but things get hinky with our investigation, we could blow the whole thing. You get what I'm saying?"

Chris nodded.

"We'll alert you if anything at all pops up." He smiled as he relaxed a bit, sat back in his chair. "You gonna get out of town? I wish I could get outta town right now."

"Yeah. I think I will, actually." Chris stood. "I really thought it'd be hard to get time off. I know we're shorthanded right now since the city cut some of our funding."

The captain nodded. "We are. But I want my officers in good mental health. That's important. You've been a great officer for me ever since you came to work here, Chris. We take care of our own. So no worries. How much time do you want?"

Chris shrugged. "A few days."

"Done."

Chris shook his hand. "Thanks, Captain. I owe you. I'll see you soon."

If he had a job to come back to.

Chris headed up Highway 95 while listening to Maecoat chatter on the other end of the phone.

"You're ditching me, man? What's that about?"

"Just for a few days."

"For time off? The captain said you needed some time?"

"Something like that."

"Dude, I think you're taking this Jules thing too hard. There's absolutely no evidence that points to her being in danger."

"I know. I just feel a lot of guilt right now." He left it at that. He knew that telling his partner what was going down would only jeopardize Maecoat's own career. If Maecoat knew nothing about what he was doing, then he wouldn't have to lie for him. "I'll be back soon."

"This is indefinite? You didn't even give the captain a return date?"

"Just a few days. I don't really know."

"Aren't you the diva of the department."

"Funny."

A loud sigh came through the phone. "Okay, man, I obviously can't talk you out of this. You're already hightailing it out of town. Just . . . relax, okay? Don't let guilt bury you alive."

"Just going to clear my head."

"While you're there, clear mine, will you?"

Chris laughed. "Will do. I'll bring you a souvenir from the clear minds resort."

They hung up and Chris looked at the dashboard clock. Two more hours and he'd be there.

He took the time to sort through his thoughts. He was convinced that Jason had been investigating the boat thefts on the side. All the documentation proved that. But the question was why. Chris's first guess was that Jason might've known someone who was caught up in it, a friend or family member, and he wanted to find out for himself if they were involved. Knowing Jason, it wasn't so he could cover up for them, either. He would probably confront them himself, ask them to turn themselves in. Jason had always had an unbelievably rock-solid sense of conviction. There were no gray areas for him—except for when it came to Jules.

Jason had loved Jules the instant he saw her, despite the fact that she didn't share his faith in God. Early on in their conversations, Chris hadn't understood what the big deal was. Jason was in love with her. So what that they didn't share the same religious beliefs? A lot of people didn't. But he knew as they grew closer, Jules's lack of faith continued to weigh on Jason. At Jason's very core, he wanted to take care of her fully, including spiritually. And up to the day he died, Chris believed Jason had every intention of doing that by showing Jules how much she was loved.

His deep convictions were annoying at times, but in some weird way, also comforting. Not very many people Chris knew stood for much of anything. It was kind of refreshing to know someone who would literally put himself in harm's way to defend the truth he believed in.

Chris had often wished truth wasn't so murky for him. He couldn't just *believe*. For Jason, it was as uncomplicated as tying his shoes. He simply had faith in the Bible, that every ounce of it was true, that it was the standard by which to measure everything.

Jason often joked that he was certain he wasn't going to

die because God put him on the earth to convince Chris and Jules to have faith in God, and it seemed like that task was going to take an eternity. As often as Jason would joke about it, though, he would also pull Chris aside, tell him things that he felt he should know. One day as they were about to dig into some barbecue at lunch, Jason said, "God loves you, Chris."

Out of respect for their friendship, Chris had not sighed like he wanted to. Instead, with a sly smirk, he'd said, "Do you have a bumper sticker to go with that slogan?"

"It's true."

"Okay, fine. Whatever. God loves me."

"I'm going to keep telling you that until you believe me."

"What makes you think I don't believe you?"

"Because there is no peace in your eyes."

Chris had shaken his head, started eating. "That's what you're going by? Peace in the eyes? I've got news for you: I'm not the kind of guy that's ever going to have peace. Too many demons, too many skeletons in the closet." And that was just his college years.

"It's achievable," Jason said. "Perfect peace. Right here on earth."

Chris had laughed it off and changed the subject, but the truth was that he actually believed it because he saw it every day in Jason's eyes, in the way he conducted himself, in the way he interacted with Jules. The man brought a sense of calm wherever he arrived. And Chris had watched him in action a dozen times. Once, they'd been the first to respond to a four-car accident. One of the cars had gone down the embankment and rolled. The wife had been thrown out of the car and was okay, but her husband was pinned and badly injured, and the car was on fire. The woman was hysterical and hindering their efforts to get him free.

Jason had grabbed her shoulders, looked her right in the eye, and said, "Pray with me." While Chris tried to get the door open, Jason leaned in through a broken window and prayed for the man. The wife prayed too, still sobbing but saying everything Jason said.

When the flames were about to engulf the car, Chris had grabbed the woman to pull her to safety. "Jason, now! *Out!*" he yelled.

Jason touched the man one more time, stepped backward, and all of a sudden, a downpour the likes of which Chris had never seen roared to the ground like a sky-wide bucket had been dumped. Bystanders cheered in awe as the firefighters peeled the door back and got the man out. It took about thirty minutes to free him. He would've never made it out in time had it not been for the rain.

It had been barely misting the hour before. No heavy rain had been predicted. Chris had checked when he got home. Yet still, he couldn't quite believe it wasn't a coincidence.

That heavy downpour was a perfect metaphor for Jason Belleno. After being around him, you felt totally drenched, in the best way possible. Since his death, it was like life was parched. A drought had struck in Chris's soul.

That's why he had to find Jules. He had to put some

meaning back into his life. Jason had always talked to him about meaning and purpose. Chris told him it was law enforcement. That's what he lived for. But then one day, it failed to give him everything he needed or protect him in a way he thought it should.

Two hours passed, filled with memories of Jason. They'd had such good times. Jason had a wicked sense of humor and loved practical jokes. His favorite was to sneak into a fellow cop's car at night, while he was handling something outside, and turn on the lights, the horn, sirens—anything that made a sound or flashed. When the officer returned and started his car, everything would come on like crazy.

Memories were cut short by the voice on Chris's GPS indicating it was time to turn off the highway. According to the computer's directions, he only had three more miles to go before arriving at Ike Patterson's home, where his widow lived.

Late last night, he'd woken up with the idea to visit her, that perhaps she knew something, knew where this cabin was. But now doubt trickled into his resolve. Was this the right thing to do? Was it even plausible that he might find a clue here? And did he have the guts to come as if on official police business? He'd already been reprimanded once.

What would Jason do?

Chris had three miles to figure it out.

21

"STAY STILL."

An odd request, since she didn't think she could move anything except her hands. And they felt like they were in gloves.

"Please. Don't move."

Jules opened her eyes. Everything was fuzzy at first. Then he came into focus but was quickly blurred again by tears.

Patrick looked at her as he fiddled with something on her hand. "You're awake. That's good."

"Why can't I move?" Her voice was hoarse. Panic surged through her as she tried to move her arms but couldn't.

"Stay still."

"Have you tied me up? Is that it?" The tears spilled down her cheeks. "I thought I was in heaven. I thought I was with Jason."

He looked at her calmly, still with her left hand in his. "You're not tied up."

Jules tried to look down to see what was rendering her unable to move. Blankets. Lots of them. Apparently wrapped tightly around her.

She was back in the bedroom. Back staring at the terrifying words on the ceiling.

"You almost froze to death," he said matter-of-factly. "I've had to treat you for frostbite. Luckily I spent some time in Alaska researching a book, so I know how."

She looked down to find him unwrapping gauze from her hands. "They hurt," she whispered.

"I can only imagine," he said. "I've never experienced it myself. Do you feel a prickling sensation?"

"Yes."

"Okay. Let's see what we have here." Patrick lifted her hand, and she could see that her skin was partly white, partly the color of a ripe peach, and her knuckles looked shiny. On her pointer finger there was a blister. He studied it for a moment. "The blister isn't a good sign." He pressed on the skin. "It's still mostly soft, except for your knuckles. Those are concerning me." He put her hand on the bed. "I believe it's superficial frostbite on your hands. You'll be in pain, but I don't think the hand will have to be amputated."

"Amputated?"

"Let's hope not." He smiled reassuringly, then began taking blankets off her. At least four. Then unwrapped two from around her body. Jules sat up, trying to assist, but was surprised at how weak she felt. And her hand hurt. She winced.

"Try not to move your hand at all," he said.

"My feet hurt too."

"Your ankles," he said, glancing down at them. "They're not as well off. You need to leave them wrapped. You're not going to be able to walk for . . . until they heal."

"Maybe I should see a doctor."

"That's not going to work out so well."

"It's not an excuse. I'm really hurt."

"I can give you more pain medication."

"No. No, I don't want any. It makes me feel weird."

"Suit yourself." He rose and went to the door. "I've got some broth heating for you. You'll want to drink, and then we work."

Jules lay back and groaned. "Work. I don't want to work. I'm tired. My ankle feels like someone took an ax to it."

He stepped back in the room. "Juliet, we are running out of time."

Jules laughed. "Running out of time? That's all we have here is time. Or the absence of time, I should say."

"By now, they know you are missing. I am not an easy man to find in the winter. But someone will come looking, someone who has the will to find you."

"Don't count on it," she mumbled.

"And when they find you, they find me," he said. "Then it will be too late."

"Too late for what?" Jules asked. But he walked away.

The home was stately, just like what Chris imagined really smart literary types lived in. It had white columns in the front, leading to two tall oak doors. The yard was enclosed by an iron fence, but the gate was open.

Chris pulled his truck into the circular drive and got out. It was never comfortable dropping by unannounced, but he felt it was better this way. Sometimes the element of surprise worked in law enforcement's favor.

He rang the doorbell. It sounded like cathedral bells.

A man in an expensive suit answered the door. Chris wiped his sweaty hands against his jeans in case there was going to be a need for a handshake.

"Yes?"

"My name is Chris Downey. I'm with the Wissberry police department."

"Identification, please."

Chris held up his badge. He was really hoping he wouldn't have to do this, but the man looked to be in a perpetual state of skepticism.

His gaze steadied on the badge for a moment, then took its time returning to Chris. "Your business here?"

"I would like to talk to Mrs. Patterson."

"About?"

Ugh. But it was the last card he had to play. "Patrick Reagan."

The man's expression flickered with recognition and concern. "I see," he said, stepping aside. "Come in. Please, have a seat in here and I will summon Mrs. Patterson. I'm Vincent Lowell, her assistant."

From the small sitting room, Chris observed a giant library the next room over, complete with a sliding wooden ladder. The house smelled like a flower garden. It was kind of making his nose itch.

Distantly he heard voices. Then footsteps coming toward the room. Soon, a woman entered. Chris wasn't sure what he was expecting, but he was surprised by what he saw.

She was dressed sharply and looked to be less than fifty years old, though she wore a lot of makeup, her eyes rimmed with so much black that it was the first thing he noticed about her.

"Expecting someone older?" she asked with a mild smile.

"Yes. Sorry. I . . . I just . . ."

"Ike's first wife died of old age. And then he married me. We were married for twenty-five years." She offered a hand. "Leona Patterson."

"Sergeant Downey, with the Wissberry PD."

"That's a ways, isn't it?"

"Not too bad."

"Still, you must have important business." She waved her

hand, indicating they should sit. "May we offer you something to drink?"

"No, I'm fine. Thank you."

The assistant left and she turned her full attention to Chris. "Vincent said you're here about Patrick Reagan."

Chris nodded, trying to find the words to explain the situation without saying too much. He wasn't sure that was going to be possible.

"We're working on a case in Wissberry, where Mr. Reagan lives, as you know. We think he may have some information, but we've been unsuccessful at locating him. Apparently he just vanishes into thin air in the winter."

Leona smiled knowingly.

"I was hoping that you might be able to help us locate him."

"Why do you think I would know?"

"I met with Mr. Reagan's current agent, Mr. Bentley Marrow." Chris smirked as Leona let out a heavy sigh of disapproval. "Obviously you feel the same way about Marrow as Patrick does?"

She lifted her chin. "For different reasons. But no, I do not care for the man."

"Do you maintain any contact with Mr. Reagan?"

She eyed Chris. "Why? Has he finally gone off the deep end?"

"Do you think he might?"

"You don't know many writers, do you, Officer Downey?"

She spoke with a haughtiness that made her seem older than she was.

"Rick Castle. But he seems stable, only a little lovesick."

"I see," she said, ignoring the joke. "You have to understand—what makes them good at writing often makes them incapable of living in the very world about which they write."

"Is that why he escapes to his cabin every winter?"

"Oh, that cabin. If I never have to hear about that again, I'll be happy."

"Is it really impossible to get ahold of this man? His home was ransacked. Not even his maid knows how to reach him."

"His house was ransacked, you say?"

"Yes."

"Well," she said after a brief moment of pondering, "that is Patrick Reagan. The man who controls his universe." She sighed. "His wife died. Did they tell you that?"

"Yes. That Mr. Reagan didn't take it well. They also told us about Ike's death."

"Sidney Sheldon once said that a blank piece of paper is God's way of telling writers how hard it is to be God."

"I'm not following."

"Writers play God, don't you see? They create their people, their creatures, and they lay out the plans for their entire lives. They then send trouble into their paths. Lots of trouble. Why?"

Chris shrugged.

"Because it is the only way to make the character grow, so that he is capable of achieving the end result. The writer, in the end, works all things out for the good of the main character. The character accomplishes more than he thought he could. He has acted heroically or solved the unsolvable. He continues on into the white space of literature, where he will live out his days in happiness."

Chris cleared his throat. "Okay."

"So you can imagine what happens to a fragile mind and soul, who has been used to creating happy endings for those he cares about, when his own world becomes uncontrollable. When he realizes that although he has created many happy endings, he will not get one of his own."

"You're saying you think Patrick Reagan is having some sort of nervous breakdown?"

"I couldn't say. I haven't spoken with Patrick since Ike's funeral."

"Do you have a sense that something might be wrong?"

She looked out a window, her eyes distant with thought. "I know that when Amelia passed away, it was very difficult. She suffered an agonizing death and there was nothing he could do. Since then, I've only heard snippets about what is happening with him, through certain circles. I imagine that he buried himself in work. Rumor was some police procedural thriller he was working on. He hasn't written well since Amelia died. And who knows? Perhaps he's not capable of writing anymore. Not without Amelia."

"Did she write with him?"

Leona thought for a moment. "It's more complicated than that."

"Can you explain it?"

"It was sometimes like she was the left side of his brain. The part of him that put the pieces together in some logical way. Patrick was notorious for being very unstructured in his writing. He'd write scenes on napkins and take copious notes on scrap pieces of paper. He'd write scenes out of order. And he'd put it all in this cardboard box. Supposedly Amelia would take it and sort it and help him figure out how to put it all together."

"Do you know anything about a writer named Blake Timble?"

"Never heard of him."

"He's not yet published but supposed to be the next big thing. There's evidence that Patrick might be upset by him coming onto the literary scene."

She smiled and shook her head. "That doesn't surprise me. Ike used to tell me how the younger writers got on Patrick's nerves. He hated their style, their disregard for true literary gumption. I remember one book in particular. It was published with no capitalizations and no punctuation. One long, run-on sentence—the whole thing. It received awards and accolades. Patrick was quite vocal about his dislike for it."

Chris leaned forward. "Mrs. Patterson—"

"Please. Leona."

"Leona. Patrick seems kind of unstable. Is there a chance he might harm someone, even inadvertently?"

"Why?"

"I can't give you the details, but there is a young woman

missing and we think Patrick might at the very least have some information that could help us find her. The problem is, we can't find *him*." Chris studied her intently. "Is there any chance you know where this mysterious cabin is located?"

Leona looked away.

"We just want to talk to him. That's all. We just need to find this woman."

Leona narrowed her eyes, watching him carefully. "Ike and Patrick had a very special relationship. A friendship that few people get a chance to have in their lives. Honestly, it was hard to be jealous because it was so genuine. Every time Ike got a chance to see Patrick, his face would light up and you could just see life breathed into him, even in his older years."

The assistant suddenly showed up in the doorway of the room, like a prompt.

"I must confess, I've been angry for quite some time," Leona went on.

The assistant stood there, making Chris nervous and distracted. He tried to focus on Leona. "Angry?"

"The publishing house has been stealing royalties from Patrick's books, royalties that belong to me. They've been holding his last royalty check until he produces the next book. Why any agent would allow that into a contract, only Bentley knows. But the fact of the matter is, I live off the royalties that Ike made through Patrick's books. And as you can imagine," she said, waving her hand about the room, "this place needs quite the underwriting. So in short, Officer

Downey, I am desperate to find Patrick Reagan myself and see what is holding him up on this book."

"Ma'am, your conference call begins in five minutes," the assistant said, slicing into the conversation as smoothly as a knife into butter.

Chris didn't believe a word out of him, and he wasn't selling it very convincingly. Leona stood, straightening the expensive material of her suit. They walked toward the front door, the only sound the clacking of her tall heels against the shiny marble floors.

"You know where this cabin is, don't you?" Chris asked as the door was opened for him.

She followed him just to the threshold. "If I knew that," she said with a wry smile, "I would be privy to one of the greatest literary secrets of our time, wouldn't I?"

"I don't know about that," Chris said, "but I sure would like to find this guy." He handed her a card. "Please call me if you . . . stumble upon any information."

She stepped back. "Best wishes, Officer Downey." And the door shut.

Chris sighed and walked to his truck. Unsuccessful. Again. Another day gone, for nothing, except to affirm what he already knew: Patrick Reagan was a guy on the verge of . . . something.

Chris got in his truck and started the heater. He saw shadows passing in front of veiled windows. His body was chilled from the brief walk to his truck. Winter was coming early and strong. The mountains already had snow. Even if he knew where the cabin was, could he get to it?

Didn't matter. He was no closer to finding Patrick Reagan than when he began.

He pulled his cell phone out of his pocket as it rang.

"Downey."

"Chris, it's Pearl."

Pearl, as they called him due to an unfortunate food poisoning incident at an oyster bar, was the guy at the department who could find the needle in a haystack and keep quiet about it too. He was the one everyone went to when their daughters started dating boys.

"Hey, Pearl, what's up?"

"Got some interesting information for you regarding a hunt for our boy Roy."

"Oh yeah?"

"Turns out there was a guy named Roy Fletcher incarcerated about a year and a half ago. And he was arrested for being involved in a boat theft ring."

"No kidding."

"Yeah. He's out at State in Warren."

Chris checked his watch. If he drove fast, he could get there during visiting hours. "Pearl, this is great. Thanks."

"One more thing."

"Yeah?"

"The captain came down this morning and asked me if you'd been asking for information regarding Jason's death."

"He did?"

"Yeah."

"What'd you say?"

"I said we hadn't talked about anything but hockey."

Chris's mind raced. "Um, thanks. You didn't have to do that."

"I figure if he was asking about it, there was a good reason you were doing it. The captain hasn't been my favorite person in the world, as you know. He stuck me behind this desk and I'll never forgive him for it."

"So he doesn't know anything about us finding this Roy Fletcher?"

"Nothing at all. Wiped my searches clean."

"Okay. Thanks, Pearl. I guess I better go find out who Roy Fletcher is, shouldn't I?"

"Yeah. And, Chris . . . watch your back."

22

JULES LAY IN BED, comfortably propped up by pillows, warmed by blankets and a delectable beef broth, watching the writer she'd admired most in her life pacing the floor while reading to her from his manuscript.

If her ankles didn't hurt so badly, she might've just rested in this moment and enjoyed it for what it was—whatever it was. She'd accepted some ibuprofen, and that had taken the edge off. But they throbbed nonstop.

"Wait," she said, and Patrick turned. "I think you're building the character up too quickly to be the hero. I think we should wonder if he is, wonder if he has what it takes."

Patrick paused, scratching behind his ear, studying his

words. "Good point," he finally said and scribbled a note before continuing.

He was reading a scene where a cop was working with a snitch, trying to find out who was stealing boats. The snitch was a guy who had his reasons for turning on his gang of bandits. Patrick just hadn't found those reasons yet.

"Maybe," Jules said, interrupting him again, "it's because he really does believe in right and wrong. He really has that sense, even though he's on the wrong side of it."

"Too easy."

Jules sighed. "I don't know then. I can't find his motivation."

Patrick smiled. "But I like that you're trying. You're working hard at this."

"Don't have much of an option."

"True." Patrick sat down in the chair in the corner of the room, stretching his legs. "What if . . . ?"

"Yeah?" she said, feeling a little giddy at the idea that he was brainstorming with her.

"What if the bad guys were too bad for him?"

Jules slumped a little. "That sounds kind of cliché. What are they, psychopathic mass-murdering boat thieves?"

"What's so bad that a thief would feel he's better off going to the other side?"

"I don't know . . . Thieves who steal from thieves."

"A given. It's part of their world. Something else."

Jules sat up a bit, readjusting her weight. Her hips were starting to hurt. She stared into space, trying to find a good answer.

Patrick began to pace again. "Blake Timble, he would overdramatize them. Yes. He would create drama where there was none to be had."

Jules pulled the covers closer to her. Was he going to start another Blake Timble rant? Her hands twisted the comforter back and forth as she watched him carefully.

"I believe he would give this about fifteen minutes of thought and throw something down on paper. He'd move on, figuring the reader is going to follow wherever he goes." He waved a finger in the air. "But we are not Blake Timble, are we? No. We are not going to settle for the easy answer."

Jules stared at him through the cold cabin air. "Maybe they weren't easy answers for Blake Timble. Maybe they just weren't *your* answers." She resisted the urge to cover her mouth as regret filled her for speaking out, but she hated the way he looked down on every writer but himself.

He turned at her words, midsentence, and froze. She locked eyes with him for a long moment; then Patrick said, "Perhaps."

Jules looked out the window. She hated feeling so vulnerable. She couldn't run even if she had to.

He was jotting something down, pausing between words, absorbing something Jules couldn't see.

"Look," she said, "my dad's a drunk, okay? Sometimes there are no easy answers in life. And sometimes what's an answer for one person isn't for another. It's easy for you to look from the outside in and judge the motives. But there's nothing easy about life. Any of it. And though many people would have you believe they've got the answers and the rule book, they don't. Not really."

"What about Jason? Didn't he have the answers?"

Jules thought for a moment. "I think Jason would've replied that he believed in the One who has the answer. He couldn't explain much, but he put his trust in Someone who he felt was worthy of it and who understood all the questions and the answers."

Patrick set his pages down and sat at the end of the bed, his eyes lit with curiosity. "What did Jason think of your father?"

"Jason always wanted to believe the best about him. But I'd lived with it, you know? I knew what my dad was capable of. More importantly, I knew what he wasn't capable of."

"But Jason, he never gave up on him?"

"He believed in prayer." Jules's throat tightened as she recalled a fight they'd had about her father, with Jules imploring Jason to stop praying for him, to stop believing things would change. She glanced at Patrick, hoping her eyes weren't too shiny with tears. "Maybe if I'd believed in prayer more, Jason wouldn't be dead."

Patrick looked torn by her words. "You don't believe that, do you? That you're responsible for Jason's death?"

"Jason was this guy that was filled with so much faith. It was like a gift that I wanted so badly but couldn't begin to even unwrap. He just believed. Plain and simple. And he always asked me to . . ." Her voice broke. She tried to hold it steady. "To pray for him while he was at work. And I tried.

But I could never get myself to trust God with him. I trusted Jason's ability to protect himself more than God's ability to protect him."

"Then I guess you were right."

"Don't say that!" Jules pounded the bed with her fist, barely noticing the pain in her frostbitten fingers. "Don't say that! You dishonor Jason by saying that, by accusing God of that."

Patrick didn't seem deterred. "Isn't he dead? Didn't God fail?"

Jules looked away. "You just don't understand."

"Then explain it to me."

"Jason would never say that. Even lying on that pavement, bleeding out, murdered by men he didn't know, Jason would never say that God failed him."

"Why not?"

"Because he believed God always had a plan. . . ." Jules let the tears run freely down her cheeks. There was no use trying to stop them. "He thought that if you trusted God, there was a purpose, and that everything worked out for good. He thought that every tragedy was used to touch someone else's life, to help someone else."

They were silent for a moment.

Patrick stirred, waking her out of the fog of grief that had settled over her. "Is this good, Juliet?"

"What?"

"Your present circumstances."

"Being held captive? My ankles rendered useless by

frostbite? My favorite author ridiculing me?" She sniffled her protest, casting him an angry look.

"Perhaps Jason's God knew that there was no reason to offer these promises if there wasn't the chance that our paths would cross with trouble. Evil, even."

Jules forced herself to look at him. "Are you evil, Patrick?"

He seemed to seriously consider it. "I don't believe so. But I've seen evil. Yes. I've seen it. Stared it down."

"Sure. In the pages of your books."

"No. Not there. Here. In this room."

There was a haunting sorrow in his voice. Jules wanted to recoil from it, but she had nowhere to go. Even though he wasn't moving, he seemed to be inching closer to her.

"What do you mean?" It came out of her in a whisper, though she intended it to sound much stronger.

"I saw evil here."

"And what did it do?"

"Not it. She."

"Evil is feminine?"

"Evil is wherever and whoever evil wants to be." His demeanor changed as his eyes flickered with a desperate pain.

"Tell me." Jules wasn't sure she even said it out loud. But something in her wanted to know.

He looked as if he might not, but then he nodded slightly as though encouraging himself that it was possible to talk about.

"It was the cancer," he said softly. "She succumbed to it quickly. I thought that might be a blessing, but it was not quickly enough for her. This woman who would not hurt a fly was so . . . vicious. She cursed me. Over and over, she cursed me."

"That was the cancer talking. You have to know that. Amelia loved you."

"She was suffering so badly. She wouldn't hear about going to the hospital. And the nurse that came and tended to her could only do so much." His voice choked. "My sweet, sweet Amelia. It was as if we'd not shared thirty-five years together. It was as if she didn't know my love for her."

"She was very sick," Jules said, sitting up even more. "That happens with cancer."

"I think," Patrick said, weariness in his eyes, "that if she had been able, she would've killed me."

Jules chose her words carefully. "For not killing her?"

Patrick didn't answer for a while and didn't look at her. "You must know for your own sake, mustn't you?"

Jules just stared at him.

"It is so clear-cut for you. You are so sure what the right thing to do was, and your trust in me relies on the notion that if I didn't kill my wife, then I can be trusted."

Jules didn't nod, but she knew he spoke the truth.

Patrick stood. He tossed the rest of the pages on the bed and they slid into a messy pile. At the door, he turned, looking directly at her. "It's that kind of thinking that got your husband killed."

Jules gripped the sheets. "What does that mean?"

"I must go prepare our dinner." He gestured to the pages.

"Read more. Read on. You're moving too slowly, Juliet. You're not getting this like I had hoped."

"That's because you're speaking in a cryptic language nobody can understand."

"I'm speaking in a language that your heart understands. Soon your head is going to catch up." He smiled mildly. "That's a quote from Blake Timble, who, despite making a mess of an otherwise-decent concept, had some worthy things to say."

He shut the door, and Jules stared at the pages. She wanted to take her hand and swipe them all off the bed. But instead, she slowly scooped them toward herself. She was becoming aware that inside these pages was the key to her release. She could no longer run to escape. She couldn't even fling herself off that balcony. She had to find this needle in a haystack. Somehow, it seemed, her life depended on it.

Roy Fletcher looked like a gecko. He had a gecko-like posture, with a long but thick neck and a mullet that barely reached his shoulders because of it. The back of his head was very flat, but his face held many angles: a pointed nose, slicing cheekbones, but thin, wavy lips, and an enlarged forehead with a scar at the top right that looked just like a bullet hole. His eyes were beady—ink black and shiny like marbles—and they weren't to be trusted. He pulled on one of his bushy sideburns like one might finger a goatee.

He approached the table carefully, taking in every detail, and sat down, still fingering his chops. His entire right arm was covered in tattoos of snakes.

"What business you got with me, cop?" he said in a thick Southern accent made harder to understand by his missing front teeth.

"How do you know I'm a cop?" Chris asked.

"I can sniff me a cop. Believe you me, I can sniff me a cop." Roy leaned back, pleased with himself. "The way you boys never sit with your back to the door. The way you always lookin' around to see what everyone else up to." He lifted his chin. "The way you look at me. I know me some cops all right."

"I'm Sergeant Downey with the Wissberry PD."

"You got a first name?"

"Chris."

"I don't like no formalities," he said. "So why you here, Chris?"

Chris leaned forward, trying his best to size Roy up without Roy feeling sized up. "I need your help."

Roy grinned. "A cop in need of my help. So greatly honored. Yes sirree."

"I'll pretend I didn't hear the sarcasm in your voice."

"It was meant to stab you right through the heart," Roy said, his tone turning cold and his beady eyes warming with anger.

Chris tried to stay neutral. This guy was obviously easily inflamed. "I believe you might have information about the murder of my partner, Jason Belleno, two years ago."

Roy's face flickered through expressions like a flame against a strong wind. "Don't know no Jason . . . What'd ya say? Bell-something?"

"When my partner was killed near a boat two years ago, he had among his possessions a scrap of paper with the name Roy on it and a phone number. I believe you're that Roy."

Roy's eyes narrowed. "Well, with an uncommon name like Roy, sure. Yeah. Sure." He laughed.

Chris sighed. "Look, we can play games here. But, Roy, I looked up your record. You're going to be in here for a long time for theft, not to mention cocaine possession. What harm will it do you now to tell me what you know about my partner's death?"

Roy seemed to consider this. "What do you know about it? The death of this Jason character?"

"I know that for two years I thought it was a random killing. But the more I dig, the more I'm starting to understand that Jason was investigating something at the time he was killed. Something about boat thefts. And right before he was killed, he got a call on his cell phone from an untraceable phone. That number was the number on the piece of paper with your name on it."

Roy pondered again. Then he said, "A boat theft ring, you say?"

"During that time our department was on the lookout for the possibility of boat thefts because of how many were being stolen from adjacent towns." Chris put his hands on the table, flat against the cold metal, spreading his fingers wide, gesturing, he hoped, in a way that showed Roy he really had no hidden agenda. "None were being stolen from Wissberry, though."

Roy, for the first time, looked conflicted. "Sometimes, you know, you don't know."

"Don't know what, Roy?"

"Who the good guy is." Roy's steely eyes softened. "Maybe I got confused. Maybe they's all bad." His eyes hardened again. "Yeah. Bad to the bone."

"Who, Roy? I don't know who you're talking about."

"Ain't you one of 'em?"

"One of . . . ?"

Roy sat back in his chair, the chains around his wrists rattling against the table. "I went to church. You know that? I did. When I was a little runt, my grandmother took me a lot. Said it was so I could always tell right from wrong. She knew I was gonna have some kind of tough life. Church—yes, that's a good place to be. I went to the one down by the shore, the one by the lighthouse. It's small. Pretty inside. Lots of stained glass and nice carpet."

Chris knew the one. It was in Wissberry. He tried not to sigh, but he wasn't sure where Roy was going with all this.

Roy looked lost in his thoughts. "I tell ya, I did my pot. I did. I'll cop to that. I did my pot. But I never did crack. And never sold any drug. Believed that was wrong to sell the stuff. I took it myself but never gave it to nobody."

"You're saying you were wrongly convicted? That you

didn't have cocaine in your possession when you were busted for theft?"

"It was planted on me."

The sigh finally escaped. "Of course it was. Look, Roy, I'm not a lawyer. I can't do anything to help you. I'm just trying to figure out what happened to my partner." Chris looked him over and then started to stand. This wasn't worth his time.

But Roy cleared his throat. "I made my peace with being in here because of what I did to your partner. Jason."

Chris slowly sat back down. "Did you . . . ? Were you the one that . . . ?"

"Pulled the trigger? No, my man. That wasn't me. But I know who did it. Yeah. I do know."

Chris felt his heart drop and race at the same time. "Who?"

"You gotta understand something," Roy said, lowering his voice. "Sometimes the killer ain't the one that pulled the trigger. Do you get what I'm talking about?"

Chris nodded, though he wasn't sure.

Roy's voice was now at a whisper. "I always knew it. I did. I always knew that Jason was one of the good ones."

"He was."

Roy lowered his gaze. "This is gonna be more than you know how to take. And it's probably gonna get me killed in here." He looked around, his eyes darting nervously from one table to the next. "But my grandma taught me things. And maybe I'm gonna make my final stand right now." He nodded. "Yeah. Make her real proud."

⌐ ⌐

Dinner was meatballs over spaghetti. Homemade, all of it. She'd been smelling it for two hours as he'd prepared the meal. Now he brought it on a tray to her room, complete with a cloth napkin and fresh Parmesan cheese.

"It looks wonderful, Patrick," Jules said. "You're quite the cook."

He smiled slightly. "It's nice to have someone to cook for. Quite boring to cook for oneself." He started to leave.

"Won't you join me?" she asked. "I hate eating alone. Breaking of the bread is to be shared. That's what Jason always said, anyway. He was big on sharing meals with family and friends."

Patrick looked surprised but left. Soon, however, before Jules had even sliced into the first meatball, he'd returned with a sturdy wooden TV tray. He unfolded it and put it in front of the corner chair. He left once again, then returned with his meal on its own tray.

They ate in silence for a while, like an old married couple. Jules tried to push the pain out of her mind. Her ankles throbbed and burned as the nerves in her skin were thawing. She'd take another ibuprofen soon, but right now she wanted to focus on him.

"I believe I figured it out," she said into the resounding silence of the room.

He looked up as he continued to twirl pasta around his fork. "Figured what out?"

"Why the guy turned into a snitch. What led him to it." Jules set down her fork. "See, he was one of those guys who wasn't all good and wasn't all bad. He still had a sense of right and wrong."

"You believe in such things? Pure motives?"

"He wasn't pure. He just wasn't all bad."

"So there's a little bit of good in everyone."

"I believe that. Yes."

"What turns people bad, then?"

"All kinds of things. I couldn't generalize such a thing."

"But aren't you good at that?"

"At what?"

"Generalizations?"

Jules eyed him as she ate her dinner. "I'm just sensing here, but I think you have something particular in mind." She smiled at him.

He actually smiled back. "I usually do. But let's get back to the character. So he turned into a snitch so that he could feel good about himself?"

"So he wouldn't feel so *bad* about himself." She laughed. "Sorry. Just messing with you. Still trying to find out if you have a sense of humor."

He chuckled, looking as though he was thoroughly enjoying the company. "That's one thing I really enjoyed about reading your work."

"My work?"

"Isn't it considered art? Blogs? Facebook posts? That tweety-bird thing?"

"Twitter."

"Stupid name." He wiped his mouth and winked. "You do have a nice sense of humor. Even after Jason died, you kept it, didn't you?"

"I guess. Jason said it was the very first thing that attracted him to me."

"I can see why." Patrick finished his meal. "So that is what I am missing. The snitch needs to have a good heart."

"No. Not like that. He needs to feel . . . a sense that he has good in him. He wants to do what is right, but he can't pull himself away from the world he's always known."

Patrick nodded and stood. He left momentarily to carry out his tray. When he returned, he picked up the pages of the manuscript from the bed. "Very good. A lot accomplished. Now I must work. It is going to be a big day tomorrow."

"Oh? More fun lost in the woods during a snowstorm?"

He looked at her ankles. "How is your pain?"

"Returning."

"It will get much worse before it gets better. You need to keep that ibuprofen in your system. I would recommend something stronger."

"I'll be fine. I'll stick to the ibuprofen."

"All right. Would you like something to read for the evening, since you must stay in bed?"

"I'd like a Patrick Reagan novel. One of the classics, please."

He smiled the smile of a man completely flattered. "I don't keep any of my books here. In fact, I don't keep any of my books anywhere. Once I am finished, I am finished. I never want to see it again."

Jules felt genuinely disappointed. "I was really looking forward to a good read."

Patrick paused, then left. After a few moments, he returned with a file folder in his hands. He approached the bed and handed it over.

"What's this?"

"My very first novel. Never published."

Jules stared at it in disbelief. "Really?"

"It's a love story, if you can believe it. Once my first suspense was published, nobody wanted a love story from Patrick Reagan. But it is quite touching, if I do say so myself." He stepped away. "Enjoy."

Jules quickly popped two ibuprofens and opened the folder to the first page.

It was simply titled *Snow*.

23

"JIM. JIM! WAKE UP!" Chris shook the Lt. Colonel as hard as he could, then tapped his cheeks. "Jim!"

The Lt. Colonel snarled and groaned. Cracking his eyes open, he grunted, "What? Get off me! Get!"

Chris backed up. "I need you to wake up! Now!"

The Lt. Colonel sat up on the couch where he'd crashed and then stood, trying to orient himself. After a moment, he went to the kitchen sink and splashed cold water on his face. Chris paced impatiently nearby.

The Lt. Colonel eyed him as he dried his face with paper towels. "What's gotten into you? Did you find Juliet?"

Chris ran his fingers through his hair. "No. Not yet. But . . . but I think I solved Jason's murder."

The Lt. Colonel looked more awake now. "Jason's murder? I thought they determined it was some thugs. That Jason was at the wrong place at the wrong time."

"That was the theory," Chris said, still pacing. "But it never quite sat right with me. And then when I found evidence of Jason looking into these boat thefts, I decided there might be more to the story."

"Is there?"

Chris nodded. "And he was right. It is more than I can take."

The Lt. Colonel frowned. "You're shaking like a leaf, son. Sit down. Over there. Before you pass out or something."

Chris sat, burying his face in his hands, trying to figure out what he believed, if anything.

"Tell me what happened."

"I traced a phone number to a guy named Roy Fletcher, who's in prison. I believed it was Roy who called Jason the night he died. I just went to see Roy at the state prison."

"And?"

"He told me the most unbelievable thing, Jim . . ." Chris's voice quivered.

"Spit it out."

"He said that he'd met Jason at a park one night when he was taking a walk. Jason sat down on a bench where Roy was eating a sandwich and started talking to him about God."

"Doesn't surprise me. The guy would talk to a tree stump if he thought he could convert it."

"So the way Roy tells it, he starts confessing that he's involved in some thefts and he's feeling bad about it. The next thing he knows, he's snitching to Jason, feeding him information about this theft ring. Jason was just about to go to the department with the information when . . ."

"Go on."

"Roy said that then Jason stumbled onto something by accident. Jason hadn't been able to figure out how and where they were hiding the boats. He found a warehouse full of them, just off the pass. You know the warehouse behind the boat factory that burned down in 2007?"

"They were hiding the boats in our town?"

"Yes. And then Jason figured out how." Chris lowered his head, almost unable to say what needed to be said next. "Our department."

"The police department?"

"They were accepting kickbacks for looking the other way. Roy came clean, told Jason he knew about the department's involvement but had to make sure Jason was . . . good. He named Perry as the ringleader—he wasn't captain back then—and named a couple of other guys. Roy didn't know everyone but felt it was far-reaching."

The Lt. Colonel's eyes were wide with disbelief. "You're telling me that our police department is corrupt? That we've got guys accepting payment to look the other way?"

"That's what Roy said."

"Is this Roy guy believable?"

"I don't know why he would have reason to lie to me. He seemed genuinely . . . remorseful."

"Remorseful for what?"

"He's the one that led Jason out to the boat that night."

"Why?"

Chris shook his head, two years of grief swallowing him whole.

"Chris?"

"Roy said because they got to him, heard he was snitching, and offered to pay him—and spare his life—if he'd do one little thing. Get Jason Belleno to that spot." Chris pressed his lips together, trying to keep his emotions in check. "Roy swears he didn't know they were going to kill him. He thought they might rough him up. Roy said he desperately needed the money, so . . ."

"The cops killed one of their own?"

"No. No, it was the guys involved in the theft ring. But you don't have to pull the trigger to be guilty."

The Lt. Colonel looked dismayed.

"Roy said shortly after Jason's death, he was arrested for theft and cocaine possession, which he claims was planted on him by dirty cops wanting to silence anyone who might uncover the truth. He said they knew he'd be discredited with a drug conviction, and even if he spoke up, no one would take him seriously."

The Lt. Colonel stood, rubbing his face. "I always knew those guys were crooked." He scowled.

"I . . . I don't even know what to do now."

"You think this is related to Juliet's disappearance?"

"I don't know. I mean, Patrick Reagan was at the police department researching a book around this time, but I don't know what one has to do with the other."

"Come here. I want to show you something."

Chris followed him over to the computer. The Lt. Colonel sat down, saying, "I was on Juliet's computer today, trying to find something, anything that might lead us to her. I stumbled onto a file called 'Writing' and opened it. Inside was this." He clicked the mouse and opened a file that popped onto the screen.

Chris felt himself gasp.

The Daring Life of Enoch Mandon by Blake Timble.

"What?"

Why would Jules have this manuscript on her computer? How could she, if it was such a closely guarded secret, according to the publisher?

Unless . . .

"She's him," Chris whispered.

"What? Who?"

"Jules. She's Blake Timble."

"Who is Blake—?"

"She's writing under a pen name. That's the only way she could have this manuscript. She wrote it."

The Lt. Colonel looked at the screen. "She *has* been writing." He smiled. "She took my advice."

A loud pounding at the door startled both men.

"You expecting anyone?" Chris asked.

The Lt. Colonel shook his head.

"Close that file," Chris whispered.

He cautiously walked to the door, trying not to let paranoia get the best of him. The door had no peephole, so he just opened it.

Jeff Walker stood there, a contempt-filled smile on his face. "Downey. What are you doing here?"

"Checking up on Jules's dad."

Walker peeked around to look at the Lt. Colonel. "Interesting. Well, the captain is upset. I've been trying to hunt you down to warn you."

"Upset about what?"

"That you're out investigating this thing without his consent."

"So he's been following me. Or someone has."

Walker didn't blink. "Something like that. Look, kid, nothing against your ambitions to find this lady, but don't double-cross the captain. Not good for the career."

"And how, exactly, am I double-crossing the captain by trying to find Juliet Belleno?"

"He doesn't like insubordination."

"Right. This is all about me disobeying orders."

The two men stared at each other. Chris didn't back down against Walker's glare.

"Look, it's just one cop looking out after another, that's all," Walker finally said, backing up with a smirk on his face. "I mean, if we can't trust each other, then who can we trust?"

"I appreciate your concern. I'll keep your advice in mind."

"You should." He walked backward, pointing at the Lt. Colonel. "And keep that nut job off the streets."

Walker drove away and Chris let out the breath he'd been holding.

The Lt. Colonel came up behind him. "What now?"

Chris turned back toward the computer. "I'm going to need a printout of that book."

It began to rain, the cold, dreary rain that scrubs the soul of joy and hope. The sky had turned dark, and with the temperature dropping, the rain would turn to snow soon enough.

He'd taken the manuscript to Perks, trying to warm himself up with a hot drink while simultaneously cooling down his temper. If Roy Fletcher was to be believed, then not only was his department corrupt, but they'd also worked very hard to cover it up. For two years. Who could be believed now? Who could be trusted? Surely Maecoat wasn't involved in this. But how could Chris know for sure? It was lie after lie after lie.

He found a corner booth away from the college crowd that finally got to take over Perks once the old folks went to bed. He tried to wipe the paranoia out of his mind and concentrate on what he was reading, flipping through the pages in an attempt to get the main idea. From what he could tell, it was the story of a war veteran who'd seen combat in two wars and turned to alcohol to cope with his grief. He had a wife and daughter at home, and he simultaneously destroyed both relationships. There was no denying how this paralleled Jules's life and the life of the Lt. Colonel. No wonder she wanted it published under a pen name. There were some emotionally brutal truths in the book.

On page 108, something caught Chris's eye as he was speeding through the text.

The daughter, named Meg in the story, sat in a car on a cold winter evening, inside the garage of her home. The car was running. The garage door was down. And she was becoming sleepy.

Chris raced through the next few pages as the character slipped away, too filled with the grief of her dad's alcoholism and her husband's death.

Surely somebody comes and saves her.

But four pages later, Meg was dead in the car.

The next morning her father found her.

Chris sat back in the booth and swallowed the fear that was emerging. Was Jules planning on killing herself?

He hurried through the rest of the manuscript to find out what happened, his finger flying down the pages. The remainder of the story was about how the daughter had left her father a note, asking him to get his life right. She wanted him to have joy and peace and live out the rest of his days in happiness.

And by *The End*, the father found his way, even through the grief of his daughter's death.

Chris held his head in his hands. What was this, some kind of final good-bye? A three-hundred-page suicide note?

Or was it just a work of fiction? Some way for Jules to cope with her grief?

His hands were shaking as he gathered up the pages and headed home, feeling as desperate as the characters in the book. He knew so much yet had so little power to do anything about it.

And he had to factor in the possibility that Roy Fletcher was lying, making it all up.

Then there was this possibility of the strangest kidnapping on the planet. How did everything connect?

It was nearly midnight when Chris arrived home. He covered the manuscript with his jacket and ran toward the porch, unable to avoid the soaking rain.

As he shook the rain off himself, he looked up to see that his front door was open. Just a crack.

He glanced toward the window. It looked like every light in the house was off. Which was strange, since Addy was scared of the dark and always had three or four lamps going even when she wasn't home.

An unsettled feeling came over Chris. He ran back to his truck, threw the pages inside the box that held Jason's files, and grabbed his gun. He couldn't tell if Addy's rental car was there. He let her park in the garage when she visited.

He listened carefully as he crept up on the porch but didn't hear anything.

He used his elbow to open the door. With his left hand, he slowly reached for the light switch. He flipped it, but nothing happened.

Chris turned, keeping his gun pointed into the dark house, and looked through the trees. His neighbor's lights were on and they always lost electricity together in a storm.

Moving inside, he let his eyes adjust as he searched for any sound or movement. Everything was quiet.

"Addy?" he called. "Addy?"

Then a noise. He couldn't identify it. It sounded like a dog's claws against a wooden floor. A tapping. A stomping?

A moaning.

"Addy!"

Chris raced through the house, knocking his shin against the coffee table and his hip against the couch. He slipped on the rug but managed to keep from falling.

"Addy?"

No reply. But as he reached the kitchen, he could see a shadowy figure in a chair that had been pulled away from the table. He carefully approached, listening for any other movement, any other sign that someone else was in the house.

As he got closer, he could see it was Addy, tied to the chair. Her eyes were wide with terror.

"Addy, Addy . . . hold on. I'll get you untied. Hold on." He opened the drawer that held a flashlight and scissors, then put the flashlight under his arm and tried to untie the knot that bound her hands behind her back and behind the chair. He tried the scissors, but they weren't sharp enough to cut through.

He went around to face her and pulled the duct tape off

her mouth. She gasped for breath, and as he shone some light on her, he could see her left eye was swollen shut.

He cupped her face. "Are you okay?"

She nodded, tears rolling down her face. "Chris . . ."

"Okay. It's okay. Stay calm. I've got to go get my knife." It had the sharpest blade on it. It would cut through swiftly.

"Chris! Don't leave me!"

"I'm not. It's okay. It's just in the bedroom."

"No . . . no, please. Please don't leave me."

Chris squatted again next to her. "Did you see who did this to you?"

"He wore a mask. . . ."

"Did you see him leave?"

She shook her head. "No. I just remember waking up, tied to this chair." Her jaw was trembling so much that her words were barely audible. "Please don't leave me. It's dark. . . ."

"I know. But I need that knife. I promise I won't let anything else happen to you, okay? Will you trust me? For once in your life?" He tried a smile.

Tears still flowed down her cheeks, but she nodded.

Chris stood and turned toward his bedroom. His gun led the way.

Once he got there, he ran the flashlight beam over the room quickly. Nobody seemed to be around, but his room had been ransacked. Drawers pulled. The closet trashed. He'd deal with that later. He had to get back to Addy.

He moved toward the dresser drawer where he kept the

knife but stopped short. There, among the clutter covering his bed—it was stabbed straight through his pillow. The only thing visible was the ivory handle.

"Subtle," he grumbled.

Within seconds, he was back by Addy's side. He cut the rope and freed her. She collapsed into his arms.

"It's okay. . . ." He let her cry for a moment before getting her attention again. "Tell me what happened."

She wiped her eyes. "One minute I'm about to make dinner. The next minute all the lights go out. All the electricity. I just thought it was the rain or something. And then . . ." She shook her head and covered her mouth like she was trying not to scream. "Then someone grabbed me from behind. And then I woke up . . . and I was alone and it was dark . . ."

Rage rose through his veins. "Did he say anything to you?"

She nodded. "He said . . . 'Tell your brother to stop sniffing around.' I think that's when he hit me." Her fingers found her swollen eye socket.

Chris put the light on her face and examined the wound. Nothing appeared to be broken, but he was no expert. She definitely needed to see a doctor.

"We have to get you out of here. Now." He took her by the arm and helped her to her feet.

"Chris, what's going on? Where?"

"I've got to send you home, Addy. It's the only place you'll be safe."

"But—"

"I don't want to hear any arguments, okay? It's not safe for you here."

"What about you?"

"I've got to figure out what's going on. But I have a pretty good idea." He took her toward his spare bedroom. "Get your things packed as fast as you can."

Then a noise. They both turned, and Chris held a finger to his lips, shutting off the flashlight.

The front door was creaking open.

Chris stepped forward, pointing his gun in the direction of the door.

"Chris Downey?" a voice shouted.

Chris rushed the door, not able to see the person who had called out his name. That didn't matter at the moment.

The tall figure that stood in the doorway was instantly flattened to the front porch. Chris pinned him with both knees and held the gun to his temple.

The man's glasses were twisted against his nose, one of the lenses cracked. He fought but with little strength.

"Hey!" he yelled. "What do you think you're doing?"

"Who are you?" Chris roared. "What are you doing here?"

"I'm a . . . a . . . courier. That's it. Just a courier."

Chris slowly climbed off him but kept the gun pointed at him. "A courier. Really. At this time of night?"

"Yeah. Really." The man took off his glasses and glanced at them before shoving them in his pocket. "I have a card and everything." He took one out of his pocket and handed it over.

"What are you doing here?"

"I came to deliver that," the man said, pointing to a manila envelope that had slid out of his hands when Chris tackled him.

Chris stooped to pick it up. "Why not mail the thing?"

"Mrs. Patterson doesn't trust the U.S. Postal Service." The man stood on shaky legs, unfolded a piece of paper, and drew a pen out of his pocket. "Sign here that you've received it," he said flatly.

Chris signed and handed the pen and paper back. "Sorry about the . . . thing here."

"Yeah, well, memories, right?"

The man walked to his electric car and drove away. Chris stared at the envelope. Addy was behind him now.

"What's going on?"

Chris ripped open the flap. "I don't know." He pulled out the contents and dropped the envelope to the ground but couldn't see anything with the electricity out. Addy brought him his flashlight. They both peered at the documents now being lit.

"What is this?" Addy asked.

Chris's breath was cut short. He held a map and a deed. On top of it all was a sticky note that read, *GET ME MY BOOK.*

"Chris?"

"It's where I can find Patrick Reagan. And if my gut's right, Jules Belleno too."

24

JULES DIDN'T REMEMBER falling asleep, but when she woke, the pages of *Snow* were neatly set on the other side of the bed, bookmarked where she'd left off, and she was snugly tucked into the covers, warm inside the shell of blankets.

But her feet were killing her. Even the slightest move of her ankles caused distressing pain. She yelped as she tried to move, and tears stung her eyes. She reached for the ibuprofen.

Although the curtains were drawn, the bright morning light reflected against the snow, bursting through the cracks like a high calling.

She stared up at the ceiling, those red, cryptic words

staring back at her. She still hadn't decided if Patrick was harmless or not. He seemed intent on helping her with something, even if his methods were slightly bizarre. But he also seemed fractured, emotionally and otherwise. She couldn't be sure of how stable he was.

One thing was for sure. If *Snow* was about his wife, then there was no doubt that he loved her. It reminded her of what she'd shared with Jason. She and Patrick had that in common, and maybe that was the way into the mystery of his intentions—that commonality.

She took a deep breath. The pain was relentless. "Patrick?"

The door to her room was shut. She wasn't sure he could hear her.

"Patrick?"

Soon the door opened. He stepped in with a tray of eggs and sausage. "Good morning." He seemed in a chipper mood.

"Hi." She tried to sit up but winced in pain.

"Your feet," he said, his face turning troubled. "I'm going to have to take a look." He set the food down and peeled back the covers. She felt his fingers pressing this way and that before he re-covered them with the blanket. "They're healing. But it's not going to be a cakewalk."

Jules opened the ibuprofen and tossed four into her mouth. Bad for the liver, but she didn't want another narcotic. She had to think clearly.

"I read almost the entire manuscript," she said, nodding toward the pages as she eased her way into a sitting position. "One of the loveliest stories I've ever read. Truly beautiful."

"Thank you." He placed the tray over her legs. "Eat up. We have a lot of work to do today." He stepped back, his expression troubled again. "You should brace yourself, Juliet. I believe you're ready for this, but it's not going to be easy."

She smiled slightly. "Nothing so far has been."

"True enough."

She ate, but her appetite waned, partly from the pain, partly from the upset stomach caused by too much ibuprofen, and partly because she continued to wonder what was in store for her today.

When Patrick returned, he noticed her food was mostly untouched. "My cooking growing old?"

She touched his arm as he started to take her tray. It was the first time she'd deliberately touched him. He looked at her for a long moment. Neither of them moved.

"Patrick?"

"Yes?"

"Take me out there. I'm tired of being in this room."

He left without saying a word, and Jules sighed. "Patrick," she called, trying to sound light though her mood was darkening. She needed to use the bathroom and she wasn't going for that bedpan again.

He returned. Pushing a wheelchair.

"That's convenient," she said with relief. His strong arms easily lifted her out of the bed and into the chair.

"Take your time," he said, gesturing toward the bathroom. "I'll be waiting out here."

She struggled to get the wheelchair through the doorway.

And getting herself onto the toilet was no easy task either. The whole ordeal took about twenty minutes, she guessed, with her feet and ankles throbbing relentlessly.

Out in the living room, the table was filled once again with all the paperwork she'd gone over a hundred times already. Her heart sank at the thought of diving into it again—or that manuscript patched together like Frankenstein's monster.

Patrick handed her a cup of coffee. She drank it eagerly.

"Juliet," he said softly, "do you believe I killed her?"

Midsip, Jules looked up. "I don't know."

"Surely you have a hunch."

Jules kept her lips close to her mug. She blew the steam, trying to kill time while she thought through her answer. "Patrick, knowing what I know of you—the brief time that we've known each other—I would say that I do not believe you killed her."

"Because I don't come across as a barbaric personality."

"Not usually."

He smiled at her little joke. He seemed to be lightening up a bit. But as he sat down, he asked, "Isn't there a time when killing is merciful?"

"I don't know."

"Sure you do."

"I don't know how to answer that."

"I believe that sometimes what seems barbaric or cruel on the surface is actually an act of mercy." He sighed as if she wasn't getting what he was saying. "I need you to believe that

I'm merciful, Juliet. Because what is going to happen today will seem . . . barbaric."

"I don't believe you killed her." Jules met his eyes with resolve, but inside, that resolve quivered. "Even knowing how much you loved her. And I do believe that. I believe you loved her more than life itself."

Suddenly tears filled his eyes and spilled over. He looked mortified but unable to stop them. Jules desperately wished she were not in the wheelchair. She wanted to drop by his side, tell him it was okay.

"I promised her I would," he whispered. "She made me promise, and I said yes because I didn't think it would . . . It was so horrible at the end. So . . . unreal." He covered his face, then tried to wipe the tears, but they kept flowing. "I wanted to ease her . . . But I could only . . . And she . . ."

"Yes? What?"

"She hated me for it." He sniffed and then regained composure. "And that's life. Life doesn't tie up all nice and neat. Some writers, though . . . some writers won't go to the necessary places to find the necessary truth. Some writers hide behind their words. Hide behind an easy way out." He stood, drank the rest of his coffee, and then looked at her. "You are to continue to work. Continue to dig. You must look harder, see everything there is to see, because when I return, it will be time for you to hear it all."

"Wait. Where are you going?"

"I must go do something."

"Please. Please, Patrick. Don't leave me here. I don't want to be alone."

"You've grown used to my company?" He grinned. "I'm glad. I've grown used to yours as well."

"I don't want to wait any longer for what you have to tell me. The time is now. Tell me now."

"At the right moment. But our time *is* running out. I must go do this, and then I will return. Then we will talk."

He walked to the rack near the door and put on a heavy coat. He wrapped a scarf around his neck and pulled on a warm fur hat. Lastly he put on his gloves.

"We know what going into the elements without proper attire can do, don't we?"

She nodded in agreement, though reluctantly.

"Now, you behave yourself and get to work. I need you to get this all sorted out before I return."

Jules looked at the stack. She was really no closer to figuring anything out than she had been before.

"Fine," she sighed.

He opened the door and a blast of air caused her to shiver. She was already cold to begin with.

"Juliet," he said, just before stepping out, "I want you to know that I know who you are."

"I love when you go all esoteric on me," she said with a small smile.

"I know you're Blake Timble."

In an instant, Jules's body stung all over. She stared at him, unable to blink or move. She hadn't been Blake Timble in a long time, and she had no intention of ever returning to him or speaking of him again. It had been a season of writing therapy that she'd impulsively sent off to a publisher to silence her father's nagging insistence that she could write. She'd assumed the manuscript would be rejected, allowing her to put to rest the idea that she might be a real writer.

Except it wasn't rejected. She'd written about her most private angst, now for the world to see.

Jules looked away, her eyes watering out of fear. She felt stripped naked of every piece of emotional cloth she'd hidden herself behind.

Patrick closed the door, and a violent shudder racked her body. She was as cold as if she'd been left outside.

⌐ ⌐

"I can't believe this," Chris said after the doctor left the exam room. "I cannot believe this."

Addy smiled, then winced. "At least it's not broken. But it hurts to smile. So don't be insulted if I don't laugh at your jokes."

"This is no joke."

She sighed. "I know. I'm just trying to . . . make you feel better."

They'd gone to the emergency room with a story that she'd fallen and hit her face on a coffee table. Everyone seemed to believe it. Right now Chris didn't need the police involved. He had no idea whom he could trust.

The bottom of Addy's eye was already turning purple.

Chris checked his watch. They'd been here for four hours thanks to a big highway crash that left them waiting for over three hours just to be seen. "Come on. Let's get out of here. We have to get you on that bus."

It took only twenty minutes to get to the station; from there Addy would take a bus to the airport.

"Listen to me," Chris said. "Do not allow yourself to be alone. Don't go to the restroom unless you see someone else go in before you. You're not totally safe until you get home, okay? Just watch everything, everyone."

"Chris, they're not after me. They're after you. You're the one we should be worrying about."

"There's plenty of worry to go around," Chris said. He pulled her into a hug. "Be careful. Call me when you get home."

"What are you going to do?"

"I'm going to make sure that those responsible for Jason's death pay. But first I'm going to find Jules."

"Be careful. That writer seems crazy, you know?"

Yeah. He knew.

After he sent Addy off, he drove to Jules's house, barely staying on the road because he was watching his rearview mirror more. The last time he was there, the Lt. Colonel had given him a key. He used it to get in when no one answered the door.

"Jim?"

"In here."

Chris rounded the corner to the small sitting area near the back of the house, with three full shelves of books, a cozy chair, and a reading lamp.

The Lt. Colonel sat there with a bottle of Jack in one hand and pages of the manuscript in the other. He cocked an eyebrow. "You don't look so good," he said, his speech slurred.

"It's been a rough night."

"Me too. Me too." He waved the pages. "Interesting reading about myself."

Chris sighed. He had wondered if the Lt. Colonel would read the book too.

"I read some of it. Most of it," Chris said.

He smiled sloppily. "It's good, huh?"

Was that a rhetorical question?

"I always told her she could write. Told her over and over. And she can. She did." He cleared his throat. "I didn't need a book to tell me I've been a screwup. I know I have failed her."

Chris sat down on the stool meant for reaching the upper shelves of the bookcase. "Jim, from what I read in the book, you've got her unfailing love."

"Don't deserve it. All this is true. Every rotten word of it. All of it but the ending. I pray to God she doesn't kill herself over a loser like me, Chris. Do you think that's what has happened to her?"

Chris didn't know how to answer that.

The Lt. Colonel's watery eyes looked genuinely at Chris. "I've been praying, Chris. Real hard for her. Real hard." He tipped the bottle back. "On my knees."

Chris smiled. "I think God answered your prayers."

"What do you mean?"

"I think I know where she is."

The Lt. Colonel set down the pages and nearly dropped his bottle of liquor. "You found her?"

"Listen to me, Jim. I'm going to need your help in this. It's getting complicated, fast."

"I'll do anything. Name it." His bloodshot eyes widened with anticipation.

"I need you to be a distraction. A big one."

WHEN SHE WAS A KID, Jules had always thought being in a wheelchair would be cool. It wasn't. She was having a hard time reaching things she needed and moving around the furniture. She already needed to go to the bathroom again but couldn't get herself motivated for all the hard work getting there.

Instead, she decided to light a fire, despite Patrick's insistence that it not be lit. This beautiful stone fireplace had been empty of flame since she arrived, and it was a shame. It was cold in the house, for one thing. And second, who didn't like to work and ponder by firelight?

She couldn't reach the matches on the mantel, but she

used a particularly long vase sitting nearby to knock them to the floor. Wood was already in the fireplace, strung with cobwebs. She got rid of those but needed newspaper or something similar.

She found a couple scraps of paper in the mess on the coffee table, plugged them into the gaps in the wood, and tried a match. It lit, but barely. The fire fought its way against a small draft. Jules didn't think it was going to sustain itself.

She needed newspaper.

She glanced to the doorway. No sound. Maybe she could . . . look around a little?

With great effort, she wheeled herself toward the other side of the cabin, presumably where Patrick's bedroom was. It seemed like a really, really bad idea to go in there, but curiosity kept her rolling along. When she came to the door, which was shut, she wondered if he'd locked it.

She listened again for any sound. Everything was quiet.

Jules reached up and turned the knob. Slowly. When she started to push the door, it made a horribly loud creak. She squeezed her eyes shut—like that was going to help.

When the door was fully open, she peeked around a small corner.

And gasped.

The entire cabin was as tidy as if it had just leaped out of *Architectural Digest*. But this room was . . . madness.

The bed was unmade, the covers twisted and turned like they'd been tied in knots. There was clutter everywhere—books stacked in corners, junk in baskets and in boxes. It looked like a basement that hadn't seen the light of day, or a human, in years.

But more alarming than the junk that accumulated were all the papers. Everywhere. In every part of the room that had space, littering every inch of the floor.

She wheeled forward, trying to comprehend what she was seeing. The papers crunched underneath her wheelchair and she bent down to pick one up. When she looked it over, her heart stung with panic.

It was one of her blog posts.

She picked up another.

Another one of her blogs.

She picked up more and more. They dated back as far as two years ago. Some words and phrases were highlighted and circled and underlined. And not just about Patrick's books. Other posts she'd written about her town were also marked, but so randomly that she couldn't make sense of it. Sometimes just a word here or a word there. Sometimes a phrase. Sometimes a paragraph.

She wheeled farther in, scooping up random pages. As she flipped one sheet over, she immediately recognized it as a page from her *Enoch Mandon* manuscript.

But how . . . *how* did he know it was her? The publisher had promised not to reveal her identity.

She eyed the rest of the junk in the room. As she looked closer, she realized it was Amelia's things—clothes, cookbooks . . . It was as if Patrick knew he couldn't keep them any longer but didn't have the heart to throw them out. So they lingered in no-man's-land, waiting for their destiny.

One box held photographs. Jules picked up a stack and flipped through them. Wow, Amelia was really beautiful. She'd radiated youth and vibrancy. There was a keenness to her eyes. They were light blue, like an afternoon sky, and her eyebrows were dark and arched perfectly. Her smile was wide and full-toothed, her platinum hair cut pixie short, fitting her thin face and her high cheekbones. She stood just a hair taller than Patrick, always with her arm wrapped around his. In one picture, she looked at him, laughing as though he'd told the funniest joke she'd ever heard.

Jules studied Patrick in his younger years. He had a full head of hair, dark brown and cut conservatively. His smile was always reserved, but his eyes showed a playfulness and even a hint of mischief, seemingly brought out whenever Amelia was by his side.

He was ruggedly handsome in the photos, not as polished as he seemed to become over the years. He sometimes sported a short beard. Wore lots of turtlenecks and occasionally an expensive-looking vest.

Jules looked around the room, trying to take it all in, trying to decide what it all meant. It seemed to be a perfect analogy to Patrick's state of mind. Mostly tidy . . . but there was a corner that was disheveled in the most disturbing of ways.

How could a man live like this? In this chaos? Especially when he seemed to crave order so much? It was a dichotomy. He was part chaos and madness and part structure and order.

His writing was pandemonium, but he ate breakfast and dinner at the same time every day.

This was where he retreated to every evening? Staring at all this junk? Staring at his wife's memories?

A noise.

She held her breath and listened.

Nothing.

But then . . . whistling?

Oh no.

Jules quickly turned the wheelchair around, her arms shaking from exhaustion already, and hurried across the floor, rolling over all the paper.

She squeezed through the doorway, using her arms to push her way through. The chair's armrests scraped against the wood. Once in the hallway, she was out of breath but raced toward the living area. The wheels moved faster on the bare wood floor.

She heard the door opening.

But she wasn't there yet.

Come on, come on. Her fingers got caught in the spokes of the left wheel, twisting one so hard that she cried out in pain.

But she had to get there, no matter what.

She could hear his boots against the floor. He was inside the house.

Jules wheeled right to the coffee table as he turned, a small smile on his face indicating that he had just now noticed her.

Her heart pounded erratically, but she tried to hold her breath. She greeted his smile with her own.

"Hi," she said, though she barely had enough breath in her.

Suddenly the smile dropped off his face, and her heart raced with a sense of danger.

But he wasn't looking at her.

He was focused on the fireplace, where the fire had actually spread over the wood quite nicely while she was gone.

Jules wheeled forward a little bit, gesturing to it. "Nice ambience, eh? Yes, I got creative with getting the matches. Didn't break anything." She grinned.

But Patrick's expression was rapidly descending into darkness. His eyes glowed as hot as the flames at which he stared. "What have you done? What have you *done*?"

He hurried toward her and Jules covered her face, readying herself for an attack. Instead, Patrick hurtled past her to the kitchen. Jules turned, watching as he pulled a large pot out and filled it with water.

Sloshing it as he returned, he'd soaked the front of his shirt by the time he tossed the remaining water onto the fire. The flames sizzled and crackled in protest but then faded into a dark-gray smoke that filled the chimney and seeped into the room.

Jules coughed.

Patrick turned and threw the pot at her. It hit her in the lap, though she managed to almost catch it. Her fingers throbbed as she grasped it.

"What is wrong?" she breathed.

"What is wrong?" he roared. "Why would you ever do that? *Why?*"

"Do what? Start a fire?" she yelled back, her whole body trembling. "In case you haven't noticed, it's freezing in here! I thought it'd be nice to—"

"Shut up. *Shut up!*" His face, as it had before, turned red with rage. He turned to the fireplace, stomping his foot into the smoke, kicking at the logs. He kicked and kicked some more.

"Stop it!" Jules yelled.

His attention snapped to her. He stood above her, teeth bared.

Then he raised his hand and slapped her across the cheek.

Jules cried out, grasping her face, tears springing to her eyes. Her skin stung, but it was the surprise of what he'd done that hurt even more. She looked up at him, shielding herself with her other hand as he raised his arm once again, high, as though he hadn't hit her hard enough the first time.

"Patrick!" she barked.

And then he blinked, frozen with his hand in the air.

"Patrick, don't!"

He stumbled backward, staring at her, slowly lowering his arm.

"Patrick, please. It's okay. Just . . . take a deep breath."

He looked at her as if to ask, *Did I hit you?*

There was no hiding what was undoubtedly a growing red mark on her cheek.

"What did I do?" he said, falling back into the chair near the fireplace. He stared into the dark, hollow, smoky pit.

Jules tried to calm herself. And him. "It's okay. I'm okay."

She had no idea where this empathy was coming from. Maybe she was just trying to keep her enemy close. And subdued.

"It's not okay," he said, his face sunken with sadness. He kept staring into the fireplace, never looking at her.

"I'm sorry," Jules said, rolling toward him, trying to appear as resolute as she could. "I didn't know that would upset you."

"There hasn't been a fire lit in there since . . ."

"Amelia?"

Tears welled in his eyes but he still didn't look at her. "One late afternoon," he began, "before dinner, I had fallen asleep in this chair after a long day of writing. Something made me stir. It sounded like there was a bear outside. Happens sometimes around here. I closed my eyes again but still heard it. Like something being dragged. I was so tired. I simply wanted to finish my nap." The tears fell, dripping onto his hands that lay limply in his lap. He shook his head as though he couldn't fathom what he was about to say next.

Jules kept perfectly still and silent. Her cheek throbbed, but she hardly noticed.

"And then I woke straight out of a deep sleep. To this day I can't explain why. It was like a hand grabbed my shoulder and shook me. I remember the hand."

He glanced at her, then averted his eyes.

"Then I saw her." He gestured to the floor in front of him. "She was right here, laid out completely flat, and she reached . . ." His gaze returned to the fireplace. "She reached into the flames. Her hand was right in there, burning."

Tears stung Jules's eyes again as she pictured the fragile woman.

"It was the only way she could think of to kill herself. She just wanted to die, no matter how painful." Patrick wept for a moment, covering his eyes. "And I stood and just grabbed her ankles and pulled her. I yanked her. And I grabbed a pillow to smother her hand. It was burned, badly. I could smell the . . ." He broke down again.

Jules was not sure she'd ever seen a more broken man. She tentatively wheeled herself closer to him.

"She died a few days later. In her bed. Without my help." He looked at her now. She was close, only about five feet away. "I might have helped her, Juliet. I might have. If I hadn't felt that hand on my shoulder, waking me. It was strong and real. Nobody was there. But I knew what it spoke to me."

"What?"

"That there is a Creator of life. He gives and takes at will. And life is the purest picture of sanctity. That's what I knew at that moment." He wiped his tears. "And why I chose to believe it rather than help my wife with her dying wish, I still can't explain to this day. But I have never lit a fire since."

Jules rolled closer. So close their knees were almost touching. She reached out slowly and took his hand. His fingers were cold. She closed hers around them and felt him instantly relax. His thumb pressed into her hand.

"Juliet," he said softly, "do you want to know why I brought you here?"

"You had something important to tell me."

"Yes. But I could've told you at your home. Or at the grocery store. Or any number of places."

"True."

"I began to understand in my solitude that I was unable to assess myself. Was I a horrible human being for letting Amelia die in agony? Was I forever damned by allowing myself to think about ending her life?"

"Patrick, it was an impossible situation."

"Most people believe we need each other to fill our lives with abundance and blessing. We believe we need people to show us all the good in ourselves. But I don't believe that's the case. We need people, Juliet, to show us our selfishness, to extract the ugliness that reveals itself in our hearts." He looked down, brushing her fingers with his other hand. "I had to know the state of my heart, how dark it was, if there was any goodness left in me at all. Everyone I trusted was dead. So I chose you."

She leaned forward in her wheelchair. "Patrick, there is lots of goodness left in your heart."

"I don't know why that hand came down to me. If I were God, I would not exert an ounce of energy toward a man who has hardly regarded Him in his life." He gazed past her, into empty space. "The hardest thing to understand about God is why He answers a prayer for a good parking space at the mall but won't hear the cries of a man desperate to save his wife. Why He wouldn't hear the plea of such a woman as yourself, that her husband might not die on a sidewalk in the darkness of night."

Jules lowered her eyes, emotion welling up in her. "I don't know, Patrick. I do know that even as he lay dying on that concrete, Jason would've trusted God that He had a plan."

"I don't think I'm capable of such blind trust."

"I don't know if I am either," Jules said, searching his eyes. "But I do believe in happy endings. I still believe in them. And I don't know if we get them here, but somehow I think that there's a way to get them there. In the next place. Heaven."

"Then what's the point of this? This life?"

"Maybe it's just what you said. We need each other to extract all the ugliness in our life." She squeezed his hand. He returned a weary smile. "I used to hate the invisibility of it all—of God, heaven. Why is heaven so unreachable from here? Why is God so invisible? Why does He make it so hard to find Him?"

Patrick nodded.

"Jason told me that God is invisible so we won't search for Him with our eyes. So we'll depend less on what seems concrete and more on the faith it takes to see without our eyes. And then when we see Him, we'll know we've also been seen."

They sat in silence for a moment, holding hands, staring into the air.

"Do you want to know how I knew who you were?"

Jules let go of his hand, backed her wheelchair up a ways. "That I was Blake Timble? Yes." Her heart pounded, wondering if he was going to throw yet another fit.

"It was rather easy. I saw patterns."

"Patterns?"

"I've read your blog every day for two years. Watched you on Facebook." He smiled wryly. "Under an assumed name. I never let my publisher know that I knew my way around social media. Playing ignorant saved me a lot of time and hassle."

Jules chuckled.

"So when I received the manuscript to read for endorsement, I saw the same turns of phrase, the same beats, the same rhythms. Do you understand? You have a particular fondness for three-syllable words that start with *e*. You tend to slip into the passive voice when you're conveying an intellectual thought. Things like that."

"Wow," she said. "That's observant." She held her breath for a second. "But why did you hate it so much?"

He thought for a long moment. "I don't hate it. Not as it seems I do. I guess my dislike arose because you believe in happy endings." He shrugged. "Maybe because you wouldn't go there."

"Go where?"

"Deep enough."

"I tangled with the hardest of subjects," Jules said. "I explored the things that ripped my guts out."

"But you let yourself die. You took the easy way out." He searched her eyes. "She killed herself in a car with carbon monoxide. She slipped away quietly, softly." He gestured gently with his hands. "Was that what you intended to do, Juliet? Slip away quietly?"

Jules held a finger under her eye, trying to catch a stray tear. "I don't know. Maybe I had thought about it. I wanted to be with Jason. I didn't want to be stuck here. But I also felt I hadn't arrived at a place where I was certain heaven would be there for me. Jason always told me heaven wasn't for good people. It was for repentant people."

Patrick suddenly rose and stood at the fireplace for a moment, remembering something. Or someone. Then he turned to her. "There won't be any meals today. I'm sorry." He walked around her wheelchair and began pushing her toward her bedroom.

"Patrick, no. I don't want to go back in there. Leave me out here. Please."

"I need to be alone."

"I won't talk. I won't do anything. Please don't put me back in that bed. I need to be out here. Looking outside. Getting some fresh air."

"I don't feel like taking care of you right now," he said, steering the wheelchair around the furniture.

"No! Don't take me back there!"

But he kept pushing.

"What about that thing you needed to tell me?"

"First things first," he said. "You started a fire, which means smoke came out of the chimney. People can see that, you know. People can find us."

"What people?" Jules asked with urgency. "*What people?* In case you haven't noticed, there's been no knight in shining armor to rescue me."

"They'll find us. Eventually."

He pushed into the room and stooped, lifting her out of the chair.

As he gently put her down on the bed, she grabbed his shirt. "Don't leave me here."

"I'm sorry," he said, batting her hand away. "I'm not well."

"Yeah? Well, I feel great. So get me out of this bed."

"Tomorrow," he said, going to the door, pushing the wheelchair into the hallway. "Tomorrow we'll talk. Right now I must watch to see if they're coming."

"Hey!" she screamed. "Don't you walk out of here. Don't!"

"I'm sorry, Juliet."

"Let me tell you something," she said, her voice in a highly emotional octave. "I don't care that you don't like my story! You think I didn't go there? Well, you're not the end all and be all, Patrick. Get it? I went where I needed to go. I bled all over every one of those pages! Spilled the blood of my soul! You didn't get it because you didn't allow yourself to get it. And that's because you're filled with jealousy. You're buying into the idea that you're a has-been, so you take your anger and frustration out on me. My book. It's *my* story! *My* soul! And you don't matter in it. You don't matter at all." Her chest heaved as the words fell out of her mouth, the last ones hanging in the air between them. He looked wounded. And Jules was glad.

"You're right," he said quietly. "You're right about every-thing." Then he stepped into the doorway, preparing to shut it.

"Patrick!"

He ignored her.

She drew in a deep breath. "I was in your room!" It flew out of her mouth before she had a chance to consider whether it was a good idea. But she was desperate.

He turned, his expression frozen in shock. "What did you say?" She knew he would know once he saw the open door. And surely she had crinkled papers as she rolled over them and then scrambled to get out of the room. There would be evidence, and something told her that it was better to confess now.

"I was in there. I saw your room." She clenched her jaw. "I saw everything. I saw *you*, didn't I? That's the real you in there. Not someone who has all the answers, but someone who is searching, someone who doesn't even really know the question."

For the first time, his guard completely dropped. He looked like a scared little boy, as if she'd seen right into his soul.

"Why did you have to do that?" he said, his nostrils flaring.

"Because you're holding me hostage, against my will. That's why. It's only fair." Her eye twitched but she kept staring him down.

"You shouldn't have done that." Patrick turned and shut the door. Jules heard it lock.

AFTER REPAIRING the breaker that cut the electricity to his house, Chris stood in front of the mirror in his bedroom, watching his chest rise and collapse with trepidation.

He'd been ordered by the captain to return to work, immediately. But instead he was risking everything on a gut feeling that Jules was with Patrick Reagan. And that there was somehow a connection to Jason's murder in all of this. How Reagan was attached he didn't know, but he did know that even before bringing the men who did this to justice, he had to rescue Jules. He owed it to Jason.

He buttoned his shirt and tucked his gun into the

waistband of his jeans. He had another weapon wrapped at his ankle.

So much of this depended on whether the Lt. Colonel could pull off the distraction necessary for Chris to get out of town unnoticed. He estimated that he had a two- to three-hour drive to get to the cabin, the best that he could tell, and that was if the weather didn't hinder him any. He didn't know who was watching and how often.

The Lt. Colonel could give him a head start, which was what he needed. But as soon as they learned he'd visited Leona Patterson, they'd get a warrant and probably find evidence of where the cabin was.

And then they would come looking for him.

By then, he'd already be there, getting Jules. Hopefully not by force.

The documents that Leona sent contained the address, which was a PO box. But she'd also sent detailed instructions of how to get there, through small, off-the-map mountain roads that led to the White Mountains in New Hampshire.

Also in the packet was a copy of a letter that Ike had sent to Patrick. Apparently Ike had signed over the deed to the cabin early in their relationship, promising to keep it a secret and to never reveal its whereabouts. The letter was written with the love one has for a brother, and Chris assumed the deep affection Ike had for Patrick went both ways. It was like how Chris had felt about Jason. His affection for Jason—and Jules—was what was driving him up that mountain.

Chris checked his watch. The plan was for the Lt. Colonel

to go to the police station in fifteen minutes during roll call and cause an uproar as only the Lt. Colonel could do. By the time they got the Lt. Colonel out of the way, they'd realize Chris didn't make lineup, but that would give him a forty-five-minute start, at least.

Chris grabbed his bag, which held some ammunition, a GPS device, and two knives. He prayed he was overreacting about the weaponry he was going to need. Literally. He'd sat on the end of his bed and prayed a real prayer to a God he was beginning to really believe in.

He checked his watch again.

It was time.

He turned out all the lights in his house, locked the back door, and headed out the front.

But as he opened the door, Chris saw him.

Greg Maecoat stood on his front porch, in uniform, legs spread in a stance that indicated he wasn't going anywhere soon. Chris momentarily froze. Maecoat kept an even expression.

"Maecoat . . . what are you doing here?" Chris said, trying to seem calm and unaffected. He was certain he wasn't pulling it off.

Maecoat looked slightly amused as he noticed Chris's clothes. Then the bag in his hand. "Why aren't you in uniform?" He made a deliberate motion of checking his watch. "It's almost time for lineup. Aren't you on your way in?"

"Why are you here, Greg?"

The two men stared at each other for a moment. Then

Maecoat sighed. "Look, the captain sent me. To . . . check up on you."

"Check up on me?"

"Said you'd been acting strangely. He was worried. Thought you might be in trouble." He nodded toward the bag Chris was holding. "Was the captain right? You going somewhere?"

"I just have some things to take care of before work. I figured I had enough time to come home and change."

Maecoat looked at his watch again. "You don't."

"You're not my babysitter. If I'm late for lineup, so be it. It's not on you."

"Now it is because I was sent here." Maecoat's eyes narrowed. "What's going on, Chris?"

"It's none of your business. Just stay out of it." Chris glared hard at him, trying to figure out if Maecoat could be trusted at all or if he was one of them.

"I can't," Maecoat said, taking a step forward. "I've got orders."

"Orders?"

"To make sure you get yourself to the station."

Neither of them budged. Chris had to think fast; his window of time was closing.

How trustworthy was Maecoat? Could Chris tell him what was going on? Could he enlist his partner to help him get to Jules?

"Greg, come in. I need to talk to you."

Chris stepped out of the way and Maecoat entered, looking around the dark living room. Chris turned on a light. "Have a seat."

"I'm supposed to make sure you're on time," Maecoat said, eyeing him and not taking the seat that Chris offered.

"There's a lot of stuff going on," Chris said.

Maecoat immediately stiffened, put his hands on his belt, opened his stance again.

"What do you know, Maecoat?"

"What do I know? About what?"

Chris balked. If Maecoat didn't know anything, then Chris was dragging him into something he shouldn't. But if Maecoat was involved, Chris had a real problem on his hands.

"What'd you want to talk to me about?" Maecoat asked with a wary expression.

Addy always said Chris had an impulsive side. Sometimes that was helpful. Other times not.

With one swift punch, Maecoat was on the floor, spun around and facedown. Chris drilled a knee into his back as he reached for the handcuffs in his bag.

Maecoat fought back but was already disoriented from the punch, and Chris managed to get him cuffed.

"What are you doing?" Maecoat yelled, his cheek smashed into the floor. His gaze cut sideways, wide and darting, trying to look at Chris.

"I'm sorry, Greg. I'm really sorry." Chris grabbed the second pair of handcuffs out of his bag, his knee now right at Maecoat's neck. "Don't struggle."

What was he going to handcuff him to? He looked around.

The pipe under the kitchen sink? Too far away. There was no way Maecoat wouldn't struggle. He was starting to already.

The coffee table was only five feet away. It was very heavy wood—two people had to lift it. Chris grabbed him by the shirt and pulled him across the wood floor. He latched one cuff to the set already on Maecoat's hands and the other to the leg of the table. Maecoat was still on his stomach. It was going to be difficult for him to get loose. Not impossible, but it would buy Chris some time.

"Captain said you were going crazy! I didn't believe him!" Maecoat yelled. A trickle of blood was running out of his mouth and down his chin.

Chris knelt beside him. "Greg, listen to me. I had to do this. For your protection."

"My protection? I need protection from *you*!"

"If you're not involved in this, then this is where you need to be."

"What are you talking about?"

Chris knew he couldn't say anything more, for both of their protection. But he could maybe throw them off a bit.

"I'm going to New York. That's where I think she is." He wasn't sure what the chances were that anybody would believe that lie, but he had to try.

"You're crazy," Maecoat said and spit on his shoe.

"They'll find you soon enough," Chris said, standing. His time was running out. "I'm sorry, Greg. I hope this makes sense to you someday."

Chris ran out the front door.

Jules couldn't find a comfortable position, and she couldn't move very much because of her feet. She'd called out Patrick's name for what seemed like hours, but he never responded.

Drifting in and out of sleep, she watched as the light faded from the window, her mind wandering to Jason and all the memories they had together. She imagined his fingers intertwined with hers. She imagined their feet in the ocean.

She'd open her eyes periodically and then be engulfed in the nightmare again. How long was Patrick going to leave her here? She wished she hadn't so impulsively confessed to being in his room. Whatever trust she'd built up with him was gone.

There was no one to help her. Certainly not Jason. She'd relied on him so much. For everything. Protection. Love. Hope. Joy. But he had not relied solely on her for those things. She'd brought him much of that, but at the end of the day, she knew he trusted more in God than even her.

She stared at the ceiling, but this time past those ugly, red letters that seemed darker than night. She stared through them.

"God . . . ," she whispered. "I need You." She swiped at her tears, but it was useless. "I need You to help me like You always helped Jason. I need hope that I'm going to get out of this. I can't do it by myself. I think he's going to harm me or keep me here for . . ." Her words trailed off into the darkness.

It didn't seem that she'd slept, but she woke to a sound

and her eyes momentarily flew open. She sensed that time had passed as she listened for more sound, keeping her eyes closed, trying to press back into sleep so she wouldn't have to face the confining darkness of the room.

But her mind remained awake, so she slowly opened her eyes again, hoping to see daylight beginning to peek through the shades.

Instead, a shadowy figure stood over her bed.

JULES JOLTED UP, causing pain to shoot through her feet and her hands.

"Shhhh," he said. "It's just me."

"That's the problem," she said. She regretted it immediately, but she felt delirious with angst.

"I see."

"I'm sorry," she sighed, trying to read his expression through the darkness. "I didn't mean that."

"Yes, you did." Patrick reached over and turned on the bedside lamp, illuminating his face. "But it's okay. You're right."

"I'm sorry I went into your room," Jules said as he sat on the edge of the bed. "That was a terrible thing to do."

"Forgiven," he said with a faint smile.

She struggled to sit up and prop herself against the head-board. "I'm in bad shape, Patrick. I need a doctor. I need you to let me go."

"I understand. But first, I have to tell you. All of it. It's time for you to know."

"About what this all has to do with Jason's death?"

"Yes."

"Okay."

"Are you prepared?"

"I don't know. But I need to hear it."

He nodded. "All right. Then I will tell you. Two years ago, I began research for a novel I was writing about a small town and a serial killer. I'd written about law enforcement before, but I really wanted a good feel for the inner workings of a precinct the size of Wissberry's. Through some connections, I gained full access to the police department. I was able to look through police records and interview some of the offi-cers. This was a few days before Jason was shot. I remember the next day, after it happened, very well. I felt I had to leave, that I shouldn't be there for the grief they needed to deal with.

"I returned a few weeks later to continue my research. Although I did conduct interviews with a couple of detec-tives and the captain, I mostly researched in the basement.

"One night as I was reading through some files, I stumbled upon Jason's case. I read through it, read the whole report, that he was ambushed by unknown assailants while he was investigating a possible boat theft. What seemed odd to me was how little detail there was in the investigation. I'd been reading police records for weeks and each case contained a lot of details that the police had investigated. Yet Jason's was bare bones. They never found the assailants. They had no good leads. End of story. I might've overlooked it, but for the fact that Jason was a cop. And cops don't leave other cops' deaths unresolved.

"So I got curious because that's what writers do, right? We're curious by nature?" he said, smiling.

Jules nodded. "Too curious sometimes."

"Yes, well, that was me. I started listening and paying attention more. Nobody talked about Jason or his death, which didn't particularly strike me as unusual, as I wouldn't expect them to chat about it. I *would* expect them to keep the file open. Yet they closed it."

Jules tried to process what he was saying. "But the captain told me they'd never stop looking for who killed Jason. That it was an open investigation."

"The file remained in the basement and it was never removed while I was there."

"So what does this mean?"

"I asked myself the same question. Why weren't they investigating this more? One night I was at the station. I hadn't been sleeping well, so I decided to do some work at night.

"It was very quiet and I heard voices upstairs. Coming through the ventilation system. I heard them shut a door.

But I could hear their voices pretty clearly if I pressed my ear against the vent. So I did. And I heard them talking about . . ."

"Yes?"

"They were talking about having planted cocaine on an informant, saying that he was locked away for good, that nobody was going to find out what happened and if he did talk, he wouldn't look credible. He'd just look vindictive."

"Talk about what?"

"Jason's death."

"What?" Jules felt all the air in her lungs escape.

"I had to piece it together, bit by bit, over a number of weeks. But what I believe happened was that several of the officers were getting paid to look the other way on a boat theft ring."

"No . . ."

"They'd exposed it, basically, but then took bribes, kickbacks, to stay silent and make it possible for the ring to continue. The thefts happened in other counties, but the thieves were hiding the boats in Wissberry, in an old warehouse."

"This doesn't make sense."

"I don't know exactly how the informant is involved. But somehow Jason stumbled upon information leading him to suspect that his fellow officers might be part of a cover-up. Someone got wind of this and I think he was lured to that remote location, where he was gunned down."

"By his own?"

"Doubtful. Probably by the thugs who were running the

ring. But the officers knew if those guys were ever caught, they'd go down too. So they tried to cover it all up by closing Jason's file. I suspect the snitch either tried to double-cross them or grew a conscience. Either way, they needed him silenced. If he was killed, that would open another investigation, which they didn't need. So instead, they framed him for drug possession and another problem went away. With time, they hoped it would all be forgotten. But I didn't forget." He sighed. "The only piece of the puzzle that's missing is the informant. I'm unable to figure out who he was or where he was incarcerated. I also thought you might know something. Anything. But you didn't."

Jules took a tissue off the nightstand and wiped her eyes. This was almost more than she could take.

"Why all this?" she asked. "Why kidnap me? Why bring me here?"

Patrick seemed to think long and hard about the answer. Jules tried to wait patiently. Finally he said, "I saw promise in you from the start, you know. When I read your first blog, after I discovered all these things, I knew you had a gift. And as I've watched you over time, I've seen you grow. I suppose as I've watched you grow in this art, I've found myself disappearing into the trappings of commercialism. Amelia always said I worried too much about it. That art was art. But when the publisher sent me *Enoch*, I felt they were trying to hint to me that my writing was slipping. I was still grieving Amelia's death. And then when I figured out it was you who had written the book, it was as though my emotions were split in half. I hated that it was you, but if it was going to be anybody, I wanted it to be you. Plus . . . I'd asked for a sign."

"A sign?"

"I wasn't a praying man, as you know. But I needed to know for sure if I was supposed to help you. So I asked for help, for a sign that I was meant to help you. And then I got your manuscript."

"Why would you want to help me? We didn't know each other."

Patrick smiled gently. "Don't you realize, Juliet, that when you put your words out there for people to read, they do know you? They know you intimately. The words come straight from our souls, don't they? And there you were, several times a week, showing me your soul, over and over."

Jules looked down. "I never thought about it that way. I did it because it seemed safe and secure."

"You cannot guard your soul when you're a writer. That is why I could not accept *Enoch* as your best. You stood guard at the gateway to your soul. Your words were precise and beautiful, and you turned a dozen phrases in the most clever of ways. But you didn't let me all the way in, and I regretted that."

Jules looked up at the ceiling. "So what was that about?"

"I hoped that as I ended my journey, I might be able to pass along some wisdom, help you cultivate your craft. Perhaps lend a little of my know-how to you."

She chuckled. "So this was all one big writing lesson?"

He only smiled.

But then she frowned. "What do you mean, 'ended my journey'?"

Patrick stood abruptly, pushing his hands into his pockets. "Juliet, it is over for me. It was the most excellent of adventures, but I cannot write. My muse, my lovely muse, is gone."

"Wouldn't Amelia want you to continue?"

"Oh yes. But what she never understood was that she was the one I let guard my soul, and she was the only one who could open its door." He leaned against the nearby wall. "Juliet, I'm sorry for all of this. I have felt for quite some time that . . . things were happening up here." His fingers tapped his temple. "I am not in my right mind very often anymore. I knew I possessed something important, a secret that I couldn't let stay hidden. And I knew as I peered into your world that you had a great destiny in front of you—one that you would never be able to see on your own."

"You really think I'm a good writer?"

"One of the best I've ever read. And that is why you will finish *The Living End*. It is yours now. And only you know how it will end. You're the only one who can decide how it all will end."

Jules tried to sit up even more. "I don't understand. What do you mean?"

Suddenly there was a loud banging on the front door. Jules jumped and gasped, so startled that she almost burst into tears.

Patrick, strangely, didn't seem fazed. "Stay here," he said.

"And be quiet, okay?" He left the room and she heard the front door open.

Jules held her breath, but her mind raced. This could be her chance to be rescued. She could scream for help right now and somebody would know where she was.

Yet just now, as he sat by her bedside, Patrick had seemed the most coherent since she'd been here. Was he finally getting a grip?

She could hear the faint sound of a conversation. Both male voices, but she couldn't make out what they were saying.

What if he fell into madness again? What if he wasn't done terrifying her?

Her hand moved to her mouth so she wouldn't inadvertently scream, because she really wanted to. It could escape at any second.

She was squeezing her eyes shut, trying to decide what to do, when she heard the front door gently close. Her hand fell to her lap and she collapsed back into the pillow. Who was the crazy one now? Her only chance out of here was gone.

Patrick returned to the room, his cheeks pink from the cold outdoor air.

"Who was that?" Jules asked.

"That was Paul Watson. Do you remember Humphrey from my book *Rage*?"

She nodded.

"I based that character on Paul."

"Who is he?"

"He's my neighbor. Kind of. He lives about fifteen minutes away, up the mountain, but he's reclusive and spends most of his time watching Terra Pass through his binoculars."

"What is Terra Pass?"

"It's the only road that leads here. There are five cabins in all that can be accessed through Terra Pass. It's unusual to see any car on it, and most people don't even know it exists. It's not on the map, if you will."

"So what did he want?"

"To alert me. It helps to have a paranoid neighbor every once in a while. He's spotted a truck on the pass."

"What does that mean?"

"It means," he said, moving to the bedroom door, "that they've finally figured out where you are."

Jules swallowed. He disappeared for a moment, then returned. With a shotgun.

"What is happening, Patrick?"

He walked to the end of her bed. "They're coming. For me. For you."

"How? Who?"

"You have to understand what is at stake here. If these cops can be implicated in Jason's death, you can only imagine the lengths to which they will go to make sure that information never sees the light of day. It was just a matter of time before they realized what I knew. But what they didn't count on was that I would tell you. You're in danger now because you're with me."

"What are we going to do?"

"You are going to stay right here. Right in this bed. Do you understand me?"

"Patrick, please . . . no. Please don't leave me. Please."

He stepped around the edge of the bed to her side, placing his hand on her shoulder. "Juliet, I will take care of you. I am not going to let anything happen to you, okay? I couldn't help Amelia, but I can help you. You just have to trust me. Stay in this bed." He looked intently at her. "I'm sorry I hurt you."

"You didn't. It's okay. I'm fine. Just don't leave me here."

"It's the only way to keep you safe." He set the gun down suddenly and pulled her into a hug, his strong arms holding her tightly. Jules stiffened but then relaxed and wrapped her arms around him. Her entire body trembled, but for the first time in a long time, she felt completely safe.

Patrick released her and took his gun. At the edge of her room, he looked at his watch. "It's time." And then he shut the door.

28

THE HEATER IN CHRIS'S TRUCK blew in fits and starts. It had never been able to keep up with the cold very well, but with the frigid air of the mountain and the steady snow, it really wasn't happy. Chris was bundled up like an Eskimo, not because of his heater, but because of his fear that the truck was going to slide off the edge of a cliff, and if he made it out alive, he'd freeze to death instead.

He'd wanted to race up the mountain as soon as he secured Maecoat, but he knew that where he was going, GPS was going to be of no help and speed was only going to get him killed before he got there. He was certain the unmarked roads Leona described were as treacherous as they were dark. Her instructions proved to be complicated to read anyway. But once he got off the main road that led up into the mountain and to the ski resorts, the roads grew narrower and more perilous. There were no guardrails or caution signs. It had taken him way longer than he expected and now the moon's light was hidden by heavy snow clouds. Maybe that's why Reagan stayed in his cabin all winter long. He couldn't get down if he tried.

It had taken him four hours just to get to the base of the mountain, which was just across the state line. From there, he took the main road up. About halfway up the mountain, he was to take something called Terra Pass. And now, as he drove twenty miles an hour and tried to navigate through the biggest snowflakes he'd seen in his life, he was not looking for a street sign. He was looking for a large boulder. That was where he was to turn.

It felt a little like he was going after the Unabomber.

His headlights bounced off the small drifts that had formed against the side of the mountain. He threw off his gloves to grip the steering wheel better. His fingers turned white and not because of the cold. Carefully, tediously, he steered around each curve. He dared once to peek over the side. If his truck went off, they'd find Jules before they ever found him.

Since he'd gotten onto Terra Pass, he hadn't seen a single car. There was a reverent, eerie quiet to the mountain. The wind howled and swayed his truck. He could hear the slight pitter-patter sound of the snowflakes hitting his windshield.

If he hadn't been on his way to rescue a woman from a madman, while driving on the edge of a cliff, he might've actually found this relaxing and peaceful. He just needed a choir singing "Silent Night" to round it off.

His mind, like the snow, drifted as he continued to circle up the mountain. He was thinking about a ski vacation he and Jason had taken before he married Jules when his headlights bounced off something large and light brown— a boulder.

He shifted carefully down to first gear, then made an immediate right onto a narrow road that went only about twenty yards before it stopped at an old iron gate like one that might be found on a cattle ranch.

He opened the map and read the instructions Leona Patterson had included. They stated there would be a lock on the chain around the gate, but that it wasn't really locked. He should pull down on the lock and then open the gate. After that, he was to continue on this road.

Chris stepped out of the truck. The cold air punched through the gaps in his coat, under his shirt, and straight to his skin. These mighty gusts of wind were immediately followed by complete stillness and silence. The snow fell steadily, and the statuesque pine trees creaked like old doors opening. He found it difficult to breathe this high up.

He grabbed the lock and pulled.

But it didn't snap open.

It was . . . locked.

"You've got to be kidding me!" Chris tromped back to

his truck and grabbed the instructions. They clearly said that it would be unlocked. In fact, they said that it remained unlocked year-round. Chris sighed and grabbed the hammer out of the toolbox in the back of his truck. He pulled on his gloves and walked to the gate. With three swift swings of the hammer, he broke the lock off. The gate swung open easily and he drove through. This time, though, he was headed downward.

According to the map, he only had a mile or so to go.

He checked his rearview mirror closely, as he had during the entire drive, to make sure he wasn't being followed.

The best he could tell, he was the only vehicle on the mountain.

But he still couldn't let his guard down because there was no way of telling what he would find once he reached the cabin. A sense of urgency mingled with the thought that he was about to encounter a place thousands of people had wanted to find over the years. He wished he could enjoy marveling at that idea.

One mile going down the side of the mountain took twenty minutes in the storm, though the decline didn't seem as steep as the incline. And as he got closer to what was supposed to be the cabin, the road declined even less.

At a fork in the road he found another gate constructed between two large trees with several signs warning that this was private property and no trespassing was allowed. At least seven more signs like this were posted nearby or hanging off the gate. Lots of pictures of guns.

The instructions said that he should take the road that didn't have the gate.

There was nothing indicating it was a road. At most it looked like a small path with no trees. But snow had fallen and the path was virtually covered. If there was a road here, he'd guess it was traveled very rarely. And not in the last hour for sure.

Chris swallowed his apprehension and followed the hidden road, mindful that there might be a booby trap hidden somewhere. Or a gunman.

As he got closer, the road became less obvious than it already was. So much so that Chris wasn't even sure he should drive forward, as it was unclear if there was an opening ahead big enough for his truck. But according to the directions, the cabin was just ahead. He might fare better on foot.

He grabbed his gun off the seat next to him and killed the engine. He sat there for a moment, trying to decide if he should kill his headlights too. It was very dark out here now, with the moon hidden by clouds. His eyesight would adjust eventually, and he could take advantage of the cover of darkness, but he was in unknown territory. If he had to chase somebody or do anything other than walk, he was probably not going to do so well.

It was such a simple decision, but he found himself frozen. *Make a choice and go with it.*

Chris shut off the truck lights and opened the door.

"Patrick?"

She'd called his name numerous times but to no avail. The cabin was quiet. The last noise she'd heard was the door leading outside opening and closing. That was it. And she couldn't fathom what he was trying to tell her. *"It's time."* Time for what? Who was after him? Her? Them?

Although he assured her he would keep her safe, she felt vulnerable in the bed, unable to walk. Even the slightest movement caused searing pain.

She tried one more time. "Patrick?"

Then something caught her eye out the window of her room. It was lightning fast, but she thought she saw a beam of light bounce off the glass. Like a flashlight. A chill ran down her spine.

She couldn't stay here.

Jules peered over the edge of the bed. It was a long drop—the bed was unusually high. How would she manage to get down without the use of her feet? Her hands might be faring better but were still sore.

She lay back for a moment, trying to keep her wits about her, trying to be strong like she knew Jason would want her to be. If what Patrick said about what happened to Jason was true, she had to get out of here. She had to expose the truth and hold accountable those responsible for Jason's death.

But she had no weapon, no way of defending herself. What was she going to do?

Her eyes fixed on the words that she'd read a hundred times by now, words written for her.

But it was what was beyond the ceiling she wanted to see. God. His mercy. His love. His strength. She needed all of it right now. So she asked.

With one resolving blink, her focus returned to the ceiling. And the words. *Terrify me.*

Jules sat up, her eyes locked onto them.

Terror.

It was a powerful weapon.

Even if she wasn't powerful enough, she might be able to stir some terror, if need be. But not from this bed. She needed a different vantage point. She needed to know what was going on. She had to get out of this bedroom.

Throwing back the covers, Jules looked down at her bandaged, swollen feet. She tried to wiggle her toes, to see how much pain she could endure, but she cried out.

"Come on," she said, gritting her teeth and staring at them. "You gotta be tougher than that. You gotta stay with me. Give me what you can."

The floor below was a good three feet onto wood. If she simply rolled out, she could land on an elbow or rib and break any number of bones. She took the pillows and blanket and tossed them over the side, next to the bed. They would at least somewhat break the fall.

With one more prayer to God, she rolled herself over the edge.

Her body hit the ground with a loud thud, and a pillow

slipped, causing her to hit her head on the floor. She winced, grabbing it and feeling it start to swell right under her fingers. Her mother had always said, *"If it's swelling outwardly, that's a good sign."*

A throbbing headache formed, but she couldn't stop now. She tried to get up on all fours and crawl, but even that movement was too intense for her feet. She dropped to her belly, then used her hands to move the blanket under her thighs and below.

She was right—it helped her slide and kept the friction off the top of her feet. They still hurt like the dickens, but she had to push the pain out of her mind right now.

Once she got to the door, she used the wall to crawl her way up to the doorknob. As soon as it turned, she dropped to the floor again, pouring sweat and nauseous from the pain. Using her forearms, she shimmied herself over the wood floors and down the hallway.

The cabin was pitch-black. Not even a night-light on.

"Patrick?" she called, this time in a whisper. "Are you in here?"

Silence.

The wind whistled and pushed against the cabin walls. Coyotes howled distantly.

"Patrick?"

She was alone. She could feel it.

Near the fireplace, Jules spotted the poker. She dragged herself over there. Her ankles were throbbing so intensely it felt as if the pain were nearly audible. She gritted her teeth and groaned with every motion.

She managed to get the poker into her hand, though she tipped all the fireplace tools over and they came crashing down, making a deafening racket. Jules covered her mouth, trying not to scream in frustration.

Then another noise.

Something she hadn't heard in days.

A car door shut.

⌐ ∟

Chris crept forward, gun drawn, trigger-happy, he knew, by the way he was jerking the weapon toward anything that moved. Surprisingly, that was a lot of things. Branches. Owls. Leaves.

"Get ahold of yourself," he said quietly. His gun steadied.

The road that would've barely been big enough for his truck made a slight curve. He followed it off-path, hiding behind each tree he could. But as he rounded the curve, he spotted it.

The cabin.

It was hard to see in the dark. Not a single light was on, not even a porch light. The cabin was small and looked to be built at the edge of a cliff because he could see that some snow seemed to continue to fall past the ground in the distance.

An SUV was parked to the side, near what looked like a

shed. Firewood sat neatly bundled against one of its log walls. Nearby an ax was sticking out of a stump.

The shadows around him were still and somber as if asleep. He was still having a hard time seeing. A small flashlight was tucked in his waistband, but whether or not he should pull it out was up for debate.

Chris stood for a moment, shielded by a tree, and tried to get a sense of the cabin's layout. There was a door in front with windows on either side—the only way in or out, if he was correct and the cabin was built at the edge of the cliff.

Snap.

The sound of a limb cracking jerked his gaze to the left, but after a moment, he was pretty sure it was his own footstep that had done it when he'd leaned forward to get a better angle. He listened. No other sounds.

The place looked deserted. What if he was wrong? What if Jules wasn't with Patrick Reagan after all? He'd spent so much time chasing this lead . . . If she wasn't here, he'd lost valuable time figuring out where she really was.

He was going to have to get a closer look. A few more trees stood in his way to the cabin. After that it was clear, which wasn't a good thing. He liked the idea of having something to hide behind. He cautiously moved forward, treading lightly, holding his breath so he could listen for other sounds.

At the last tree before the clearing now, he stopped for a moment, his senses on alert for anything unusual. His hair was already wet from the snow, and his exposed skin was paying the price. He couldn't linger out here much longer.

"Don't you move."

The words were so close that Chris could feel the breath in his ear. Something sharp pressed against his throat, with an arm squeezed tightly below it. Chris struggled to breathe, trying to stay still.

"Drop your weapon."

Chris opened his hand and the gun dropped into the snow. The grip loosened a bit and he gasped for air.

"I knew you were coming," the voice whispered. "I know what you're coming for. You can't have it. Or her."

29

CHRIS FOUGHT to keep himself still and calm. If he was going to get out of this, he couldn't afford a mistake. And right now, it seemed that there was a chance he could underestimate the strength of the man with a knife to his neck. One wrong move and his throat could be sliced right open, even unintentionally. But he had a feeling whoever this was, he was very intentional.

He couldn't be sure it was Patrick Reagan, but the chances were good. He had a low, rumbling voice, like a powerful motor under the hood of a Mustang, and it ordered him to pull his second gun out of his ankle holster.

"I'm not here to harm her," Chris said carefully. As he

spoke, he felt the blade of the knife press into his skin again. "I came to find her. She's missing. People are worried about her. Is she okay?"

"Shut up."

"I can't do that. I have to make sure she's okay."

"Who are you? A cop?"

He said *cop* with heavy disdain. Chris took a moment, trying to decide how to answer.

"I'm a friend. I was her husband's best friend."

The man let out a small laugh. "Yes, well, I've seen what Jason's friends have done to him."

Chris tried not to swallow. The knife, just above his Adam's apple, was very close to cutting him. How did Patrick Reagan, if this was him, know about Jason?

He spoke slowly, carefully. "That's why I'm here. I found out what happened to Jason. And there are men willing to silence me. By any means possible."

"Not men. Cops."

"Yes. I don't know how many are involved. But I'm not one of them."

"How do I know that?"

Chris stared forward, into the snowy darkness, locking eyes on the cabin. "Look, when I began investigating Jules's disappearance, I came across some information at Jason's house. Information that led me to realize he knew something was going on. I found a piece of a boat hull. And a box full of information on the boats that were being stolen. That led me to a phone number, which eventually led me to an informant named Roy Fletcher."

Suddenly the knife left his neck and he was pushed to the ground. His cheek hit a small stick that scraped his skin. Blood trickled over his chin. He quickly flipped onto his back. The man was now pointing a shotgun at him. Chris recognized him as Patrick Reagan. Though it was dark, his eyes had adjusted enough to see that Patrick's eyes were lit with adrenaline. He looked a far cry from the stoic picture in his publicity photos.

Chris lifted his hands into the air. "I'm Chris Downey. Jules knows who I am. She can vouch for me. Is she here?"

"Tell me what you know about this informant."

"He's in prison. He claims he was set up by the cops. Had cocaine planted on him. They knew that once he was convicted for drug possession, his testimony was going to be worthless."

"You talked to him?"

"Yes. He told me the entire story, how he'd been working with Jason to bring down this theft ring, only to be persuaded by the other side to shut up and tell them who he was working for. The cops weren't stealing the boats. They were given kickbacks every time they looked the other way. Thugs murdered Jason, but the cops involved knew that an investigation could lead back to them. So they did what they could to cover it up, including closing the investigation on Jason and shutting down the informant by putting him in prison."

Patrick stared at him through the darkness. Jason could see puffs of frozen breath rapidly blowing out of his mouth. His own body was turning cold and he shivered.

"Is Jules okay?"

"She needs medical attention," Patrick said solemnly. "She got frostbite trying to . . ."

Chris nodded. "Okay. Then let me take her off this mountain."

Patrick kept the gun pointed directly at Chris's head. "She knows. At least some of it."

"About Jason?"

"Yes."

"How did you know? Is that why you took her?"

Then, faster than Chris could process what happened, a shot blasted through the night's silence and Patrick Reagan dropped to the ground. The gun fell from his hand, just a few feet from Chris. Chris crawled through the snow, grabbing at the cold metal of his own gun, which lay right under Reagan's hip. Another shot was fired, coming from behind him. He reached up and shot twice into the darkness, the sound shattering the still, cold night. He turned back to Patrick, who'd been shot through the leg.

"They're here," Patrick whispered, wincing in pain. "Don't let them get to her."

Chris randomly fired into the trees where he thought the shots came from. "Where is she?"

"Inside. In the west bedroom."

Patrick began trying to crawl to take cover behind the

stump with the ax. Another shot was fired, but this time it sounded like it came from a rifle.

"There's more than one!" Chris yelled.

Patrick squeezed his eyes shut and gasped through the pain. "One's on our side. The one with the rifle. Go. *Go!*"

Chris tossed him the gun that had been at his ankle. "Cover me."

Patrick nodded. He pulled himself completely behind the stump, and Chris stumbled after him, crouching behind the firewood. "Who else is out there?"

Patrick peeked over the stump. "A friend. On the count of three. One . . . two . . ."

Chris prepared to run, but then Patrick said, "Wait."

"What?"

"She's going to be scared. And she gets irrational when she's scared."

"Okay."

"Stay in the cabin until we can take care of things out here."

"I can't promise that. My number one priority is to get Jules out of here safely. Whatever that takes."

Patrick raised his gun. "Three."

⌐ ∟

Jules cried out in pain with each movement, but she had to know what was happening. Patrick was out there somewhere in the dark, and now there were gunshots. Lots of them. Scooting over to the door that led outside, she managed to pull herself to her knees to see through the small window next to it. From what she could make out, everything looked quiet.

Then movement. A shadowy figure darted into a grouping of trees. The build was tall and thin. She knew it wasn't Patrick. Her stomach turned and any hope she felt drowned in utter dread. How was she going to defend herself? She'd have to hide. It was her only hope.

Jules ducked below the window at the sound of a shot firing and grabbed the poker. Where could she hide? She didn't know the cabin well enough to get creative.

Another shot. She was going to have to move quickly, which was the one thing she couldn't do.

⌐ ┕

Chris ran, firing simultaneously, until he reached the door. He grabbed the knob, turning it easily. As fast as he could, he slipped in and slammed the door shut. He wondered if he should lock it. Patrick might need to get in. But that would leave access to whoever was out there. He couldn't take a chance. He turned the lock and it clicked.

He kept his back against the door and felt for a light switch but couldn't find one. He looked right, toward what should be the west bedroom. It was even darker in the cabin, and it took his eyes a few moments to adjust well enough that he could see the outlines of furniture.

"Jules? It's Chris. Jules?" He listened for sound. An answer. There was nothing.

Outside, another round of shots was fired.

Quickly he scooted against the wall toward the hallway that supposedly led to the bedroom. He tripped over the edge of a rug and hit his knee on a windowsill but kept going. "Jules? It's Chris." It had been a while. Too long. "Downey. Chris Downey. I'm here to get you, to get you out of here safely. Call out to me."

Nothing.

If she knew what Patrick knew, she might be leery of him, too. He wasn't sure how he was going to convince her he was on her side, but first he had to find her.

Once in the hallway, he was only a few feet from a closed door, which he assumed was the bedroom.

He grabbed the doorknob.

Then he heard it. The front door he'd just come through opened with a loud crack, like it had been kicked in.

⌐ ∟

Chris Downey? That's what she thought she'd heard. His voice was muffled by the doors that stood between them. But it sounded like Chris. What was he doing here? Was he here to help her? Or kill her?

If he'd made it this far, either he'd gotten past Patrick, by some awful means, or Patrick had let him in. There was no way of telling. Before, she could've never believed Chris capable of something like this. He was Jason's best friend. He would've never hurt Jason or been involved in a cover-up.

But now she didn't know. Everything she thought was true turned out not to be.

Besides, why would Chris be up here? Why would he be looking for her? She'd sent him away a long time ago after he'd reached out to her. She'd been bitter and angry and hadn't wanted any reminders of Jason. It had ended with her yelling at Chris to get out of her house. They hadn't spoken since.

And her father . . . well, he wouldn't be capable of finding her if he tried. He'd been drinking more than ever lately. There was a good possibility he didn't even know she'd been missing.

She heard her name called again. This time it sounded closer. She pushed herself farther back in the closet and pulled the small piece of luggage in front of her. It didn't completely hide her, but in the darkness she'd be hard to see.

"Jules?"

This time the voice was closer.

Her head swirled with dizziness from the pain. It was getting worse. But adrenaline could do amazing things. She could hold on. She had to—

A loud sound from the front of the cabin startled her into clarity. She gasped, covering her mouth. A scream desperately wanted to escape.

And then gunfire. But this time it was very close. She heard a thud, right outside the closet.

Jules squeezed her eyes shut and prayed as loudly as silent prayer would allow.

The bullet struck his shoulder, burning as it tore through his muscle. Chris heard it hit the wall behind him and knew it had gone straight through. The force of it threw him back. He stumbled, then fell, hitting his head against the edge of the bed, which was thankfully just the mattress. He collapsed onto the ground. His gun hit the floor and slid to the other side of the bedroom. He started to scramble for it, but his arm buckled underneath him. And then a foot stomped on his hand.

"Not so fast."

Chris looked up. Through the darkness, Jeff Walker was pointing a gun at him.

"You . . ."

Walker smiled a little. "Yeah. Me. Where is she?"

"I don't know. She was supposed to be in this bedroom but she's not here."

Walker slowly lifted his foot off Chris's hand, then stepped toward Chris's gun while keeping his own pointed at Chris.

"Don't do anything stupid," Walker said.

"Yeah. Because I'm the one doing stupid things."

Walker smirked. "Now you're going all self-righteous on me."

"You're responsible for Jason's death. His blood is on your hands."

"We didn't kill Jason," Walker said, frowning. "We didn't know that was going to happen. Jason was snooping around and got himself killed."

"You might as well have pulled the trigger yourself."

"I sleep fine at night."

"You have no honor."

"Yes, well, I have a house in Aspen, so I'm doing okay."

Then, at the same time, they both heard it. A small bumping noise coming from the nearby closet.

Walker's face expressed delight. "Juliet," he called, "it's Detective Jeff Walker. I need you to come out of the closet right now before someone really gets hurt."

Silence again. Chris tried to think of what to do. Walker was thinking just as fast. He moved to a wall and found the light switch, but when he flipped it, nothing happened. Patrick must've cut the power.

Walker cursed. "Juliet, I don't want anybody to get hurt! Get out here now!"

"Don't!" Chris said.

"Shut up, Downey, or you're going to get both of you killed."

"What's your plan, Walker?" Chris said, trying to stall him from going to the closet. "How are you going to get this all cleaned up? They're going to find us eventually."

Walker smirked again. "Really? Because as far as I can tell, this place is off the map."

"You found it. How?"

"I followed you. Had Maecoat put a tracking device on your truck. Sold it with an 'It's for his protection.' Nice, by the way. Handcuffing your partner to your coffee table."

"You're not going to get away with this. You know it.

What'd you do with Patrick? Do you think it's going to go unnoticed that a famous novelist is missing or dead?"

"I think I'm going to be able to sell the idea that he went completely out of his mind."

"Like Roy? Just set people up who get in your way?"

"That's the idea."

"Patrick knows the truth, Walker. He's probably already told people."

"Yes, well, one problem at a time. Juliet, if you don't come out right now, things are not going to turn out well for you."

Walker kept his gun pointed at Chris and walked to the closet. It had sliding doors and he opened one, his gun steady on Chris but his gaze peering into the darkness. He pushed his hand into some of the clothes.

"Juliet, get out here!"

He stepped into the closet a little more and leaned forward. But suddenly he cried out, the gun falling from his hand and hitting the floor. Jules screamed and Walker stumbled backward. Something was sticking through his front and out of his back, on his left side under his rib cage. Something sharp, almost spear-like. Blood drained out and he fell sideways. He moaned and Chris could now more clearly see an iron-like stick coming out his front, near his belly. Was that a poker?

"Jules!" Chris said, grabbing Walker's gun.

"In here," she cried.

Chris hurried to the closet, his shoulder burning.

Jules scooted to the opening. "I can't walk," she said. She

looked at Walker and covered her mouth with her hand. "Oh no . . ."

"Don't worry about him." Chris retrieved his own gun and tucked Walker's into the waistband of his jeans.

Walker moaned again.

"Come on. I can help you with my good arm. Can you stand?"

"I don't think so."

"Okay." Chris stooped. "Put your arms around my neck."

Jules complied and Chris stood, using his good arm to lift her. She cried out.

"Hang on. I just want to get you out of this room. Then we'll figure out how to get you to the truck."

She clung tightly to him, and he managed to lift and drag her, with her toes barely touching the ground, out of the room and down the hallway. He got her to the couch and set her down.

"It hurts so much," she cried. "You're . . . You've been . . ."

"I'll live," Chris said. "First I need to stop the bleeding." He laid his gun on the coffee table and went to the kitchen, rummaging through the darkness for a rag or towel. Once he'd found several, he went back to the couch. "Can you tie these around my shoulder?"

Jules nodded. Her hands were shaking but she managed to tie two towels together and then tie them around his shoulder. His forehead was dripping sweat and he felt dizzy, but he tried to shake it off.

Tears streamed down her face. "What happened to Patrick?"

"I don't know. I'll help him as soon as I get you to a safe place. I don't know who else is out there."

"You saw him?"

"Yes. He was trying to protect you. He told me he knew about what happened to Jason."

Jules nodded. "We can't let them get away with it."

"I know. We won't. But first we have to get off this mountain. My truck is parked about fifty yards away, through that clearing. Before we move, I have to determine if there's anyone else. I heard another gun being fired. Sounded like a rifle."

"That might be Paul."

"Who is that?"

"Patrick's paranoid neighbor. He's the one who knew you were coming before you arrived. He's a little bit crazy, I guess, but I think he's on our side. At least . . . mine and Patrick's side."

"Okay." Chris took a deep breath. His heart was pounding fitfully. He needed a drink of water. He went to the kitchen for a glass and splashed his face from the sink. He couldn't afford to pass out.

"I think the only way I can get you out of here, since I can't carry you, is for you to ride piggyback. Can you do that? Your arms are okay?"

"Yes."

"Okay, then let's—"

Chris was knocked down by a figure he only saw briefly before he hit the ground. Chris managed to get to his feet, but Walker was on top of him again, shoving him against what Chris thought at first was a wall. But something pressed against his hip and he realized it was a doorknob.

Chris pushed against Walker's face, but Walker had him around the throat, his face like a bulging red blister, his eyes wild with hate. Chris was choking and losing breath quickly. Screaming, Jules threw something that hit Walker in the back. With that short distraction, Chris managed to turn the doorknob. The door opened and he fell backward, out into the cold.

They were on a deck, one that looked like it was suspended over the side of the cliff. An iron guardrail went all the way around it. Chris felt wet and sticky at his belly and realized Walker had been bleeding all over him. He'd pulled the poker out at some point.

Walker lunged forward and pinned him against the railing. Chris felt the gun at his back but he'd never be able to get it. He began to tip over the edge. Below him, he could see the vast valley, hollow and sweeping. There was no way to survive the fall. And Walker knew it. He pushed harder, grabbing Chris's waist, trying to throw him over.

Chris was losing his footing fast. Neither man, as they bled out, was particularly strong at this point, but Chris had only one good arm to work with. Walker was pale, his lips turning blue. But his eyes were wide and erratic; Chris knew it was adrenaline that kept this guy moving. He wanted to kill Chris if it was the last thing he did.

The edge of the iron railing pressed against his back, slicing with every movement. Chris had to get the upper hand—and fast. His only hope was to bring Walker to his knees, and at the moment he had one weak spot: a hole through his abdomen.

Walker got a good grip on Chris's coat and ripped it sideways, throwing Chris off-balance. And with that, Walker managed to get his arm hooked under Chris, who felt himself being lifted off the ground. The only foot still touching the deck was slipping and sliding in a pool of blood.

Inside, he could hear Jules screaming his name.

Walker moved his arm and Chris took his shot. With his hand balled into a fist, he pushed it into Walker's side, right at the wound. Walker screamed and Chris tried to use the momentum to push him off-balance. But with one hard strike, Walker punched him in the stomach and Chris lost all his breath.

He could still hear Jules screaming, but now it sounded distant, as if it were in a tunnel. Walker was shouting and cursing at him, but it was delayed in his head, echoing around like his mind was a cave.

Chris found himself turned around, lifted off the ground. He tried to grip the railing, but his fingers slipped. He tried again and caught it, but he was halfway over and there was nothing but black, jagged rocks below. His vision blurred and he closed his eyes, trying to fight but losing momentum.

And in his mind, he could hear himself calling for God. He listened, fascinated by how urgent he sounded. How he sounded as if he knew to whom he was calling. And strangely, he heard his name called back, by a voice saturated with all that was good and right. It was a strong voice, yet strangely intimate—a voice he'd never heard but always known.

He found himself laughing and floating, feeling a perfect peace. Jason had spoken of this peace before. He called it the peace that passed all understanding. Chris never knew what he meant by that, until now. Dangling over a cliff, about to lose his life, he felt that somewhere on his way down, trusted hands would at the very least catch his soul.

I'm ready. I believe.

Through the peace that had swept over him like a lullaby, a noise sounded around him. It was a familiar noise but he couldn't place it. Before he could figure out what it was, he felt weight drop off him.

Chris opened his eyes. Walker fell to the ground as he clung to the railing. Then Chris fell too, nearly on top of Walker, and rolled off him onto the icy deck.

"Jules!" he called. "Are you okay?"

"Yes," she cried. "What happened?" He couldn't see her. He guessed she was still on the couch, unable to move.

"Just stay there." Chris was on his belly. He glanced back to see if Walker was moving. There wasn't a chance. He had an inky-black bullet hole through the side of his head. Chris craned his neck up, to see where the shot had come from. Off the side of the deck about fifteen yards, the cliff jutted out and there was a small area of dense trees. As Chris stared hard through the darkness, he could see a figure standing near one of the trees.

"Patrick!" Chris called. "Are you okay?"

There was no answer. And the man disappeared into the shadows.

"Patrick!"

"Chris?" he heard Jules call.

"I'm coming." Chris tried to get to his feet. It took three tries. The towel that had been tied around his shoulder was soaked in blood. It dripped through his fingers as he held his hand against it.

He took a few tentative steps. He managed to grab the doorway and make it inside.

Jules gasped when she saw him. "Chris . . . hurry. Come over here. We've got to stop the . . . the . . ."

"I know." Chris stumbled and collapsed onto the couch.

Jules untied the drenched towels. "You've got to go find something. A T-shirt. Something like that."

Chris nodded.

She pointed to the opposite bedroom. "In there. That's Patrick's room."

Chris stood, his legs wobbly underneath him. Using the furniture and walls, he stumbled forward. It was still hard to see, but the bedroom looked abnormally cluttered. He found a chest and pulled open two drawers before finally finding undershirts. He grabbed four and made it back to Jules.

"How do you feel?" she asked, quickly tying one around his shoulder. "You look pale."

"I don't feel good. But I can make it to the truck." He wiped the sweat off his forehead. "The question is, how do we get you there?"

Jules looked through the doorway that opened to the deck. A cold breeze was blowing through. "Is he dead?"

"Yes."

"Leave me here. Go down and get help."

"I'm not leaving you here. There is no way. We'll figure something out."

Jules tied two more shirts around his shoulder.

"Okay, that's good enough for now. I'm going to open this other door, look outside for a bit, see if I can figure something out." The cold air might also keep him from bleeding as fast. And keep him alert.

Jules nodded.

He picked his gun up off the table and opened the door. All was quiet in a night that had been filled with so much chaos. The clouds had cleared and the moon was shining some light into the darkness. He stepped outside, wondering if it was safe enough to leave Jules to drive his truck all the way up to the cabin. And there, right in front of him, was a shiny, silver sled . . . as if someone had anticipated his needs. He looked around but saw no one. He couldn't shake the feeling, though, that he was being watched.

Chris hurried to grab the sled's rope. The sled was lightweight, made of aluminum. He pulled it to the step of the cabin with ease. The cold air had done him some good. Back inside, he went to Jules on the couch. "Okay, put your arm around my neck. I just have to get you to the door. There's a sled right outside to pull you to the truck."

"What about Patrick? Is he dead? Did you see him dead out there?" Her eyes filled with desperate tears.

"I didn't see him."

"Who shot that guy?"

"I don't know. Now let's go."

Together they hobbled toward the door, both of them growling through their own pain. He got her to the sled and nearly dropped her into it. She bit her lip as if holding in a scream. But after a moment, she nodded that she was okay.

Chris picked up the rope in one hand and pointed his gun outward with the same hand, whipping it back and forth, looking for any small movement. He would probably shoot first and ask questions second, but he couldn't pull her and point the gun at the same time. He was going to have to make a choice.

In the snow, his toes had gone completely numb. A lot of things were going numb, including the arm that had been shot. He was having trouble holding the gun. Within moments, he had to drop it. He looked ahead, focusing on the truck.

"Jules," he whispered, "grab that gun."

She nervously reached for it and tucked it close to her.

He moved them swiftly down the small hill and toward the truck. Once they reached it, Chris gasped for breath that was harder and harder to get. His lungs felt like they'd shrunk to half their size. He leaned against the passenger door for a moment, his body shivering from the cold and shaking from the blood loss. Jules looked up at him, as if wondering how she was going to get in the truck.

He took as deep a breath as he could and stooped. "Put your arm around my neck." It felt like the muscles in his back were going to snap right out of his skin as he lifted her. He accidentally banged her against the door but she managed to reach around him and open it. With fingers he could barely feel on his other hand, he grasped the edge and opened it wider.

He practically dumped her inside. With his good arm he helped her sit up and get situated.

"You okay?"

She touched his cheek gently and smiled through tears. "Yes."

"Okay. Hang in there." He shut the door and moved around the back of the truck, holding onto the rim of the bed, to get to the other side. His eyes were fixed on the dark wilderness, searching its shadows for Patrick or anyone else. Nothing moved but the lightly falling snow.

He got into the truck. Jules was leaning forward, searching the darkness too.

Chris touched her arm. "We have to go."

"What about Patrick?"

"I don't care about Patrick. I care about you."

He turned the truck on and the heater blew through the cold, relaxing them both a little. He gripped the steering wheel so his hands wouldn't shake.

Jules turned to him, putting her hand on his shoulder,

seeming to understand more than she could say. "Thank you . . ."

He smiled at her. Frankly he couldn't believe they'd made it out alive. "We'll drive down until we can get a cell phone signal, then call the police, okay?"

"I'm not going to press charges against him," she said resolutely.

Now was not the time to argue that point.

"I know it sounds weird, but I think . . . I think this was all a gift."

"I don't know what that means. But I have to disclose everything in the report. We're witnesses. I can't lie for him. Or you. I hope you can understand that."

"I understand," she said, and she really seemed to.

The darkness seemed to grow thin against the emerging moon. Only wispy, haunting clouds floated by. He watched Jules. She was far away but peaceful.

"We need to get you medical attention, okay? We need to go."

She nodded, whispered a quiet good-bye as if Reagan stood right there in front of the truck, and then she gently slipped her hand into his.

THE KIDNAPPING HAD become legendary overnight. As soon as the police got to the cabin, so did the press. Finally they had found Patrick Reagan's secret retreat. Pictures leaked out. It was breaking news on every channel. The private man she knew him to be was spoken of every five seconds every day for weeks.

Jules refused to do television interviews about her experience as Patrick's hostage. But she hated the things that the news reported about him. So much of it was untrue. Speculation. He was grossly misrepresented in every way.

She wanted people to know the truth. And she had the perfect platform for it too.

When *Enoch* released with more fanfare than it could've ever had on its own merit, Jules decided to speak about Patrick, on her terms and in controlled environments. As she did readings and speaking engagements, she began to refer to him. Without giving much detail about her time with him, she spoke to his character. His kindness. His immense love for the craft of writing. And his knowledge of it too. She spoke of the changes she made to her manuscript, how she found her way to a deeper truth. She never took questions and maybe that added to the mystique. But like him, she had no interest in entering into the New York writing scene. She didn't attend the many parties she was invited to. And since *Enoch*, she had not written another book.

But she wanted to.

It was an itch that wouldn't go away. And it made her smile because she knew then that she was a real writer.

It was June and the weather hinted that it was ready to spread its warmth more consistently. Jules had been writing since before sunrise and had gotten up to stretch her legs and get coffee when she heard her father's truck pull in. She opened the door and greeted him as he walked up the sidewalk.

"There's my genius, famous, brilliant daughter!" His face lit with pure delight, and she wondered if there was anything better than seeing delight on a father's face. He'd aged what seemed like ten years while she was gone that one week. But what she got in return was much better.

He hugged her tightly. "How's my baby girl?"

"I'm really good, Daddy."

"You got a signing or anything today?"

"Not today. Just speaking at the library this evening."

"Glad you mentioned that. I won't be able to make it to that one. They moved my AA meetings to Tuesdays for the rest of the month."

She smiled. "It's okay. I told you, you don't have to come to everything. There's too much!"

He cupped her face. "Don't you know that it's my favorite thing to do?"

"Come in," she said, taking his hand. "You want some coffee? I was just taking a break."

"Nah. I'm on my way to pick up Carla." He grinned widely. He'd met Carla at one of her book signings. She was very different from Jules's mother. Kind of homely, with long, gray hair that hinted there might be a hippie in her somewhere. But she was kind, and they shared a love for adventure and travel. They had a special connection, and Jules couldn't even begin to resent it.

She winked at him. "Don't let me stand in your way."

"Just wanted to come by and check on you." Inside his blue eyes, watery now with age, she saw that there would always be a fear in him that she might not be okay. She supposed that was the price of love. Along with it came constant fear that it would be torn from your arms. She'd risked it once, and all of her fears had come true. Somehow, she was still standing.

"All is well, Daddy."

"I'll call you later, okay?"

"Okay."

She waved at her father as the FedEx truck came rumbling down the drive, passing her father's truck on his way out. The deliveryman hopped out, carrying a medium-size box. "Good afternoon. Sign here," he said, handing her a digital signature pad. Jules took the box from him, wondering what it could be. She hadn't ordered anything that she could remember.

At her kitchen counter, she pulled the tab that opened the box. Inside, neatly bound, was a manuscript titled *The Living End*. By Patrick Reagan.

She stared at his name, breathless. She had hoped—prayed, even—that he would contact her. But as Christmas passed and winter faded into spring, she'd heard nothing and assumed that he had permanently disappeared.

The manuscript was thick. The paper, a heavier stock, was crisp, pure white. She put her hand on it as though she might be able to feel its heartbeat.

An envelope, sealed with a burgundy wax stamp with the fancy letter *R*, peeked out of the edge of the box. She'd almost missed it. Opening it carefully, she found a handwritten note.

Dear Juliet,
I was delighted to hear that you decided to release your
novel under your real name. I was not certain Blake
Timble and I would ever be acquainted as friends. But
you, dear one, will always be my friend. I hold you in

high esteem and have resigned myself now that there are better writers in the world than I. Your talent is immense. I know you've found your destiny.

My destiny has come and gone. I know you will respect that I must go away. I want to live out my days alone and in peace, writing for myself, writing for the pure pleasure of it again. I realized over these past few months that I was attempting to write about a world I no longer understood. And maybe I no longer wished to understand it. I've become good at hiding from it. I thought that Amelia and I could live in solitude and enjoy each other and be everything to one another. Even if she had lived, I realized that she could never fulfill every need in my soul. It seems we were created to be filled by something—Someone—greater than ourselves. As much as Amelia loved me, she could not reach the bleakest corridors of my being. Perhaps more than the cancer, I ate away at her life by trying to keep her all to myself, by hiding from the very thing I sought to write about.

I suppose we understand each other, as your own journey took you to a closed and confined space where you peered out into the world through a tiny window. But maybe we can learn from each other as well. Maybe, unlike me, you can summon the courage to live openly, alongside this world, leaving the imprint of your existence on its dewy grass.

I hope I am one of those people you hold close to your heart when you sink below the surface of the ocean and delight in the way the light looks from a different perspective. I hope I have helped you not fear the waters of the deep.

Enclosed you will find my final novel, The Living End. I finished it to honor Jason. It is dedicated to you. There is nothing more raw or real than the unfinished and unpolished work of a writer. The world will see it clothed, but you have seen it laid bare.

I wish you the very best. You won't be able to find me, but I will always be nearby. Warm regards.

Your biggest fan,
PR

"Jules?"

She gasped, looking up to find Chris standing in the doorway.

"Sorry . . . didn't mean to startle you. The door was wide-open."

Jules suddenly realized there was a draft, slightly fluttering the edges of the manuscript. She hadn't even noticed. "Oh. Sorry. Come in," she said, beckoning him with her hand.

He walked in and closed the door. "You look nice."

"I feel a little haggard. I've been writing since 4 a.m."

"*Haggard* does not and will not ever fit you." He grinned and pecked her on the cheek. "You ready for lunch?"

She nodded but pointed to the manuscript sitting on the table. "It's from Patrick."

Chris looked at it, worry flickering through his eyes. "You didn't think you'd ever hear from him again."

"No, I didn't." She glanced at him. At the beginning of a relationship that started soon after he rescued her, they'd had to agree to disagree about Patrick. Chris didn't understand what happened in the cabin. As far as he was concerned, Patrick Reagan was a lunatic.

"Have you read any of it?" he asked.

"No. Not . . . in a while. The letter says it's his last book. That it was written to honor Jason."

Jules looked at Chris for a long moment. They'd been through so much in the last six months. The cops involved in the theft ring were charged, which later led to the arrest of the men who shot Jason. Patrick had disappeared before the police got to the cabin. He would be arrested if they ever found him, even though Jules never pressed charges.

Jules had met with the prosecutor and agreed to testify on Jason's behalf if they needed her. The ADA, Robert McKinnel, told her they had enough evidence to put them all behind bars for years, thanks to Jason's work before he died and Patrick's work after. Chris had been relieved to know that Greg Maecoat had not been involved in the ring. They returned to being partners after internal affairs cleared them both.

"You okay?" Chris asked.

She smiled through tears. "I am."

Chris pulled her into a tight hug.

"Thanks for being here for me," she said, burying her face in his shoulder.

"Look, don't misunderstand. I'm totally in this for the cool factor of dating a famous writer."

Jules laughed. She loved his sense of humor. She was beginning to love even more than that.

"Why don't we go get you some comfort food. How many calories do you burn per page, you think? Enough to justify clam chowder made with real cream?"

"Enough for ice cream!" she said, clasping her hands together hopefully.

"Depends on how many times you hit that heavy Delete button."

"Too many times to count."

"Then it's a double scoop for you!"

She laughed and he grabbed her hand, leading her toward the door.

"I'll be out in a sec," she said. "Let me get my purse."

Chris walked out and Jules passed by the table on which the manuscript sat. She paused, the tips of her fingers brushing the top page, finding their way to the middle, hovering over his name.

And he was right.

She felt him nearby.

ACKNOWLEDGMENTS

I'D LIKE TO THANK all the people at Tyndale who continue to be teammates in this wonderful world of writing. The entire fiction team, the sales team, the support staff are incredibly gifted, dedicated, and professional and a joy to be around. Special thanks to Jan Stob, Sarah Mason, and Karen Watson for continuing to believe in my stories and writing.

I'd also like to thank my agent, Janet Kobobel Grant, for her constant guidance and encouragement. She is a fountain of wisdom from whom I draw much. Also, thanks to Ron Wheatley, my constant writing companion and technical adviser, who makes my stories read authentically.

My family—Sean, John, and Cate—bring such joy to my life and fill my days with deep meaning and purpose. It's easy to come back from my imaginary world and dwell in the moments that are real.

And as always, thank You to my heavenly Father, who allows me to work out my faith in my stories and ask the hard questions, never harshly rebuking me but always dealing with me kindly and attentively.

ABOUT THE AUTHOR

RENE GUTTERIDGE is the author of nineteen novels, including *Heart of the Country, Possession, Listen,* and the Storm series from Tyndale House Publishers and *Never the Bride,* the Boo series, and the Occupational Hazards series from WaterBrook Multnomah. She also released *My Life as a Doormat* and *The Ultimate Gift: The Novelization* with Thomas Nelson. Rene is also known for her Christian comedy sketches. She studied screenwriting while earning a mass communications degree, graduating magna cum laude from Oklahoma City University and earning the Excellence in Mass Communication Award. She served as the full-time director of drama for First United Methodist Church for five years before leaving to stay home and write. She enjoys instructing at writers conferences and in college classrooms. She lives with her husband, Sean, a musician, and their children in Oklahoma City. Visit her website at www.renegutteridge.com.

DISCUSSION
QUESTIONS

1. At the beginning of *Misery Loves Company*, Jules writes in her blog that Patrick Reagan has lost his spark as a writer. In what ways can any of us lose our spark? Can that loss be prevented or a spark restored once it's gone? How?

2. Jules copes with the loss of her husband, Jason, by retreating from the world and looking forward to seeing Jason in her dreams. What do you think was healthy or unhealthy about her response? Have you ever turned to your dreams or imagination to cope with grief?

3. Jules's father, the Lt. Colonel, says in chapter 1 that "instinct can carry you an awful long way, but full analysis can save your life." Explain what he means by this. When have you had to put "full analysis" into practice?

4. In chapter 5, Jules considers the purpose of death: "What was this life for if not loving and living and changing and breathing? What was the point of it all if death took it away?" Have you ever struggled with similar questions? Were you able to reconcile your thinking about death, and if so, how?

5. In chapter 6, the Lt. Colonel says that technology is ruining our society. Considering the story line in *Misery Loves Company*, is there some validity to his concerns? How should we apply wisdom in our use of technology? What are the pros and cons of social media in our culture?

6. When Patrick asks Jules if she told the truth about his writing on her blog, she answers him honestly despite being his captive. Have you been in a situation where telling the truth was risky or costly? Explain.

7. In chapter 8, Patrick asks Jules, "Did you intend to harm *me*?" in reference to her blog post about his writing. If you were writing a review about someone's work on your blog and knew the author would read your words, how would that knowledge affect your writing? How much responsibility do you think reviewers have to consider the feelings of the author?

8. Have you ever found yourself in a terrifying situation? If so, please share, if you feel comfortable, how you coped.

9. Jules describes herself as someone who only functions in a well-ordered environment, as opposed to Patrick, who is "fond of chaos." Describe how you best function and discuss why you believe God formed you this way.

10. "You can't find peace because there is no peace without truth," Patrick says in chapter 17. What does he mean by this? Do you agree that there's a relationship between peace and truth? Explain.

11. Later Patrick says, "Writing is about finding truth. But you can't find the truth if you don't see everything," describing how writers closely observe their world. Do you need to look more closely at your world? What would change if you did so?

12. Leona Patterson tells Chris in chapter 21 that "writers play God, don't you see? They create their people, their creations, and . . . then send trouble into their paths." In literature, obstacles are essential to good storytelling. What would our lives be like without trouble? What purpose do our problems serve?

13. Consider Patrick's words in chapter 25: "We need people, Juliet, to show us our selfishness, to extract ugliness that reveals itself in our hearts." How do people play this role in our lives? Can you think of a time when you either allowed someone to play this role or prevented someone from doing so?

14. Patrick asks Jules if there is a time when killing is merciful. How would you answer him? How would you handle an end-of-life situation if you were in the place of Patrick's wife? What would you do if you were in Patrick's position, watching someone you loved suffer?

15. As Patrick and Jules consider God's role in their lives, Patrick remarks that "the hardest thing to understand about God is why He answers a prayer for a good parking space at the mall but won't hear the cries of a man desperate to save his wife. Why He wouldn't hear the plea of such a woman as yourself, that her husband might not die on a sidewalk in the darkness of night." Have you wrestled with similar questions about answered and unanswered prayers? How would you answer Patrick?

Also by Rene Gutteridge

THE STORM SERIES:
The Splitting Storm
Storm Gathering
Storm Surge

THE OCCUPATIONAL HAZARDS SERIES:
Scoop
Snitch
Skid

STAND-ALONE TITLES:
Listen
Possession
Never the Bride
(with Cheryl McKay)
My Life as a Doormat
Troubled Waters
Ghost Writer

NOVELLA:
Escapement
(part of the 7 Hours series)

THE BOO SERIES:
Boo
Boo Who
Boo Hiss
Boo Humbug

NOVELIZATIONS:
Heart of the Country
(with John Ward)
The Ultimate Gift